FLIGHT
OF THE
ARCHANGEL

By Isabelle Holland

FLIGHT OF THE ARCHANGEL

A DEATH AT ST. ANSELM'S

THE LOST MADONNA

COUNTERPOINT

MARCHINGTON INHERITANCE

TOWER ABBEY

THE DEMAURY PAPERS

GRENELLE

DARCOURT

MONCRIEFF

TRELAWNY

KILGAREN

FLIGHT
OF THE
ARCHANGEL

Isabelle Holland

DOUBLEDAY & COMPANY, INC.
GARDEN CITY, NEW YORK
1985

Library of Congress Cataloging in Publication Data
Holland, Isabelle.
    Flight of the archangel.
    I. Title.
PS3558.O3485F5   1985   813'.54
ISBN 0-385-19296-7
Library of Congress Catalog Card Number 84-28685

In memory of
AMANDA
who delighted my days

FLIGHT
OF THE
ARCHANGEL

PROLOGUE

Many years later, I realized I came to the city to find Joris, even though at the time I knew he was dead.

Ten years is a big difference between half siblings, and I was only twelve the night Joris walked out of a party and was never seen again. As the search widened, the police questioned us—my mother, my father and me—many times, trying to find, in some detail of his life, thinking, writing, friendships, the clue that would reveal what had happened to him. They had even talked to me. I remember sitting on the front porch of our farm in my riding clothes talking to two detectives from New York.

"So there's nothing at all," one of them finally said, "that you can think of that would help us find your brother?"

"Half brother," I corrected. It wasn't that I didn't idolize Joris. I did. He was the epitome of everything I loved and admired. In some of my moods I wanted passionately for us to be whole siblings. In others, I wanted equally passionately for us to discover we weren't siblings at all. When that happened —in my soaring fantasies—he would admit that he had always adored me, and would sweep me into his arms . . . When he went to Princeton when he was eighteen and I was eight, the main part of my life stopped functioning—at least for a while.

"Kit darling," Mother said finally one morning, "I know that Joris's departure means that for you the sun, the moon and the stars aren't functioning. But the horses have to be fed and the stables have to be cleaned."

She had, of course, used the one lever that would push me back into life. After all, I confided to Buttercup, my horse, even Princeton couldn't last forever. But, in a sense, it did. The party from which Joris never returned happened just before his graduation. So he never again lived at home.

I had told the police everything I knew, or could think of, or could remember—or almost everything. The trouble was, there were so many things Joris had said, most of them (if I were honest with myself) I only partly understood, or didn't understand at all.

Sometimes, when he caught sight of my rapt but rather uncomprehending expression, he would burst out laughing. "Never mind," I remember hearing him once say, "one day you'll understand."

I wasn't even sure what I was supposed to understand. His words were beautiful, like poetry, I used to think.

"But then, I am a poet," he said when I told him this.

"Do you write poems?" I asked him. If Joris dwelt in the brilliantly colored world of the abstract, my mind and understanding was grounded in earth.

"In my head and consciousness," Joris replied.

"Yes, but I can't read them there."

"I'll recite them to you."

"Recite me one now," I pleaded. As far as I was concerned, now was where it was at.

But he just smiled. "Later."

If "What do you mean?" was my favorite question, "One day you'll know" was his favorite answer. Then he'd pull my hair, "when you grow up."

Finally I took to writing down things Joris said in those golden times when he came home from school. I thought it was very bright of me to have thought of doing it, so I could mull over his words when he was away. But he caught me once.

It was the only time I ever saw him really angry and it frightened me. My mother could be exasperated and my father could be severe. But that was all part of life. Everybody I knew had parents who gave them problems from time to time.

But when Joris saw my book of his sayings, something happened to his face. Curiously, I don't remember too much about what occurred then, except that he took away my book. He left to go back to school after that, and when he came home it was as though nothing had happened and once again I was his adoring acolyte.

When the police came, trying to find out what had happened to Joris, why he had disappeared, I didn't tell them about the book or his anger. For some reason, I felt it was a terrible shame that I had to bear alone: I had betrayed his trust.

Eventually, of course, as the years passed and the investigations produced nothing, we had to accept that Joris was dead. At the end of seven years this became a legal fact. I was in college by then, and that year, the year I was nineteen, produced a double blow: one was the harsh legality of Joris's death; the second happened during a weekend when I was visiting a friend in Connecticut. Our farm in Virginia burned. My parents and some of the horses were killed before the fire engines from the nearest town could reach them.

After I graduated I came to New York, mostly because it was the most exciting city in the world (or so people said) and was the center of everything that interested me.

But a small part of me, perhaps the child that still lived in me, chose to come to New York because it was there that Joris had last been seen. Irrational as it might be, and in defiance of everything the police said, I thought he might still be there. And if he were there, then I wanted to be there too.

1

By the time I was thirty-two, I had worked on several newspapers and magazines and had become a moderately successful free-lance writer, and my byline, *by Kit Maitland*, was seen increasingly above stories about the city and some of its people and families and lore. Always a loner, I had many acquaintances but few—if any—close friends. I had also been married and was now separated.

About my marriage: like everything else that took place after I let Joris be dead, it seemed second-best, a substitute. If I had married someone totally unconnected with Joris, with the family, with Virginia, then perhaps my life could finally have found the first-best, the right way to function for me.

But I married Simon Warfield, Joris's first cousin on his mother's side and his near twin. The Warfields were among those arrivistes whom my father deplored and married into. They were manufacturers from New Hampshire who had made their money in the mills of New England and then come down to Virginia to become country gentry. Simon was, in every way, Joris's echo, and he followed the more brilliant Joris like a faithful shadow. Even nature made him seem second-rate, an afterthought. Joris was six-one in height, Simon not quite six feet. Joris was muscular and well made. Simon was skinny. Joris had brilliant blue eyes that drew one's own like magnets, Simon's eyes were a light gray. Joris was a born athlete. Simon tried to be and often fell on his face, to the unkind laughter of both Joris and me. We finally came to call him "Mr. Me-Too."

"Just like a Japanese," I said, giggling, when Joris suggested it.

"Ah so," he said, which drove me into giggles again.

Simon was about a year younger than Joris, but he went off to the University of Virginia the same year Joris left for Princeton. Simon had tried for Princeton but was not accepted.

"Naturally," I said to Joris.

He grinned.

Then Joris failed to come home that summer night. During the intervening years, as long as I was home, I couldn't bear to see Simon. Both the resemblance and the differences were too great.

But finally, after I was working in New York, he called me one day out of the blue and asked if I'd like to have dinner. Since I'd last seen him he'd been in the Army for three years, gone to law school and was practicing with some firm on Wall Street. He looked far less like Joris than before and was infinitely more attractive than I remembered him. The skinny boy had become a lean, hard man with deep-set light-gray eyes which, when not compared with Joris's, were compelling in their own way. I knew from the family grapevine that he had graduated Phi Beta Kappa, and learned from one of his friends when we'd gone out in a foursome that he had made the law review.

Away from Joris, away from all the unfavorable comparisons —which Joris and I had been all too happy to point out— Simon was bright and funny, with an offbeat sense of humor that served as much to keep him at a distance as to amuse. Except, of course, when we drank. With Simon, as with all drinkers (I later learned), liquor served as a bridge to intimacy. He could consume more martinis than I thought the human frame could hold, without (as far as I could see) visible effect.

Unlike me. I tried to keep up, because, besides Simon, the group of writers and journalists I ran around with were not noted for their abstemiousness. But as a drinker I was a failure. At some point I came to an end of my ability to soak up any more alcohol, and after the disaster of the marriage I returned with relief to my natural, unadventurous social drinking.

But in the months that I was discovering how wrong Joris and I had been about Simon, I drank enough to be blind to the amount Simon could put away.

At the end of three months he asked me to marry him and I accepted.

Was I really in love? Even then I wasn't sure. With all the differences and the passage of time, there were still moments with Simon when, achingly, I saw flashes of Joris. When that happened I knew then I couldn't be sure whom I loved—or if I loved anyone.

I remember waking up in the middle of the night after a rousing party. I had a terrible head, but I was no longer high, because a sober, cold little voice in the middle of my head asked in clear, flat words, "Do you love him?" The trouble was, I couldn't be sure to whom "him" referred.

I didn't come up with an answer, and the next night was another party and at the end of it Simon proposed in what I had come to think of as his characteristic, off-center way. In fact, the whole thing was typical of his less than romantic approach to our relationship.

He said, looking down into his umpteenth martini, "You know you couldn't have married Joris anyway, not unless you felt the laws of incest were outdated. He was, after all, your half brother." Curiously, this was the first time he'd mentioned Joris, but that didn't occur to me till later.

I'd had a drink or two myself, or I wouldn't have so easily fallen into talking about Joris. Also, I wouldn't have said what fell out of my mouth then. "I'm sure we weren't. I'm *positive* we'd have learned somehow that we weren't."

He put his head back then and laughed. He laughed and laughed until everyone in the restaurant stopped talking and turned around.

"You're drunk," I said disgustedly, knowing I was far from sober myself.

"How true! Although I think that's a case of the pot calling the kettle black. But since, despite your best efforts, the road to an incestuous marriage is closed to you, why don't you marry me? Much healthier! We aren't even related."

"Certainly not!" I was still miffed. "I wouldn't think of it."

Nevertheless, a week later I accepted, and the partying went on till the day I found myself standing with Simon in front of a clerk down at City Hall, and left, a few minutes later, Simon's wife.

I knew within a month what a stupid mistake I had made. There were, in the first week or so, moments of tenderness, glimpses of something I'd never before experienced. I was probably both as knowledgeable and as ignorant as the average young woman of my age. I knew the techniques, the approaches. What I had always been short on were the feelings. Briefly, Simon aroused these. He touched in me an inner core, a level that I hadn't known existed. But I wasn't ready to have it touched, at least not by him, and I reacted accordingly.

It was then his drinking increased, or, as I came later to think, perhaps it had simply abated temporarily while he courted and married me. Whatever the reason, he came home drunk more and more often, and when I objected, came home later and later. There were titanic rows in which terrible things were said, dreadful accusations made. At the height of one of these he struck me, and we both stopped, appalled. But it happened again, and then again. The next day he was always aghast and penitent. But there came a time when there was no next day, because I had left and gone to stay in a furnished room. I left behind no address or phone number and arranged with my then job to be sent out of the city on assignment.

The trouble with leaving like that, and being too afraid to return, was that I had abandoned clothes, furniture and a suitcase full of personal mementos. It was the latter that I mourned. Twice, during the day, I had tried to go back, but I had had the forethought to ask our super if the apartment was empty. That was when I found out that Simon was upstairs, drinking his way to oblivion. So I didn't go back. Mentally I let go the pictures of Mother and of Buttercup, of our home, "Percy's Walk," and of the stables and some of the foals. I hated to lose them, but it was better than being beaten again.

In the first few months after that, I relived those beatings in my dreams, night after night. No one had ever struck me before. When my mother was angry with me, she told me why and by the time we'd finished with our conversation the anger had gone. My father, never very close to me, his girl child, simply put an icy distance between us when he was displeased.

So Simon's stinging blows were so far from anything I had known that it was easy for me, for a while, to pretend they hadn't happened—like his being drunk.

When I left him, my unconscious, or whatever part of me it was that refused to believe what he was doing, played the scenes back in my dreams. I would wake up soaked in sweat, crying, my heart racing with fright. When I was traveling, I looked carefully before I entered a room for the first time, in case Simon might have found out I would be there. It was absurd, irrational, and I knew it. But for many months there was nothing I could do except accept my fear and trust that it would recede. Which, of course, it eventually did.

Finally, with all of my addresses new, I went to a lawyer to see about a divorce. But, by that time, it was Simon who had disappeared.

For two years my lawyer tried to find him. He learned that Simon had drunk himself out of his law firm not long after I left him. Since then, there had been several more jobs, all ending the same way, and of shorter and shorter duration each time.

"He arrived drunk and left drunk," one former employer told my lawyer. "After three days I fired him. I can't imagine why I waited even that long, except that I'd known him way back and knew he had a first-rate legal mind."

"He must have been talking about someone else," I said to my lawyer when he reported it to me.

"Other people have said the same."

"Little Mr. Me-Too," I countered angrily, reverting to my old child's image of him that now seemed prophetic. "He never had a mind of his own at all."

"Why did you marry him?"

I had to realize it was a fair question. "I'll give you the true answer, but you'll either not believe it, or, if you do, you'll consider me a greater idiot than ever."

"Go on." The lawyer was clearly fascinated.

"I married him because he resembled . . . he was so much like somebody else that I thought . . . I don't know what I thought. But that's the reason. Also I didn't see any reason why not to."

"That's probably no more irrational than a lot of people's reasons, if truth were told," the lawyer said. "However, it doesn't seem a very reliable base on which to build a marriage —even without his drinking."

"Now what do we do?"

"Keep on trying to find him, advertising and so on. We could launch a thorough investigation, but it would be expensive, and I'm not sure you want that."

I shook my head. "I wish I could afford it, but I can't."

"Then, we'll just have to keep on searching. Eventually, either we find him so we can serve the papers, or he can be declared legally dead. In which case you will be free."

"Maybe he *will* die," I said, the memories of his blows still sharp.

"Perhaps. In the meantime, get on with your life. Are you in a hurry to marry someone else?"

"Good God no!" The thought was appalling.

"Then there's no great urgency."

"What if he turns up and starts making husbandly demands?"

"In that case you will call the police immediately, and we may induce them to keep tabs on him long enough for you to serve papers."

With that I had to be satisfied.

But the years passed and Simon did not return, nor did any of the lawyer's inquiries bring information about him. He was as gone, I realized, as Joris, and his departure was as maddeningly ambiguous.

But, for a variety of reasons, some of which I didn't want to examine closely, I stayed clear of alliances that were too emotionally entangling or demanding. It was not a trait in myself that I liked or approved of. But when things got beyond a certain point with any of the men with whom I went out, then, without thinking, almost without volition, I backed off. I think what I mostly felt at that point was not free—not because of Simon, but because, in some way, I had never been free.

I worked, I wrote, I traveled. And then one day, one of the magazine editors who had often assigned me articles asked me to do one on Rivercrest, the van Reider mansion up on the Hudson. Only it was no longer known as the van Reider place. An Episcopal church in the city, St. Anselm's, had bought the old robber baron's palace and turned it into a study, conference and retreat center, and renamed it St. Cuthbert's.

"You shouldn't have any trouble," the editor said. "I want you to concentrate on the architecture of the place, and you ought to be able to get it from any local pamphlet or potted history."

But he was wrong about my not having any trouble. I had a lot.

The robber baron's great-grandson did everything in his power to prevent me from examining any of his family documents, even those concerned with nothing but the designing and building of his family home. And while I was struggling with him I was also trying to get the church's permission to examine the house close up and inside. It didn't seem an extraordinary demand, but I was never able to find anyone who could actually give me written consent and a key. Only the rector could do that, I was told, and either he was always away, or the church was between rectors, or he was out. A letter asking for the necessary paper went unanswered.

It was while I was stewing about this, making endless phone calls to anyone I thought could help me, that I began to notice, each morning, a man standing on the corner opposite my apartment house, his eyes fixed on the windows of my building.

For a moment I felt a convulsive spasm of fear. Six years had passed since I had walked out on Simon, and there'd been no sign of him.

Even as I stared at the man, though, I knew it was not Simon. But the fear did not go away. Having come back, it stayed. Morning after morning, after I put the kettle on for coffee, I would go to the window facing the front. The man would be there, his face turned to my window.

You're being paranoid, I told myself, staring out my front windows at the figure in jeans, a leather jacket and a wool cap. Since my apartment was on the top floor of my walk-up brownstone, I couldn't judge his height or the color of his hair, which was covered by his cap. And by the time I had twice run down three flights of stairs and flung open the front door, he had gone. That he had left just as I was tearing down the stairs to confront him could, once, be taken as coincidence. That it happened twice made it less coincidence and more spooky.

The next morning and the morning after he was not back at his station. I decided happily that I had been mistaken, that his business, whatever it was, had nothing to do with me, and turned my attention once again to trying to get permission to see the house that was now called St. Cuthbert's, the former Rivercrest, that had once been the van Reider mansion.

If, of course, it had been designated a landmark, I could have obtained the permit with no trouble. But the church that owned it, St. Anselm's, had been remarkably clever and farsighted in seeing that it had escaped the clutches of the landmark commission, and getting into the grounds and into the house without their permission and help was impossible— as a variety of public and private agencies were busy telling me. Even the church was less openly hostile than Hilary van Reider, who simply replied to my politely worded note with the words "No, you may not see the van Reider documents" scrawled across my civil phrases. So there I was. The van Reider documents were still in Rivercrest, owned now by St. Anselm's and to which I was forbidden access.

I had seen Rivercrest at a distance many times. From the road it reared, a Victorian gothic monstrosity made of gray stone, its long windows topped by ecclesiastical-looking arches. "Prince" van Reider had built it in 1870, lavishing on its size and grandiosity a portion of his huge fortune made in newspapers, shipping and mining. The van Reiders, of course, had been part of the New York scene since the earliest Dutch settlements, and Rivercrest replaced what old drawings showed to be a smaller, prettier, altogether more tasteful house.

The first Jan van Reider had set up a printshop and printed one of Nieuw Amsterdam's earliest newspapers. Ever since, there had been van Reider newspapers—one in New York, one in Chicago and one in San Francisco. They alone would have made the family rich. But with the money from his newspapers, Hilary's great-grandfather branched out into shipping by investing money in a small company owning freighters. After some fierce trading and dubious dealing on the stock exchange, the van Reiders owned the shipping company, and one of the van Reider sons was made president of the company. Fortunately for all concerned, he managed it well and brought more millions to the family trust. Some of those millions went into South African mines, which paid several hundredfold.

But Hilary's grandfather lost three quarters of his fortune in the crash of 1929 and died of rage and chagrin a year later. By the standards of those selling apples on street corners the family was still wealthy, but, in the long run, not wealthy enough to manage and pay for a house like Rivercrest. Hilary's father hung on as long as he could, cutting staff, closing wings. He was a humane, philanthropic man who disapproved of both his father and his grandfather, and brought up—or tried to bring up—both of his sons to be ashamed of the practices of their piratical forebears. He wanted to sell the house and its land above the Hudson to the state as a monument. But that was in the depth of the Depression, and no official felt he could justify the expenditure of millions on a state preserve when people were starving.

When Jan van Reider III was almost in despair about getting rid of the house, St. Anselm's, then New York's wealthiest church, made a surprising offer. It was not as much as Jan van Reider had hoped for, but it was a great deal more than nothing at all. So he sold the house, its contents and the land to the church with the proviso that he and his two sons could occupy one portion of one wing. Jan's second and extremely messy divorce had taken place when Jan IV was sixteen and Hilary eight. When Hilary was in his first year at Yale, both his father and his older brother were killed in an airplane crash. Since then, Hilary had lived mostly in a New York apartment and was a partner in a small law firm. By agreement, he could occupy a suite at Rivercrest, and I assumed he spent some time there, although neither he nor anyone else had actually said so.

When Rivercrest, renamed St. Cuthbert's by the enthusiastic rector of St. Anselm's who had overseen the negotiations, became church property, he and everyone else in the congregation took for granted that it would be a center of spiritual activity, a retreat house, a perfect place for conferences on theological and social matters, a pleasant vacation site for weary clerics and their families. They also hoped it would be an ideal location for groups of underprivileged children during the summers, where youngsters from the asphalt jungle would come to learn about nature's cycles and the relationship between the carton of milk at the supermarket and the friendly cows who were pastured on the hillside.

That experiment lasted only a few years and was discontinued with—I discovered as I tried to track down the history of the place—remarkably little publicity.

In fact, nothing at all was heard of St. Cuthbert's by the public until there was a rumor that the rector before the present one, the Reverend Norbert Shearer, was trying his best to sell St. Cuthbert's for what he considered far more important uses of the money spent on its upkeep and to finance his own romantic vision for feeding the world's poor. The most likely buyer was the guru of a vaguely Eastern cult based in California who wanted to open headquarters on the Atlantic coast and had offered a handsome amount of money. And that's where the matter rested. Mr. Shearer* had been unable to get permission from the vestry and the congregation to sell St. Cuthbert's, and, before he could defeat the opposition, the church and its staff were wracked by a scandal that included a murder and a near murder.

* *A Death at St. Anselm's*

During that period the guru's financial representative made further approaches. But no one at St. Anselm's had the time or inclination to listen.

So St. Cuthbert's, né Rivercrest, sat up above the Hudson, unused and, as far as I could find out—except for the van Reider suite at the end of one of the wings—empty.

"You know, I honestly think I could get into the White House more easily than I could Rivercrest," I said to the editor who had asked me to do the piece.

The Public Eye was a part-news, part-activist magazine that had started out in the sixties but, unlike many similar journals floated in that turbulent period, had survived. This was mostly due to the editor who inherited *The Public Eye* from its founder, Brian Monahan. Before he died, Monahan had rested his mantle on his nephew, Piers Somerville, who combined Monahan's crusading instinct with a superb news sense and had served his apprenticeship at one of the national newsweeklies.

"So it would seem," Piers said now.

We were having lunch at The Grenadier, a self-consciously British eatery, specializing in shepherd's pie, mixed grill and kippers.

Piers pushed away his plate and lit a cigarette. "Bother you?" he asked, as he had often asked before.

I smiled. "As I've frequently said, no. If you want to cultivate lung disease, that's your problem."

"Don't be such a puritan, Kit. Anyway, it's now universally considered dangerous to breathe. I'm surprised you don't arrive with your own oxygen cylinder."

"Moderation in all things. What do you want me to do about St. Cuthbert's, or Rivercrest? I only ask because getting the church's permission to go there has taken a lot longer than I thought it would, and I wasn't sure how keen you were on it."

He blew three smoke rings out of his mouth and then said, "What do you want to do?"

"I'd like to go on with it. While I've been waiting for the church and the rector, I've been spending time in the New York *Times* morgue and the Public Library reading back issues of every journal and magazine published then or since containing anything about Rivercrest and/or St. Cuthbert's. Mostly

they were pieces oohing and aahing over the splendor and opulence and all the money spent in importing curtains and wall coverings from old French châteaux. There were frequent references to the huge staff that kept the place in apple-pie order ready for a van Reider to descend bringing forty guests. The usual social drivel.

"You don't sound impressed."

"I'm not. As a subject for an article for *The Public Eye* it's not up to your usual standard. For one thing, the portrait of the evil robber baron and his palazzo has been done to death. There isn't a well-known name whose marauding ancestors haven't been hung out naked in print in all their greed, oppression and union busting. It's certainly not a news story. More to the point, while you're not above social natter, your pieces usually have bite, and your historical studies only bother with that kind of snob study when there's a strong and contemporary point to make. But," I went on slowly and clearly, "if there's any of that here, you certainly didn't share that knowledge with me."

He didn't say anything. In fact, his good-looking face had all the studied lack of expression that filled me with suspicion. "What's behind this?" I asked.

"Well, we do have a big ad on fin-de-siècle American architecture in the offing. And we're not so rich that we can afford to be cavalier with it. I did just mention to the ad people that the piece on Rivercrest is coming up."

"Come on, Piers," I said. "If anyone has ever been the banner holder for separation of advertising and editorial content, you are. In fact, you once got fired over it. Are you selling out now?"

"No, I'm not selling out, Kit dear, but even with an angel we have to watch our pennies and not spit in advertisers' faces."

"I didn't know you had an angel. Who is he? Or she?"

"Nobody you know."

"How do you know I don't know him/her?"

"You're right. I don't know. But he—it's a he—insisted on total confidentiality. So don't ask me any more about him."

"Okay. But if you have an angel, why are you insisting on this story? It sounds boring beyond words. And I don't believe for one minute your tale about an advertiser for turn-of-the-century Americana. I'm supposed to be a good investigative reporter, right? That's why you hired me, right?"

He sighed and lit another cigarette. "There's a rumor of a rumor of a rumor that more is—or was—going on in that derelict mansion than anyone will talk about. You remember the reporter who committed suicide last year?"

"The one from *The National Investigator?*"

"Yes."

"Since when does *The Public Eye*—right up there with *The Nation* and *Esquire*—concern itself with the goings-on of one of the supermarket tabloids? Their specialty seems to be 'How I made love to a UFO—' "

"—and found God," Piers finished.

"Exactly. That's precisely their level."

"Tabloid or not, a suicide is a suicide. This gal—I've forgotten her name—somehow got into the house. Nobody, including the police, knows how. But she did get in. Or was let in. Anyway, two days later she was found dead of an overdose of some lethal drug in her motel room. There were papers on the bureau in her motel room—old-looking, innocuous letters, or at least they seemed to be letters—maundering on about balls and gowns circa 1902. Van Reider gave evidence that they looked like they came from some family papers, but swore up and down nothing else was missing.

"The letters, by the way, if that's what they were, had no end and no beginning," Piers continued. "There was no salutation, no name, no addressee. And there was no sequence between the pages. Chemical examination of the paper and the ink placed them somewhere at the turn of the century. The writing's almost undecipherable. They may not even be letters."

"Then how did they know they had anything to do with the van Reiders?"

"Because the word 'Rivercrest' occurred once in one of the papers, and there was evidence that the reporter or someone had been in the house: a cigarette of the kind she smoked in an ashtray, a towel used in a bathroom. Van Reider made no bones about admitting that the papers probably did come from his family, but said the last time he saw anything like them they were lying loosely around a desk somewhere in the wing the family still occupied. He said they were of no particular value except to the family."

"I can't think why I didn't read any of this in the papers I've been going through."

"Wasn't the death of the reporter reported? I seem to remember it was."

"Since I was cross-referencing Rivercrest and St. Cuthbert's, there must have been no mention of the house in the report of the girl's death. Odd. How did you hear about it?"

"From somebody who knew the girl. Two other papers have tried to dig loose further information. None has succeeded. You know, it's hard to remember, but in the old days the prominent families would hire public relations people to keep their names *out* of the newspapers. The whole thing's turned around now, but, for whatever reason, the Rivercrest-van Reider-St. Cuthbert's connection to the girl was never printed."

"And that's the real reason you're sending me out to do so-called research on that otherwise boring mansion. Why didn't you tell me the truth in the first place?"

2

There was a long pause, then Piers said, "Oddly enough, because you *are* a good investigative reporter. I wanted you to start from scratch—no preconceived ideas, no suspicions to bore in on. I just didn't envision all these obstacles that the church and van Reider have put in your way."

"You do realize, of course, that if your fears were realized, and there was hanky-panky of some kind by some person or persons unknown, I, too, could end up dead of an overdose in a motel room. Thank you."

"Kit, you have a lot more brains and a hell of a lot more clout than that poor kid who died."

"You sound like you knew her."

Another pause. "I did, once."

"Then, it wasn't just the report of someone who knew the girl whose name you couldn't recall."

"All right, Ms. Prosecutor. I wasn't the only person to know her, by a long shot. I hadn't seen her in a long time, but I did know her once."

"Who was she?"

"Her name was Crystal Mahoney. She was a kid from nowhere who could write a story and was building herself a modest career in the news world when the high life got to her. It was the usual story of pot and coke and liquor, and she went down fast. And being half related to some mafia families didn't help. She did some hooking—high-class kind, with a phone and an answering service—but nevertheless hooking. Then she met a guy she liked and made a huge effort to get out of that and go back into reporting. About the only place that she could find a job was—as you charitably put it—on one of the supermarket tabloids. The police and everybody else with any right has talked to her boss, who swears she simply told him she was on to a good story and was going to chase it. When the police suggested that they search his files, he talked nobly and at length about the sanctity of the First Amendment. So did his lawyers. Whether or not he knew what the story was, he certainly didn't say, and he isn't saying now."

"And you wanted me to go and do a simple piece about this old monstrosity without a word of warning about the girl, the papers, the tabloid and so on."

"Yes. I don't know what she knew, or if she knew anything. But I wanted you to start from scratch."

I got up. "Next time let's have a little more background material. I feel like I've been had."

He stood up and put out his hand. "I'm sorry, Kit. I went about it the wrong way. I can see that now. And I'm not holding anything back—truly I'm not."

I looked at him. "I can't get rid of the feeling that there's something more you know about this. However, at this point, wild ponies wouldn't stop me from going after the story."

This time, I decided, I would go to the church and see if I could wrest something out of them in the way of a key or at least written consent to see the place.

For a moment or two I toyed with the idea of telephoning and making an appointment. But that would mean stating my purpose, and such had been my luck so far, I thought I'd do better simply turning up, so that whoever felt like being uncooperative would have a live body to contend with, not just a voice over the phone.

St. Anselm's had once been the most fashionable church in the city, but although some of its original aristocratic membership still remained, time had moved most of the upper crust farther uptown to the eighties and nineties.

Staring now at the finely carved stone front, I wondered how full the huge church might be on any given Sunday, especially in view of the fact that after the recent scandal another segment of old-time members had possibly transferred to other parishes.

I glanced at my watch. Five minutes past noon. The great doors were open, although in the few moments I had been standing outside on the pavement, no one had gone in.

To go in myself would take effort. For what felt like many years I had made a point of not entering any church, most especially an Episcopal church. The memories were too painful, the anger I felt, still, after all this time, too easily aroused.

My father, who was an Episcopal priest, was the old-fashioned sort, and he had an intense dislike of the emotional, the experiential, the subjective and the personal in worship or the life of the spirit. "What about St. Paul?" my mother, no biblical scholar, nevertheless asked.

"He was a saint. That was different."

"He didn't begin life as a saint," Mother objected. "After all, saints are not that different from the rest of us."

"That's a ridiculous statement," my father said angrily, two red flares of anger on his thin cheeks. "I grant you all the knowledge in the world about horses, their capacities and how to ride them. But please grant me my own area of expert scholarship . . ."

The scene came back to me vividly. We were at lunch in the dining room, Mother and I in riding clothes, a breeze coming through windows, and outside the sound of horses whinneying and the smell of newly cut grass.

Standing on the Park Avenue sidewalk, I was back in Virginia. And then, swift on that memory came another, this time of Joris, and I felt the old grief . . .

This is getting me nowhere, I said to myself, and walked briskly to the corner and along the length of the block to the parish house.

Walking through the huge double door on Lexington Avenue, I went up the short flight of steps to the information desk just beyond.

After I had explained to the elderly receptionist why I wanted to see the rector, she said, "I'm terribly sorry, he's away at a conference in England and won't be back until next month. Would anyone else do?"

"From what I can gather, only the rector can give permission for me to go up to your St. Cuthbert's building in Dutchess County." I realized I sounded hostile, but I could have kicked myself for not, after all, telephoning.

"You really should have phoned," the lady murmured, adding to my self-criticism, and therefore my ill temper.

"I tried phoning several times in the last weeks, but with all the goings-on here no one would even talk to me."

"We've certainly been through our dark night of the soul," the woman said.

"I don't think murder and mayhem were exactly what St. John of the Cross had in mind when he coined that phrase."

The cool blue eyes looked at me. "Is there anything I can do for you now?"

"Yes, find me someone who can give me written permission to go up to that mansion, so that I won't be arrested for breaking and entering. I gather that no one is there, so that if I did get in it would be considered a felony."

The woman and I stared at one another. Then she pushed a button on her elaborate phone system. After a minute she said into the receiver, "There's a . . . young woman here—" She paused as I pushed my card at her. She picked it up and read, "A Ms. Catherine Maitland. She wants permission to go up to St. Cuthbert's to do an article on the place." Pause. "I told her the rector was away, but she says she wants to speak to somebody else." Pause. "All right."

She turned to me. "Mrs. Aldington says you can go up to her office."

"Who is Mrs. Aldington?" I wasn't about to be pushed off on another, slightly more senior, flunky.

"The Reverend Claire Aldington is an assistant rector."

"Oh. All right. Where's her office?"

"You can take the elevator and then walk down the hall to your right, or you can go up the stairs there. Her name is on the door."

I took the stairs, and when I got to the top went on walking in the general direction the receptionist had indicated. Eventually I got to the door, and there, in white letters on a black plaque was indeed her name: Rev. Claire Aldington. I had been out of the city when all the brouhaha regarding the church scandal broke, but I did vaguely recall seeing her name in some account of the events.

"Come in," she called as I knocked on her door. I turned the knob and opened the door.

A young woman in clerical collar, black front and gray suit got up from behind the desk and came forward. "I'm Claire Aldington," she said. "Won't you sit down?" And she indicated a chair and sofa in front of her windows.

She was shorter than I, and slight, with dark red hair and hazel eyes. I knew, of course, that for several years women had been ordained in the Episcopal Church. I had seen their pictures in the newspapers and occasionally on television. I had never met one in the flesh, and was surprised at my faint sense of shock. My next thought was a certain grim satisfaction at how much my father would have hated the idea.

"Something tells me you've never before encountered a woman priest," Mrs. Aldington said pleasantly as we both sat down.

"I'm sorry it showed. It's just that I've never actually met one before, although I think it's high time the church climbed out of its stuffiness."

"So do most of us. Tell me why you want to see St. Cuthbert's."

"I've been assigned to do an article about it for *The Public Eye.*"

"Why?" She frowned for a moment. "I've read the magazine. I wouldn't have thought a piece about one of the old robber-baron mansions would be of interest to its readers. The magazine's more political, isn't it?"

"Yes. Usually. But sometimes they do something off the beaten path, like this story."

It sounded lame, and I, of all people, should have realized just how weak it was. After all, that was what had made me pin Piers to the wall. On the other hand, I found the church's reluctance to let me go into the mansion profoundly fishy.

"Why is the church so reluctant to give me permission? What is so private about the place? From what I've heard, St. Anselm's is fairly anxious to sell what amounts to an expensive white elephant, and my article may help to find an interested buyer."

"It may. On the other hand, we have an obligation to the van Reiders, who, by agreement, still occupy part of one wing, and I or the rector or anyone else in charge is answerable to the vestry about who gets in there and who doesn't."

And there we sat, neither of us (I was suddenly convinced) being entirely candid. "I truly have no intention of writing anything derogatory about the house itself, the church, or any future owners, and in view of that I find the church's foot-dragging about giving me a key and/or permission to go there a little puzzling."

"Ms. Maitland, do you swear to me that architecture and period decorative art are the only things you're interested in?"

They weren't, of course. I discovered that Mrs. Aldington had unnervingly penetrating eyes. "No," I heard myself say, to my own surprise.

She grinned, looking younger and less clerical. "Okay. So what's the real reason?"

I took a deep breath and told her about the reporter from *The National Investigator.*

"And the police seem to feel that she was in St. Cuthbert's?"

"Yes. There were the pages or letters that had been in a drawer in the private wing, and there was a cigarette stub that seemed to be the same kind she smoked and a towel had been used in one of the bathrooms. Not iron evidence, but suggestive."

There was a pause. Then Mrs. Aldington said, "What was the reporter's name?"

"Crystal Mahoney." I knew from the way she looked up suddenly that the name had some meaning for her. "Do you know her, or know of her?"

"Yes. She was once a client of mine."

"A client?"

She nodded. "I'm an ordained priest, but my main area is counseling."

"You mean she was a member of this church?" It seemed so unlikely as to be dazzling.

Mrs. Aldington smiled. "Our parish is a lot more mixed than it was even ten years ago, let alone twenty or thirty. Many of our members are from the outreach program, which brings in all groups and economic levels. However, in answer to your question, Crystal Mahoney was not, strictly speaking, a member of the parish, but she was part of the community outreach program with which we work, and she did come to me for counseling for a while."

"Then you must have been aware that she died of an overdose of some lethal substance in a motel room not far from St. Cuthbert's."

"Yes. The police asked me about her. They wanted to know if she was, as they put it, 'the suicidal type.' "

"Was she?"

Mrs. Aldington looked at me for a moment. I felt in her a slight withdrawal. "You know, if members of our staff have been less than totally cooperative, it could be because we've had more than our share of attention from the press and have learned to be leery of reporters. I dislike the descriptive 'the suicidal type.' A policeman once asked me if somebody was the kind of person who could commit murder. And I gave him the answer I'm about to give you. Given certain circumstances, almost all of us could be either violent or suicidal. But if you mean was Crystal Mahoney a depressive with a list of failed suicide attempts behind her, then the answer is no."

"Then you think it was murder?"

"That's for the police to answer. I hadn't seen Crystal in more than two years. She was, as I'm sure you know because it was in the papers, part of one of our drug rehabilitation programs. And she was a successful graduate. She had a hard time finding a job on a newspaper after that, but I'd heard she'd succeeded in landing something on some scandal sheet, which is certainly not like being on the New York *Times*, but she had to begin somewhere." She sighed.

"Did she stay in touch with you?"

"No. She wasn't the world's most attentive client. She did get herself clean, off both drugs and alcohol, which is certainly to her credit, but she wasn't too keen on therapy."

"Do you think she committed suicide?"

"Again, that's for the police to find out." She hesitated. "If she went back to drugging, then it could have easily been an accident. God knows, we know enough figures in the entertainment world who seem to have gone that way. But I have no idea what the police may have found when they went digging around. They haven't been back since that original question."

There was another pause as Mrs. Aldington and I sat silent, she behind her desk, her hands folded, I staring out the window while I tried to find a place to begin a probe. Well, I thought, first things first.

"Will you give me a note of written consent to go up to St. Cuthbert's, and a key to get in?"

There was a moment's hesitation, then Mrs. Aldington said, "All right. I'll type one now."

She turned to a typing table beside her desk, inserted a sheet of notepaper bearing the church's letterhead and typed for a moment or two. Then she pulled the paper out and signed her name at the bottom of the paragraph.

"Okay," she said. "This should prevent you from getting copped for breaking and entering. Let me run this off on the copier so that we have a record too." She was about to leave the office when she looked back. "You might as well come along. I have to get a key from the rector's office, and the copier is in his secretary's room."

Mrs. Aldington walked ahead of me down the long hall, turned left and went into a room opening off the right. Straight ahead was what I could see was part of a much larger office. Visible were a leather sofa and a portrait of a man in turn-of-the-century clerical garb. His face could only be described by even the most charitable as "God-fearing."

"Hello, Sally," Mrs. Aldington said as she entered the smaller room ahead of me. "Can I use your copier?" She glanced at me. "This is Ms. Maitland. She wants the key to St. Cuthbert's. I've written out permission and would like to run it off." She waved the sheet of paper.

Sitting behind a large desk was a woman of around forty with gray-black hair pulled into a neat knot at the back. The effect was chic rather than drab, due, most likely, to the woman's finely arched cheekbones.

"I take it you feel sure Douglas would approve," the woman said. Douglas, I remembered, was the Reverend Douglas Bartlett, rector of St. Anselm's. Was there a tinge—more than a tinge—of reproof in the woman's cool voice?

"I see no reason why he wouldn't," Mrs. Aldington replied. "It's not as though we'd used St. Cuthbert's for the past several years."

"Keeping it up was simply too expensive," Ms. Hepburn said. "We had better uses for our money."

There was a silence while Mrs. Aldington fed her consent form into the copier. I had a feeling of, if not hostility, at least tension between the two women.

"Here," Mrs. Aldington said, handing one of the two copies of her letter of consent to Ms. Hepburn. "You'd better have one of these for your files. Now, can we have the key to St. Cuthbert's?"

"I'll get it." Ms. Hepburn rose. "It's in the rector's office."

While she was gone I said, "Ms. Hepburn doesn't seem too happy about my going up there."

Mrs. Aldington didn't say anything for a moment. Then, "To some extent I'm going out on a limb in giving you this consent, because the whole subject of St. Cuthbert's is a rather sore one. The previous rector put it on the market, as you know, and as you also probably know, in the teeth of considerable church opposition. The only really good offer we had was this guru from California, and then when the recent scandal blew up, everybody just wanted to forget about the whole thing. My concern is what you told me—about a possible connection with Crystal Mahoney. I hope that whatever the connection was, it had nothing whatsoever to do with Crystal's death. The short squib in the paper about Crystal never mentioned St. Cuthbert's, and, until this morning, I had no idea there *was* a connection. Until that white elephant is sold, it's ours and therefore comes under the heading of our responsibility. Which is why I have given you the permission." She paused. "I wonder what's keeping Sally." She got up and left the room.

I sat there, staring at the oak-paneled walls, the wall-to-wall dark red carpet, the view across the roofs of the low Lexington Avenue buildings opposite. And then I heard the two women's voices.

"It's always been here, since before Norbert's time. The rector before him kept it in that particular slot in that particular drawer." That was Ms. Hepburn.

"Are there any other keys?" Mrs. Aldington asked.

"The custodian who kept an eye on the place has one, as does his wife, who does whatever housekeeping has been done for the past few years. As far as I know, those are the only other keys."

The two women came back.

"I'm afraid the consent Mrs. Aldington gave you is not going to be worth anything without a key to get into the building. And the one we've always had has been mislaid," Ms. Hepburn said, not, I thought, without satisfaction.

"Or stolen," Mrs. Aldington added in a matter-of-fact voice.

"Oh, come now, who on earth would want to steal a key to St. Cuthbert's? There's nothing there to attract anybody."

"I wouldn't say that, Sally. There's quite a lot there—furniture, paintings, expensive knickknacks, to say nothing of whatever valuables the van Reiders have kept there."

"Well of course I realize that. I mean, who on earth here would steal the key?"

"Sally, if something is missing, there are two explanations: one is that the last person who used it failed to put it back in the right place, which would be called misplacing it. The other is that it's been stolen. There isn't the slightest possibility, is there, that someone who might have borrowed it could have slipped it in one of your desk drawers if the rector's office was locked, is there?"

"Are you suggesting that I may have been the one to misplace it—or steal it?"

Ms. Hepburn radiated anger. She might, of course, be paranoid, I thought, watching the scene with interest. But I was
more inclined to believe my earlier impression that all this was
simply a manifestation of friction between the two women.

Mrs. Aldington took a deep breath. "You must be . . . well
. . . nuts, to think such an idea would occur to me. You know
as well as I do that when Doug's office is locked people stick
things in your drawers rather than leaving them about on top
of your desk. You've told me so yourself."

The bright red spots under Ms. Hepburn's admirable cheekbones faded. "I'm sorry, Claire," she said stiffly. "It's just . . .
just that this kind of thing has never happened to me before.
And the whole last year has been upsetting."

"Of course." Mrs. Aldington's eyes were guarded but kind.
"Do you think we could look, anyway? Just in case somebody
did slip the key in one of your drawers."

Ms. Hepburn sat down and yanked open her top left hand
drawer. She was meticulously neat. There were two keys in a
small slot in the front of her drawer.

"This one," she said, holding up one of the keys, "is to the
rector's office. And this," she held up the other, "is to the safe
in the wall over there behind the painting." She opened all her
drawers, wide, so that neither Mrs. Aldington nor I could fail
to see everything in them. "Now," she said, "I'll check the safe,
just in case."

But there were no keys in the safe.

"Can you remember if anyone mentioned anything about
going up to St. Cuthbert's recently? I mean anyone from the
church staff."

"No. Or I would have mentioned it right away."

"I see. Well, thank you for looking. Sorry to have bothered
you. Ms. Maitland, let's go to my office. I seem to remember
you left your coat there.

"Well," Mrs. Aldington said as she handed me my coat from
the back of the chair in her office, "good luck about getting
into St. Cuthbert's. The custodian Sally was talking about is
named Krause. He and his wife live in a dilapidated farmhouse
on the road to St. Cuthbert's and you certainly have my per-

mission to see if you can get a key out of them. In fact—do you have my letter there?"

I handed her back her consent. She inserted it in her typewriter, wrote a line or two, typed her name underneath again and then initialed the P.S.

"Strictly speaking, I should go and stick this in the copier, too. But I'm just going to gamble that we won't need proof that I told Krause to let you have his, or his wife's, key. Here." And she handed me back the letter. Beneath her first signature she had typed: "Mr. Krause, we haven't been able to find the St. Cuthbert key here at the church. I know you and Mrs. Krause each has one. Would you please lend one of your keys to Ms. Maitland, who will return it to you when she has seen the main building."

"Thanks," I said.

"Please note this is trusting you not to run off and have a copy of the key made."

"I thank you for your confidence. No, I wouldn't do that. I might raise all kinds of public hell if I thought you were interfering in the public's right to know, but illegal copying of keys is not, I think, part of that."

"I'm glad to know it. Let me know if you need any help. By the way, you'd better leave me your address and phone number."

"Just in case I run off with one of the art treasures at St. Cuthbert's?" I said, scribbling them on a piece of paper from my notebook. "Here." I handed it to her.

She grinned. "Thanks."

I could see the fake turrets of St. Cuthbert's a good twenty minutes before I arrived there. Half hidden from me by trees lining the road, and two miles away across the valley, their pointed roofs shone in the slight drizzle. Obviously, whatever van Reider built it, he thought it a thing of beauty, an architectural treasure. Halfheartedly I tried to allow for the difference in era making for difference in taste, but didn't succeed in convincing myself. Anybody who spent all the money it took to create such a huge monstrosity was surely lacking not only in taste, but in any other values. But then, I admitted to myself, I was prejudiced against the rich.

Growing up, I had been surrounded by them, by their newly built or renovated stables, their splendid stock, their old houses with new bathrooms.

"Nouveaux riches," my father had said, forgetting his Christian charity.

"Not entirely," Mother countered. "There are a few of the old families who've simply managed to hang onto their money —good luck to them."

"It's not your fault that you haven't," my father said loyally.

Our house, "Percy's Walk," had come down in Mother's family from a Percy Moorman who had come over to Virginia in the eighteenth century. The Moormans were good at anything to do with horses: they could ride, hunt, train and show. They were not good at profitable pursuits, and what little money had been brought into the family through careful marriages and experiments in tobacco growing, had dwindled to a trickle.

And Father was right. Our section of Virginia had become a mecca for the possessors of industrial fortunes who had wanted to acquire squirarchies. Most of them were extremely nice and very helpful, always ready to lend a hand or one of their stablemen. But the fact remained that while our house was old and beautiful, it was also in an advanced state of disrepair, the plumbing was anything but up to date, and the kitchen was built for a team of servants, not one overworked housewife. Not that Mother cared very much. Mother loved me, the horses, the house and Father, in that order.

My father had come as rector to the small local Episcopal church. He was a widower with a son and badly needed a wife. Why Mother married him I was never quite sure. He had no money of his own. Mother was loyal and affectionate, but even as a small child I knew she was not in love with him. As time passed he withdrew into his books, where he could indulge his endless passion for family genealogies and the writings of seventeenth-century Church of England clerics. After his first stroke when I was twelve, he retired from the priesthood and simply lived at home. Our relationship contained almost equal amounts of love and dislike. He was a handsome man, fastidious in his tastes. More than anything in the world I wanted his love and approval, gifts he conferred on only one person, his son, Joris. I think he thought of me in some way as a "mistake," a sport, a maverick, a deviant.

"You have common tastes," he once told me, when I became best friends with Cindy Repton, a daughter of the most arriviste of the nouveaux riches. Despite her family's ambition for her, she remained terrified of horses. We'd hide in the attic and she would tell me her favorite dirty stories, as passed on to her by her brother. My other best friend was the son of one of the stablemen.

"Here you are in the heart of some of the best society in the country," my father said from time to time, forgetting that he had just described them all as arrivistes, "and who do you pick as your particular friends? The son of a stable boy and the common child of a common family . . ."

"I think Christians stink," I once said to my mother.

"You mustn't . . ." I could have almost finished the sentence for her, You mustn't judge other Christians and churchgoers by your father. But her voice stopped, because there was no way she could have finished that sentence without being disloyal to my father. And disloyalty to anyone or any institution she believed in was, to her, unthinkable. "And don't jump so quickly to judgment. It's a bad habit you have." Then she kissed the top of my head and sent me out to exercise Buttercup . . . In those days I loved Joris, Mother and Buttercup, in that order.

And why was I thinking about that now? I wondered, staring through the mist across the gray-green valley seen through the filter of the roadside trees now bare of all but the last autumn leaves. The answer seemed to be the horses I had seen grazing in the various paddocks lining the road and belonging, most likely, to the horse farms whose signs I had noted on the way here.

I turned left off the main road, as the instructions had said, and then left again onto a narrow road, really little more than a track. This ended at pretentious-looking gates with heraldic creatures holding up shields on top of the gateposts. Now rust covered most of the iron and almost all of the lock. The two gates weren't closed, in fact. The sides hardly met. But I had to drag one of them back through overgrown grass to be able to get the car in.

Suddenly the guru—beard, beads and all—looked much better to me. Whoever and whatever he was, he'd do something about this collection of rust and metal—preferably remove them altogether.

After I was through the gate I drove for another mile and a half to the bottom of the valley, passed the farmhouse on the way up and stopped. I had tried to call Krause before I left New York, but repeated calls got no answer whatsoever. I knew it was foolish to come up without having reached him, but I was tired of waiting around. Somehow I would find him—or his wife—and get one of them to give me a key.

It was therefore something of a shock to find no answer to my rings on the farmhouse's doorbell. In fact, with the blinds drawn, the place had an empty feeling.

"Mr. Krause," I called out. When there was no response, I pounded on the door and called louder. Nothing. Silence. I waited a moment—the Krauses might be out in the back somewhere—then knocked again. This time all I heard was the deep-voiced barking of a dog, a dog that was coming nearer, quite rapidly, around one side of the gray stone house. I turned. I had one glimpse of a brownish-gray wolf of a dog, then I was on the ground, trying with my arm to keep the savage teeth away from my face.

"Akela! Down!"

The teeth that had been closing on my arm through, luckily, a sweater, a suit jacket and a raincoat, suddenly relaxed. The dog scampered away towards a tall man in a raincoat and rain hat, carrying a cane.

I got up feeling stunned, bruised, badly frightened and furious. "You have no right on earth to let that dog loose," I said angrily, brushing off my arm. "I could sue you for damages for this."

"How?" he asked in an even voice. "There's a sign on the

gates saying, Private Property, Keep Out. Plus another, saying, Beware Savage Dog. You were well warned."

"There was no sign on the gates I've just come through."

"Then they must have fallen down. Or been knocked down by vandals. Are you hurt?"

"I don't even know."

"Well, find out, so if you are, I can tell you who to sue."

I stared at the man. Logically, since this was the farmhouse occupied by the farmer, Krause, then this should be Krause. But I was very sure it wasn't. I did some rapid eliminating and came up with a name.

"Hilary van Reider, I suppose."

"You suppose right. What are you doing here?"

"I'm trying to get the key to the house from the custodian."

"I haven't seen him or his wife for some time. I came here to see them myself. They're supposed to be caretakers. The house—the main part—hasn't been cleaned since I don't know when. It's none of my business since it's no longer mine, but the church should certainly be informed."

I thought of Claire. "Yes, they should. Mrs. Aldington expected them to be here. In fact, I tried to phone them. I wonder what happened to them. The place looks deserted."

"Probably just took off. Typical! Nobody today has any sense of responsibility."

I examined the indentations in my raincoat. If it were torn, I'd be even angrier than I was now. Fortunately, the material was not damaged. Nevertheless I said, "Do you always set your guard dog on people?"

"Not when they have any business being here. But with the Krauses gone and the house falling to pieces and nobody giving a damn, to say nothing of all the noises around, it's just as well to be careful."

"What noises?"

"How the hell should I know what they are? I merely hear them. For all I know, people could be stealing the paintings and the silver to their hearts' content. No longer anything to do with me."

With the laudable object of getting as much information as I could out of this man, I knew I should be tactful. But my arm still hurt.

"I thought you just criticized people for not taking responsibility. It appears you don't either."

"As I've said before, it's private property—not that that stops any busybody from trying to get in."

"I have permission to go into it."

He paused. "What's your interest in the house?"

I hesitated, reluctant, for a moment, to answer. Then, "I want to do an article on it."

His face, which had been starting to relax, stiffened. "Not if I can help it."

Several comments, none of them polite, rose to my mind. Finally I said as pleasantly as I could, "I'd like to remind you that this property belongs to St. Anselm's Church. And as I told you before, I have permission—" I pulled the paper out of my coat pocket—"*their* permission to look over this monstrosity."

"It is still, and by contract with that church, my home, albeit one small area of it. And will remain so as long as I can manage to prevent them from selling the place to that outfit of crazies."

"You can't, because you don't own it."

"Perhaps not. But I can at least hold up the proceedings on the grounds that a suite of rooms has been granted to me and my family in perpetuity, and that the church cannot sell those rooms without securing my family's use of said rooms. I don't know why I'm bothering to explain all this to you."

"Because I have every intention of getting in that mansion with or without your aid. I'll grant that you can make it hard for me to examine your part of the house, but I have been given permission to look over the main part of the house and I will."

"Have you decided yet whether you're going to sue me?" he said sarcastically. "Shall I put you in touch with my lawyers?"

I hesitated, brushing off my coat and pants legs. Then I straightened. "I definitely will not if you'll just let me see your family documents—at least all the ones concerning the house." It was only a trial balloon. The documents I was interested in were those from which came the pages found in Crystal Mahoney's motel room. But I didn't want to go into that without being a lot surer of van Reider's attitude and possible involvement in Crystal's death.

"You must be demented," he said in the same even voice, "to think I'd show family papers to any prying journalist who's out to make a name for herself by digging up old stories and destroying a family's privacy. There's some newspaperwoman . . ." He frowned suddenly. "I wonder," he said. "Your name wouldn't be—er—Catherine Maitland, by any chance?"

"Yes, by some chance, it would be my name. I've written you at least two pleasant and polite notes asking to see your part of St. Cuthbert's, and have received for my pains nothing but your ill-mannered refusal scrawled across my request."

"A variety of historians with unimpeachable credentials have written asking to see various documents relating to family affairs, and I have refused them. Why on earth would I give my permission to someone who probably writes for some near-comic-book of a so-called newspaper."

I'd been brushing the remaining grass from my pants leg, but at this, abruptly, I straightened.

"I think you have me confused with Crystal Mahoney—the late Crystal Mahoney, who was indeed from a gossip tabloid, and who died in a motel room with some of your family papers scattered around the bureau there."

There was a longish silence while we eyed one another.

Then he said, "As I told the police, those were completely inconsequential pages from a journal that must have been lying in a drawer in one of the pieces of furniture in Rivercrest." He paused. His face, narrow and pale anyway, seemed drawn. "I have never found the press—even the so-called respectable press—to have the slightest conscience about pawing through other people's drawers, desks, closets and stealing whatever they think will sell their wretched sheets."

"You should move to Russia," I said pleasantly. "The press there is completely controlled."

"There's a vast difference between wanting a controlled press—which I don't, and never have—and a responsible one, something we seem to have lost."

"You know," I said, still amiable, "anyone, not just someone from the hated press, would think you had something to hide either about your family or about Crystal Mahoney's death. If those pages were unreadable, or innocuous, why are you so angry about the whole thing? You're sounding more like a guilty man than anyone I've heard in a long time."

"Guilty of what?" His eyes were like two dark holes.

I reminded myself that I should not antagonize this man. "Let's start over. As far as I'm concerned, you're not guilty of anything. But I don't understand why you're so resistant. A girl dies in a motel room. Scattered around are pages from some portion of the van Reider documents. Isn't it natural that people—the police, the press—would want to know the connection, if any?"

"It was not in the paper that she had papers belonging to my family. How did you find out?"

"Because I was told by my editor, who knew the girl, and who probably found it out from the police. And before you blow your stack about that, a crime was committed, and unless it hinders the investigation, such matters are for public record."

Akela, the dog, looking remarkably peaceful, trotted back and rubbed his nose against van Reider's hand. Somewhat to my surprise, van Reider leaned down and patted him. It was a surprisingly gentle gesture in such a hostile man. As for Akela, his tail now waving back and forth, it was hard to believe he was the same savage creature that had had me on the ground.

"Yes," van Reider said finally. "It is a matter of public record that she had papers from my family scattered around. I was rejoicing that it had somehow missed the newspapers and television news, but I can see that I was congratulating myself too soon." The strange part was, he no longer sounded hostile or angry. He sounded resigned . . . even defeated.

"Could you tell me what was in those papers?" I asked.

"No."

"Do you mean no you can't, or no you won't?"

"I don't think I'll answer that, either."

"Then, I'll have to find out some other way." I waited to see if he would respond. When he didn't, I said, "Wouldn't it be better if you told me yourself?"

I had really meant that as a friendly inquiry, although even as I spoke, I could see how it could be taken as threatening. Which it was.

He straightened. "A subtle form of blackmail? I tell you what you want to know, and then you'll be easy on me and the van Reiders? If not—well, Ms. Maitland, as everyone knows, any old and formerly rich family is now fair game. I can't stop you going to the house. But I don't have to help you in your demolition job. Now if you'll excuse me."

He limped off, Akela in tow, and disappeared behind some trees. In a few seconds I heard a car start up and speed away. I felt angry, frustrated—and determined. I was going to find out what was in those family papers, I decided, if it took an act of Congress to enable me to do it. With this admirable purpose, I got back in the car and drove slowly along the tree-lined meandering path that led to the house. The path proved longer than I had imagined. In fact, with twists and turns it covered several miles. The house itself remained hidden by the trees and woods around the path. Then, abruptly, with no preparation, the path burst through the woods and out onto what must once have been a giant lawn. Now it looked like an overgrown field.

There was a small folly to the left, round, its clapboard sides sagging, its little wooden stair crooked. Great, shapeless yew trees, one on each side of the drive, bespoke a one-time ambition to adopt the characteristics of an English manor.

The house itself was made of stone. In the center was an enormous door with gothic-type arches above it. On either side of the door were stone posts that rose over the general roof of the house to turrets, seen more on French châteaux than English manors. The whole effect was rather that of a keep or gatehouse. Beyond this center portion on each side spread wings, rising three stories, topped off by gabled attic windows. Below, each window was surmounted by a rather forbidding gothic arch, like an eyebrow. On the outside, the house did not seem in poor repair, but there was a hollow look to the windows where one might expect to see curtains.

I parked the car and got out. Only when I was at the front door did it occur to me that in the heat of the quarrel with van

Reider, I had forgotten that to get into the house I needed a key.

"Hell and damnation," I said aloud, and simply out of reflex action, turned the huge door knob and pushed.

The door opened.

3

Having effortlessly entered, I stood there for a moment, feeling foolish—especially when I remembered my battle with van Reider. It was, in fact, so ludicrous, that I laughed, and the sound seemed to echo in the tall, vaulted hallway that ran the width of the house. At the opposite end was another door, and beyond that, visible through the glass panels of the door, more trees, overgrown lawn and, rimming the edge, some water—most probably a pond, I thought.

Still amused by my easy entry, I glanced over my shoulder to see if van Reider and his faithful hound were anywhere in sight. Even the irascible Mr. van Reider, I thought, might be amused by the open front door. But there was no one in sight, so I closed the door and stood staring around me.

The hall was wide and paneled in dark wood. On each side were three portraits. Underneath the center portrait on one side was a chest, on the other, a table with its legs curved back onto a pedestal. On the floor were two oriental carpets.

Half an hour later I had been through most of the downstairs rooms: two huge drawing rooms, an even larger dining room, a small dining room, two studies sandwiched between larger rooms, and a library. The inside of the house was—or would have been—far more attractive than the outside, probably because much of the furniture came from an older, more graceful era than the building itself. But the effect was marred because, as van Reider had said, the house's interior had been shamefully neglected. Dust, dirt and debris lay everywhere. The large pieces of furniture had been dust-sheeted. But the dust sheets themselves were covered and pocketed with dirt. Curiously, considering how long the church had owned and used it, there seemed very little evidence of church meetings, conferences or study groups. Here and there I saw dust-covered pamphlets, usually on the church's role in society, but they were an aberration—a bit of reading material brought in after church meetings, conferences or seminars. The van Reider presence seemed stronger and more enduring. This was undoubtedly due to more family paintings in almost every room: a few older than those in the main hall, most of more recent vintage.

Rivercrest was not, I found myself thinking, a happy house. Having allowed that thought to enter my mind, I found it, quite suddenly, overwhelming. Only once in the past had a conviction gripped me in quite the same way: Twelve years before, I had waked up in the middle of the night, frightened and desolate, filled with an overpowering sense of something terrible about to happen. The following day I heard that my parents had died the night before in the fire that destroyed their home.

Now I stared around the small study I had come into from the drawing room behind me. There was nothing alarming about the study, perhaps because none of its contents had been dust-sheeted. And it was considerably cleaner. The room contained a desk and chair and love seat opposite. There was also, in one corner, an armchair with a small table beside it. Shelves of books rose almost to the ceiling, always for me a comforting sight. Yet even here I was filled with a depression I could not account for and which, for me, was rare.

"Come off it, Kit!" I said aloud to myself. Nevertheless, somewhere, in some offbeat book, I had read that extreme emotions, both good and bad, were forms of psychic energy and as such could impregnate the walls of rooms. And that there were, in fact, machines of some kind that could take those imprints or vibrations from the walls and interpret them.

I knew that my grandmother, my mother's mother, had been a clairvoyant, a "gift" that had brought her considerable unhappiness. I also knew that my father had scorned anything to do with the psychic and forbade it to be mentioned in his presence. "Superstitious rubbish" was his name for it.

I was finding it hard to breathe, so I opened the study door opposite the one I had entered by, and found myself in the library.

It was, without question, the most cheerful room in the house, partly, no doubt, because it contained so many books—tiers of them, rising to the ceiling. And because it had most obviously been dusted fairly recently.

Magazines covered one end of a center table. There was a flat-topped desk and a fireplace. Thinking to find, now, some reminder of the church's ownership, I glanced at the journals. There were several issues of a scholarly history magazine, two or three old copies of the London *Times Literary Supplement*, some American literary journals and various other magazines, all considered important in one field or another. There was nothing whatsoever that seemed specifically churchly or theological.

Strange, I thought. This library could belong to any wealthy, literate American. Here the name Rivercrest suited its ambiance perfectly. The name St. Cuthbert's had no relevance at all.

On to the next room, I told myself. I had thought the library would be in the end of its wing, but there was a small door at the other end which I did not think led outside.

I crossed the carpet and turned the knob, looking in. This was plainly one of the studies that seemed to serve as a buffer between larger rooms. The room itself appeared to be an extension of the library. There were bookshelves to the ceiling and a library ladder resting on rollers and suspended from the top shelf on casters. A small spiral staircase in the near corner led up (I assumed) to another floor. Half the room was hidden by the door, so I stepped all the way in, expecting to see a chair and table of some kind.

They were there, but I paid them scant attention, because also there, lying in the middle of the floor, was a man. He was lying on his side, one arm flung out. The side of his face was covered with blood.

"My God!" I said aloud. The words, loud in the small room, seemed to mock the man's stillness. Fighting revulsion, I knelt down on one knee beside him, and became aware of and furious with my own inexperience. Putting a hand inside his denim jacket, I felt his chest. There was no movement, but for all I knew that meant nothing. Quickly I put my fingers under his jaw where I did know there was a pulse. There was no movement there, either. Finally, I felt for the pulse in his wrist: again, nothing. Gingerly, gently, I pushed him and he flopped over on his back. Then I put my ear to his chest. There was no sound and no vibration. When I straightened, I saw one eye, open and staring. The other was caked in blood. The sight of it made me shudder.

"He's dead," I said aloud. And at that, the reality of it hit me. He was indeed dead.

Slowly I stood up, but remained where I was, looking down at the man. Then I took a deep breath. You're a reporter, I told myself, not a Victorian maiden. Now *think!* Staring down at the blood-clotted eye was not as easy as I knew I would have pretended it to be if I were giving counsel to someone else, or writing an article on crime.

Finally the obvious occurred to me. The police had to be called. At once. I looked around. A phone was on the end table beside the chair. I picked up the receiver and waited for some kind of a dial tone. There was none. In fact, there was no sound at all. Then I jiggled the bar on which the receiver rested. The line was dead.

I put down the phone. It was at that moment that I heard the sound of a car.

The study faced the back, and the sound of the car, coming from the library next door, seemed to emanate from the front. I rushed into the library and over to the front window, and caught sight of the back end of a car—not much more than its bumper—disappearing among the trees of the woods lining the drive.

Where in God's name did that come from? I wondered. It was certainly nowhere in sight when I drove up to the front of the house. However, a narrower version of the front drive led around both ends of the house, so the car could have come around from the back and then speeded up more noisily in the front. Quickly I ran to the library's back windows, opened one of them and leaned out. I saw then, cleverly concealed against the far end of the building so that it looked like part of the left wing, a structure that could have been, among many other things, a garage.

Walking back to the middle of the room, I became aware of other disquieting facts. I had assumed I was alone in the house, an assumption that didn't hold up under examination. I knew little about bodies, but this one was warm to the touch, and not stiff, which would argue that he had been killed in the very recent past. And if that were the case, I had not only not been alone in the house, I had been sharing it with a murderer who had obviously killed his wretched victim shortly before I started meandering through the various rooms picking up impressions. No wonder the house has bad vibrations, I thought grimly.

And where was the murderer now? Still in the house? It was not a reassuring thought. I stood there, as though trying to read a message in the silence around me as to whether or not I was alone. Then I remembered the car speeding into the trees before I could see it properly. Was that the murderer? It seemed likely. And in addition to all this, the phones in the house appeared to have been disconnected, so that I was unable to reach the police or, for that matter, any help.

For a moment I stood there, in the library, immobilized by various fears that seemed to come at me like guided missiles: if whoever it was who had left in the car was not the murderer, then the murderer might still be here . . . or murderers. Turning, I looked at the opposite end of the library, the direction from which I had come. Beyond it, I knew, was another study, then another drawing room, then the dining room, then another small room . . . Nor had I noticed any garden or french door that led to the outside. Which meant that to leave, I would have to get through all those rooms to reach the front door and my car . . . *my car.* I could feel my insides freeze. Was it still parked on the side of the driveway? I hadn't noticed when I was trying to spot the car driving out . . .

Quickly I ran back to the front window. Yes, thank God, my car was still there, and my fingers closed comfortingly on the keys in my raincoat pocket.

For a moment, I stood there hardly breathing. I was listening. Were there other slight noises that I had ignored but that meant others were in the house, on another floor?

It was at that point I remembered Hilary van Reider.

Of course, I thought, he *lives* here—certainly part of the time. He had stalked away from me down at the Krauses' cottage, and then I had heard him get into a car. There could be a short cut I didn't know about and he could have got here ahead of me, in time to commit the murder.

Would van Reider have been in the car I'd just heard? More to the point, would he have been the killer of that man lying in the study? Where was he now?

At that moment I nearly jumped out of my skin, because the telephone resting on the library desk rang. I plunged across the room with my arm out, relief flooding through me. I could now phone the police. But as I was on the point of picking up the receiver, I stopped. Now was the time to find out if there were anyone else in the house. I stood, my arm to my side, as the phone continued to ring. On the fifth ring I picked it up.

"Hello."

"Is Hilary there?" a female voice asked.

"I don't know. I don't think so."

"Who is this?" There was more than curiosity in the tone. There was a hint of hostility.

"This is Catherine Maitland. I am a reporter. I was given permission by the church to examine the house." (Why was I explaining all this? I wondered.) "Who are you?"

"I'm a friend of Hilary's." The upper-crust voice was cool.

"Then, as a friend of Hilary's, would you hang up so that I can phone the police? There's a dead body here in the study beyond the library. I thought the phone had been disconnected, because when I picked up the receiver in the study to call the police, the phone itself was dead."

"A dead body? Hilary's?" There was a rising note of anxiety in the woman's voice.

"No, not Hilary's."

"You know Hilary?" This time the suspicion was evident.

"I've met him once," I said calmly (and added mentally, and you can have him). "Now would you please hang up. I don't want to stay here alone with this body longer than I have to."

"But—"

"*Please.*" I didn't exactly shout, but I didn't whisper, either.

"Very well. But I'll call you right back."

"Who are you?" I asked again and received the same reply.

"I told you, I'm a friend of Hilary's."

"Because I know the police will want to know when I tell them about our conversation."

It worked like magic. She hung up immediately. I then called the operator and asked her to connect me with the local police.

I explained to the man who answered the phone about the dead body.

"Somebody will be there in a second. Don't touch anything."

"I already have. I turned the body over on its back. I wanted to make sure he wasn't alive."

"Don't touch any more, then. Did you know who it was? Could you identify the body?"

"No, I—" At that point I became aware of something that had been nagging at me in the back of my mind. "I don't know," I said. "I thought I didn't recognize him, but when you asked me, I wasn't sure."

"You mean, you think you may know him?"

"I told you. I'm not sure."

There was a silence. Then, "Like I said, don't touch anything else. Just wait for the officers to get there."

They arrived in less than ten minutes. Two police officers got out of the car and started toward the house.

I realized then I had to run the length of the wing to let them in.

Unlatching one of the windows, I opened it. "Officer," I yelled.

They both turned and started towards me.

"Are you the woman that found the body?" one of them asked as they came within voice distance.

"Yes. I am. I'll let you in, but I called out to tell you that I have to get through this wing to the front door to do it. So don't think I'm not coming."

"Okay," one of the officers said. He was a tall young man with a somewhat wooden face.

"Are you alone?" the other one inquired. He was shorter and fairer, but he looked a little older than the tall man beside him.

"As far as I know, I am. I haven't seen or heard anyone else in the house. But I must tell you that someone drove out of here a short while ago."

"Since you found the body?"

"Yes."

I could see the officer measuring with his eye the distance from the window ledge to the ground, as though thinking about coming through the window. But he finally said, "Well, open the front door as soon as you can. We'll go over there and wait. If you hear anything at all between now and then, open another window and shout. Break it if you have to."

"All right."

I walked quickly through the rooms and pulled open the heavy front door. Then I led the two officers back through the rooms to the study where the body lay.

They both bent down.

"How long ago would you say you found this?" the shorter officer asked.

"Maybe five or seven minutes before I called you."

He stood up. "And what were you doing in those five or seven minutes?"

"Reacting—it's not every day I stumble on a dead body." If the officer appreciated my irony he gave no sign of it.

"And?"

I took a breath. "I felt his heart, then the pulse under his jaw, then his wrist. Then I leaned down and put my ear on his chest, just the way I've seen them do in the movies and on television. But I could find no pulse and no movement. However, I did register that his hand, when I touched it, was warm, so I don't think he can have been dead that long."

"I agree with you," the officer said. "And after you finished trying to find a pulse, did you call then, or did you do anything else?"

I was beginning to get a little annoyed, as much at the cop's attitude as anything else.

"As I told the officer on the telephone, I turned him"—I indicated the body—"over. When I found him, he was lying on his side."

"Too bad you moved him."

"I was trying to find out if he was alive."

"Okay. You turned him on his back. So then what?"

"Then I tried to call you, but the phone in here was dead."

The cop turned. "That phone over there?" He indicated the phone on the side table.

"Yes. That phone over there."

He went over, lifted the receiver, listened for a moment, jiggled the bar up and down, then put it down. "It's dead," he said, and then picked up the cord from the floor. "Somebody forgot to put it in the jack."

I felt like the idiot I was supposed to feel.

The other cop asked, "How could you call the station if the telephone wasn't connected?"

"I called the police from the library, where the phone was working."

"What made you try the phone in there—if you had already tried it here and found it dead?"

"I didn't, as you call it, try the phone. As I told you before you even came into the house, I heard a car start up somewhere in the front. This room looks to the back, so I knew the sound must have come through the library which stretches the width of the house with windows both front and back. I had run into the library and was looking out the front window when the phone in there started ringing."

"You didn't mention that before."

"You haven't given me a chance."

"Okay. So the phone started ringing and you answered it. Did you answer it right away?"

"No. It suddenly occurred to me . . . if the body was so recently dead . . . and with the car belting out of here, I thought somebody else might still be in the house. I let it ring five times. Then I answered it. It was a woman asking for Hilary, Hilary van Reider. I asked her twice who she was, but beyond telling me she was a friend of Hilary's, she wouldn't say. I told her please to get off the phone and let me call the police. She resisted doing so at first, but when I told her that I would, of course, tell the police about our conversation, she hung up immediately." I paused. "One other thing, when I said there was a dead body here, she said, on a sort of rising note of anxiety, 'Hilary?' I would say she is a fairly devoted friend."

"Did you get her name?"

"No, she wouldn't give it to me. After that, I called you."

The cop looked at me for a moment, then said, "The desk sergeant said you thought you might recognize this guy. Do you?"

I looked back down at the dead face, the blood coming down half of it like a flow of lava, tracking straight across the eye. I knew that there was something about his appearance that seemed to catch on a hook in my mind. But when I tried to think what it was, all ideas vanished.

"I don't know," I said finally. "I have a vague sense that I've seen him before. But seeing him like this now . . ." I made a gesture. "I'm sorry. I have a feeling I know him. But at this moment I can't tell you from where."

The two policemen conferred for a moment. They spoke in low voices, so I couldn't make sense of what they said. Then the younger went off into the library and towards the phone. The other turned back to me.

"We've sent for the coroner and the photograph and lab people. They'll be here in a minute. In the meantime I'd like to ask you some more questions."

As a reporter, there were some questions I would have liked to have had answered also. Who was the man lying on the floor of the study? Who was the woman who had telephoned asking for Hilary? And where was Hilary now, and where had he been for the past half hour? "Okay," I said to the cop. "Do you mind if I ask you something?"

"What?"

"How long ago would you say that man has been killed?"

He looked at me for a moment. "I was hoping you could tell me that."

"If you mean, you think I killed him, then why on earth would I call in the police? Surely I'd get away as soon as I could."

"You might have your reasons."

"That's reaching some, officer, isn't it?"

He was a little shorter than I—probably about five foot seven, which was exactly my own height without heels. With two-inch heels, I stood at five-nine. Somehow I felt that the fact he had to look up to me was not to my advantage.

"Now," I said, "could you answer my question as to how long he has been dead?"

"The doctor can tell us that when he comes."

"But you're experienced, and you were here sooner than the doctor."

"Look, Ms. . . . Ms. . . ." He glanced down at some notes in his hand.

"Maitland," I finally said. "Catherine Maitland, free-lance writer living on Charles Street, in the Village, in Manhattan."

"All right, Ms. Maitland. The face of the body was already stiff when we arrived. Rigor can set in anywhere from ten minutes after death to several hours, depending on the condition of the body, the warmth of the room, et cetera. And it begins with the face. When you found him, did you notice if his face was stiff?"

I hesitated, thinking back. "I don't know. I didn't touch his face, if that's what you mean. After I turned him over, I . . . I saw that the blood had caked down half his face, covering one eye, and that the other eye was open. And they were just staring. But I didn't touch him."

"We'll let that go for the moment. Tell me why you're here."

"I'm here because I've been assigned to do an article about this house by the magazine *Public Eye*. I was given the assign-

ment by the editor, Piers Somerville, who will certainly con-
firm this if you call him"—I glanced at the still-expressionless
face of the policeman—"which I am sure you will do."

"We always check the statements given to us," he said. "So
you came this afternoon to examine the house. Have you been
here before?"

"No. I've spent several weeks trying to get permission from
St. Anselm's Church in New York to go over the place. They
kept saying that the only person who could give me permission
was the rector, and he's been away. Finally I went over there
and saw a woman priest, who gave me permission . . . Here it
is . . ." And I took it out of my pocket. "But she told me that I
would have to get a key from a custodian named Krause, who
lives down the road. Apparently he and his wife both have
keys. He's a sort of caretaker and his wife cleans the place. Or
did."

"So you got the key from the Krauses?"

"No. While I was knocking on their door I got mowed down
by a guard dog belonging to Mr. Hilary van Reider, who followed around the house immediately."

"What happened after that?"

"I guess you could say we had a fight."

For the first time, the ghost of a smile appeared briefly on
the officer's face.

"I take it his fights are not unknown," I said boldly.

"I wouldn't know about that." The cop had his facial expression back under control. "So how did you get the key?"

"I didn't. In the general heat of the battle, I forgot that I
needed it, and I didn't remember until I brought my car up
here. So I didn't expect to be able to get in, but when, just out
of curiosity, I tried the door, it opened."

"In that case you could have told us just to come in, couldn't
you?"

Again I felt the complete idiot. Then, without thinking, I
laughed. "Yes, if I hadn't forgotten all about it."

His expression didn't change. "What did you and Mr. van
Reider fight about?"

"About my having permission to look over the house, which
he still seems to regard as his own, about the group of crazies

—as he described them—that want to buy it from the church and whom he is afraid the church will sell it to unless he can stop them, and about the girl, Crystal Mahoney, who apparently committed suicide at a motel up here, with pages from his family papers strewn around the motel-room bureau."

I added on the last in the same matter-of-fact voice I was using. Whether I could get anything from this stone-faced cop about Mahoney I didn't know, but I was fairly sure that if I made a big thing of it he would clam up.

"What do you know about her?"

"Not a lot. What I've told you. Plus the fact that she worked for some cheap tabloid."

"Does her death have anything to do with your being here?" He spoke sharply—not at all in his usual manner.

I hesitated. My instinct was to be as uncommunicative about this matter as I could get away with. The local press had already shown a remarkable lack of interest in Mahoney's death and the papers in her room, which would argue that someone had made it worth their while to look the other way. But who? And how could I find anything out by being cagey?

"Yes, it does. My editor knew her slightly, and was puzzled by her death and its surroundings, and why there wasn't more in the papers. That's why he sent me here."

At that point, we heard a couple of cars drive up. The officer went into the library and I followed. Through the library window we could see men getting out of two cars.

The cop said, "I'd like you to wait in here while these other men do their jobs. And then we can talk some more down at the station."

"Do I understand that I'm under arrest?" I really didn't think he had a reason on earth to charge me. Even so, a nasty little chill went down my back.

"Nobody's said anything about an arrest. I just want to ask you some more questions, and that'll be easier when these guys finish their work and we can take you to the station. Why don't you sit down and wait."

He walked towards the other men as they came through the library door at the other end. For a moment they all stopped and conferred and then moved across the library into the study. I was sure that the policeman had talked about me, because at least two of them threw me a sideways glance as they passed. But then, I thought, trying to give common sense a chance, they probably would have anyway.

After they were all in the study and I could hear their voices, although not what they were saying, I debated tiptoeing up behind them to listen to their comments, or doing what had been in my mind for the past few moments: go upstairs.

If this house were to become a subject of police search, I was by no means sure that I could get to look over it—at least not for a while. Sooner or later I, or my editor, could make noises about a reporter's First Amendment right of access. But as long as the police had any reason to think the house itself was involved, they could put a guard around it. And I was extremely aware of the fact that Crystal Mahoney's connection with this house had not been mentioned in the brief news accounts of her reported suicide in a nearby motel. Since van Reider papers were found there, this could not be explained under the heading of sloppy or lazy reporting. It was a reasonable certainty that pressure had been exerted and that the local police were involved in some way, if only passively.

All of which meant that they could—at least for a while—prevent me from coming back. I decided that my need to know something about the rest of the house was greater than my need to know what the doctor and various other police personnel in there were saying.

Quickly I bent and took off my shoes. There were large areas of parquet floor between the oriental carpets that seemed to occupy the centers of the huge rooms. Then I moved as quickly as possible down the side of the library fronting the house. The door to the study was very near the back wall, so I would not be in sight until I had to go through the door from the library opposite, or unless one of the cops poked his head back into the library to see what was happening.

But none did. I managed to get out of the library without their noticing; then I ran as fast as I could through the small living room, through the dining room and into the central hall. There was a cop standing outside on the stairs leading up to the front door, but his back was turned.

Luckily for me, the staircase clung to the right wall of the hall, going up behind the door through which I had come. At the top was a landing, behind which were windows, and then another flight to the floor above. It was when I ran across that landing that I could be in the most danger from the cop on the steps outside, because I would be easily visible if he should glance around. And then, of course, there was always the possibility that one of the cops examining the body would discover I was missing.

I went up as fast as I could, aware that the moment they knew I had gone, they would be fairly sure that I had come upstairs. I could not run outside in front of the cop. Was there any other door leading outside I could use? It was as I crept across the landing that I found an answer. One of the landing windows was a french door leading out onto a terrace formed by a porch over the back door. Praying that the bolt would slide easily, I touched it, pushed a little, and found that it did. In a few seconds it had slipped all the way back. Then I turned the door handle, and the glass door opened. I left it open. It was by no means a guarantee that they would not search upstairs immediately. They would, of course, look through the house anyway before they left. But by that time I hoped to have searched on my own. For now, I depended on their wasting time thinking I had run out through the french door, because the ground rose a little at the back, and the drop from the porch roof was not too formidable for a reasonably active person. Surely, I told myself, they would think I would try to escape, particularly since the cop who questioned me seemed to think I might be his best suspect.

The policeman standing on the front steps, his legs apart, his thumbs in his belt, hadn't turned. I paused for a moment, listening. There wasn't a sound from the library wing. Perhaps they hadn't even discovered my absence. Still holding my shoes, I ran upstairs.

At the top I hesitated, remembering the small winding stair leading out of the study where I found the body. But prudence dictated that I look through the wing opposite to the library. Even without shoes those downstairs might hear me. So, after glancing quickly over the wide graceful hall upstairs, decorated, like its counterpart downstairs, with six portraits, I turned to the right into the first room.

It became obvious that there were eight rooms per wing, four facing front and four back. Most of the rooms were bedrooms, and there were a number of connecting baths. Two of the rooms had been made into upstairs studies. The entire assembly bespoke old wealth. The furniture was exquisite, some of it European, much of it early American. The curtains and wallpaper had once been beautiful. But several decades of spotty care and outright neglect had had their effect.

I moved quickly, but at one window, attracted by the heavy damask-rose curtain, I paused to touch it. Then, aware of having to hurry, I moved on and caught my foot in the edge of the rug. I grasped the curtain for support. There was a ripping sound, clouds of dust billowed up and several inches of curtain pulled away from the rest of the fabric. Hastily I pushed it back, then stood, finger against upper lip, fighting a sneeze, waiting to see if anyone had heard. After that, I continued my way through the rooms. My interest was first to see if anyone was upstairs, or if it looked as though someone had been there within the past few hours. I was also intensely curious to see the part of the house that Hilary van Reider still considered his.

Plainly, though, I thought, coming back into the central hall, his quarters were not in that wing. For all my caution, I had been quick. Not more than five or six minutes had passed since I had tiptoed out of the library. As I moved back across the upstairs central hall towards the opposite wing, I heard the sounds I had been listening for:

"Joe's standing in the front, she can't have gotten outside . . ."

It was a man's voice, although not, I thought, that of the officer who had questioned me.

I ran even more quickly down the hall of the remaining wing. Unlike the hall in the right wing, which led at the end to a window, this hall ended with a door. The rooms on either side were duplicates of those I had seen in the other wing. I opened and closed the doors quickly, hearing the voices from downstairs get louder. The rooms were empty and they looked as unused as those I had already been through. Then I opened the door at the end of the hall and found myself in a good-sized study, on the other side of which was another door, leading, I suspected, into a bedroom.

There were footsteps coming up the main staircase now. A voice said, "Look, she got out here onto the porch . . ."

I then heard an entirely unexpected and incongruous noise from the room ahead: the snarling of an angry cat. For a moment I hesitated as something—some memory, perhaps—slipped in and out of my head. Whatever it was, it was unpleasant. I gave a slight shiver. But I pushed myself forward, even though I knew that any moment I would undoubtedly feel the policeman's hand on my shoulder. Then I thrust open the bedroom door.

The cat, a big, striped reddish ginger, was standing on the bed, facing the door, his back arched, hissing. Beside him, half under a quilt, was a boy of about twelve, his eyes closed, his face white. He was so still and so white that for a moment I thought he, too, like the man downstairs, was dead.

"Oh my God!" I said, and ran over. Out of the corner of my eye I noticed, on the far side of the room, the top of the winding staircase that went to the study below. As I moved towards the bed, the cat arched its back. A low growl hummed from its throat, and then it hissed at me, leaped off the bed and disappeared down the winding stair.

"What the hell—?" said a voice behind me.

"Dad?" the boy muttered, and I saw his eyes open.

"What the blazes are you doing with my son?"

I turned. Hilary van Reider, backed by the police, was moving across the room as fast as his limp would let him.

"The police must have been dim-witted indeed to let you out of their sight," van Reider said, reaching down towards the boy.

"Oh we're not that stupid, Mr. van Reider. We knew she was upstairs. We were just coming to get her to take her down to the station."

4

The whole thing rapidly became a muddle and then degenerated into a nightmare. After a lot of talking and shouting, I gathered the boy's name was Bart, for Bartholomew, and that he'd been reading in the study adjoining when something hit him on the head.

"And you have no idea who it was?" the policeman asked.

He shook his head, then winced.

"Can we leave any other questions until after I can get my son to the hospital?" van Reider asked curtly. He turned to his son, who was sitting up, and said in a far kinder voice than I'd thought he was capable of, "Come on, Bart, I want Dr. McCormack to look at your head."

Bart slid off the bed, and they left, van Reider's arm protectively around his son's shoulder.

"Okay now," the officer said, turning his attention to me. "For your information, the doctor says the man downstairs has been dead probably about forty-five minutes, give or take ten minutes. It's at least possible for you to have knocked the kid on his head here, and then gone down and killed him, too."

"But why would I do it?"

"I don't know. And furthermore, I don't have to know your motive. I do know you had opportunity, and there doesn't seem to have been anyone else around at the relevant time."

I was not unacquainted with the feeling of being trapped; it certainly had happened during the days of my disintegrating marriage when Simon was knocking me around. But I had never had it before in quite such a chilling way.

"And what about that car that I heard and saw speeding hell-for-leather out of the grounds here?"

"We only have your word for that. The garage has Mr. van Reider's car in it, and according to him, that's the only car here. No one else has reported seeing the car you talked about, even though we've managed to make a few inquiries."

"But since I don't know either of the people—the man who was killed, or Bart van Reider—I do insist that that makes your suspicion pretty weak."

"But you told the guy on the phone in the station that you thought you might know the man. That something about him was familiar."

"I know I did. But I couldn't get any further than that with it. I still have the feeling, but I can't pin it down. Has he been taken away?"

"He's being put into the van now."

I went over to the window facing the front and saw the covered stretcher being put in the van.

"And now, Miss Maitland, if you'd just come with us to the station."

At the station house in the nearby town I went over the story with him and with a detective again and again. Their suspicion of me struck me as so ludicrous that I still couldn't take it seriously. At the end of two hours I was beginning to.

"I'm not answering any more questions until I talk to a lawyer."

"If, as you've been claiming for the last several hours, you're innocent, then why are you thinking immediately of calling a lawyer?" That was the detective.

"In the first place, it's not immediate. In the second place, innocent people need a lawyer just as much as the guilty. Where is your phone?"

The detective shoved the telephone toward me. "Too bad," he said. "I was about to tell you to go home."

I got up. "In that case, I'll go. I'd rather talk to a lawyer from my own phone anyway."

"Don't leave the New York area or anything. We still have a lot of work to do and questions to ask."

In the days when I was married to Simon I knew a lot of lawyers. But in my three-year headlong flight away from New York, I had lost touch with them, and when I came back, something—painful associations, remembered humiliations when we were together at parties and Simon was drunk—kept me from getting back in touch. The divorce lawyer who had tried to track down Simon for me was now retired and in Florida. However, I thought, finding another lawyer would be no problem. Piers would almost certainly know one.

As I opened the front door of the brownstone on Charles Street in the West Village where I had my apartment, I glanced at my watch. It was long after office hours. I knew Piers's home phone, but experience had taught me he was seldom there. I wanted to talk to him, but I could certainly wait till morning.

I fished the mail out of my box and went upstairs to the fourth floor. When I walked into my apartment I was confronted by Topaz, my long-haired marmalade cat, who was sitting erect, waiting for me to come through the door. A friend who once stayed with me said that when I came through the front door downstairs, Topaz got up from wherever he was and took up his stance. Since my apartment was three stories above the entrance, I could never figure out how he knew I had come in. But I believed her, because he was always there, with a look about his tilted gold eyes and his whiskers that seemed to say, "It's about time."

"All right, Topaz," I said as he rubbed against my legs, "it's nice to see you, too, but don't pretend to me you're starved." For a moment there flashed into my mind the memory of the big red cat on the bed beside Bart van Reider. Did the van

Reiders own the cat? I wondered. And then dismissed it from my mind.

I bent down and stroked Topaz's heavy fur and rubbed his head. A feline expert told me that when cats rub against their owners' legs, then turn around and rub the other way, then back again and again, they're marking the owners as theirs; that if they could talk they'd be saying, "Mine, mine mine," with each rub.

I glanced at his dish, which still had some of the dry food I had left for him. So it wasn't hunger. It was love and/or loneliness. Yet the one time I had brought a cat in to be a chum for him when I was out all day, Topaz had half killed it. I had been assured that two weeks would see the end of hostilities. So after two and a half weeks, instead of leaving the new cat locked up in the bathroom, I left them together in the apartment when I went off to an all-day conference that I was covering. When I got back, the second cat was jammed under the bed and wouldn't come out.

I scolded Topaz. I wouldn't talk to him, or touch him, and when he tried to rub against my legs, I removed him. Later that evening I went in to discover that he had expressed his anger at me in a very feline way on my favorite quilt.

The new cat went back to its original owner. The relevant portion of the quilt went into a basin where it soaked overnight, then it went to the cleaners.

With his enemy gone, Topaz turned himself into a moving, walking, rubbing, miaowing valentine. For two weeks I ignored him. Then he stopped eating. It was a long, tough battle and he won. There'd been no more four-footed interlopers.

"Who do I know who's a lawyer?" I asked Topaz as I sat down on the sofa to examine my mail and he settled himself in my lap. His loud rattling purr filled the silence. I was still thinking about this when the phone rang.

When I picked up the receiver, a female voice said, "This is Claire Aldington. We were told by the police that there'd been a murder up in St. Cuthbert's and that you'd been held for a while for questioning."

"You heard right on both counts. I was walking from the library into the study at the end of that wing when I walked into a dead body. Since I gather he was very recently dead, I couldn't convince the police that I had not done it."

There was a short silence on the telephone, and I found myself saying with a rising anxiety, "Don't tell me you harbor the same idea of my guilt as the police do!"

"No," she said. "That silence was really sympathy and a sort of astonishment at the coincidence. I, too, was an object of police suspicion when we had a murder at the church here. And I, too, found the body. Somehow you don't strike me as a murderer any more than I strike myself as one. I'm sorry . . . I'm sorry that happened."

I hadn't realized how much being a suspect had been a strain, until I felt a slight swelling in my throat. It was amazingly gratifying to talk to someone who trusted that I was not a killer.

"Are you all right?" she asked.

"Yes. Yes, I'm fine. I was just . . . just a little overcome at your taking it for granted that I hadn't beaten the wretched man over the head. I've discovered the hard way how much you take other people's good will and trust for granted until you suddenly find it isn't there."

"Yes, I know." She hesitated. "I don't want to put pressure on you now, when you must feel exhausted and drained, but I would like to know just what happened. Do you think you could come by the church tomorrow morning?"

"Yes, of course." It suddenly struck me that I would welcome a talk with her, too. "By the way, this may seem an odd question, but do you know a lawyer? I feel at this point that I ought to have one."

"There are several in the church. I'll try to have a list for you when you come tomorrow."

The next morning I went to her office and, helped by a few questions, told her what had happened. After this she produced the names of some lawyers. "I don't know any of those, myself. But there are trial lawyers, or criminal lawyers"—I made a face—"who are known by the lawyers who are members here."

"All right. Thanks."

I took the list from her and put it in my pocket.

"And then," she said, "there's Hilary van Reider. I think he's a lawyer."

"*Hilary van Reider!* I can't think of a quicker or more efficient way to make certain I'll be behind bars for life. He does *not* like me and I do *not* like him. Since it was not part of my bumping into the body, I didn't tell you about my encounter with him before I got to the house." And I recounted what had happened in front of the Krauses' house. "He's arrogant, rude and thoroughly unsympathetic," I finished.

"Oh," she said. "Well, I don't know why I would have thought otherwise. Heaven knows, he's done everything he could do to prevent our selling the wretched place to the Swami Gupta Nanda."

I thought for a moment in silence. "You know, if I weren't so involved, I'd be covering this case like mad. There's something odd and fascinating about it. And when you add the whole thing about Crystal Mahoney and the van Reider papers strewn around the motel room, and the fact that that part never made the papers . . . I wonder if van Reider bribed the police."

"To keep them from reporting about the papers to the press?"

"Yes."

"I don't know van Reider well, and I can see that you have a good reason to dislike him. He's never been exactly famous for his warm, toasty personality. And that divorce of his dragged through the tabloids in such delicious detail for so long—I guess that embittered him, especially toward anyone in the press."

"What divorce?"

"I don't see how you can be a member of the press and not know it."

"Wait a minute. Yes. I do remember a few details. I was abroad on assignment that year, but I read about it in the newsmagazines. 'Aristocrat sues model-TV-actress wife for adultery,' that kind of thing, wasn't it?"

"Very much that kind of thing. But what really made it juicy was the custody battle. Van Reider wanted complete custody of his son, but the judge was one of those who firmly believed that a child's place is with its mother, no matter how inept the mother may be. So all van Reider got was visiting rights and an occasional weekend."

"That may explain his hostility towards me as a reporter."

Mrs. Aldington was staring out the window with a vague frown on her face.

"Something bothering you?" I asked. "I mean, anything to do with me or the murder or whatever?"

She took a breath. "I haven't seen the morning paper yet. But I did listen to the television news last night—both early and late. The murder was all over both, of course, including your part in it. I tried to monitor as many TV stations as I could by switching channels, and there wasn't a reporter who didn't point out that this was the second murder connected with this church—which is not the kind of thing that makes anybody connected with the church happy."

"I can imagine. You know," I went on, "a few moments ago I commented that if I weren't so involved, I'd be madly covering this. Well, I think I will anyway, and find out as much as I possibly can while doing so."

"I wish you would. My devout hope is that it has nothing whatsoever to do with the church. But since the murder occurred on our property, then we're involved whether we like it or not." She paused. "What I guess I'm saying is, we're inevitably involved, simply because the body was there in St. Cuthbert's. But it would be much better for us if it were an accident."

"A murder isn't an accident. And since he was killed only a few minutes before I found him, then he wasn't dispatched somewhere else and brought there—at least I don't think it would have been possible."

"And that was only a few hours after you were here, getting our permission."

"That's right, although I'm not sure I see any connection in that fact . . ."

"I don't either. I'm stretching or, I guess, free-associating . . . You came here to get permission, got it, went up to St. Cuthbert's and found the body . . ."

Just as she finished saying that, something slid together in my mind. I had gone to the church to get permission, but before that I had looked out to see if the man who stood across the street and watched my apartment was still there, and he was. *And that was the man whose body I found several hours later* . . .

"My God!" I said. "It was that man. I'm sure of it . . ."

"What man?"

"Off and on, for the last month or so, I've seen a man standing on the street opposite my apartment house, staring at my apartment. But it's three floors up, so that my view of him has only been from that angle, because whenever I tore downstairs to confront him, he was gone by the time I reached our front door. I live in a brownstone on Charles Street, in the Village. There's no elevator, so it takes a few minutes to get down, no matter how fast I go. What's always baffled me is how on earth he knew I was coming down to look."

"But you think it's that man."

"Yes. I think so. But I couldn't make what I'm sure the police would call a definite identification. He was dark, with short straight hair, and a rather large nose with a sort of aquiline bump to it. But again, how that would look from three floors up and lying on the floor are two different things. Especially as blood was running, or had been running, down half his face."

"Would what he was wearing be similar?"

For the second time I felt that "click," as of something sliding home, or into a slot. "Yes. Yes, Claire"—I used her first name without thinking—"he always had on the same clothes: jeans, with a sort of dark T-shirt and a denim jacket. That's what he had on when he was watching my house, and that's what the body was wearing. Of course, they're not exactly uncommon garments for a man to wear these days."

"Was there any mark on them, or any part of them that was unusual? Like a badge, or a decoration or a stripe?"

I shook my head. "I was too far above in my apartment to notice anything like that. And if there were any on the body in the study, I was too busy being questioned by the police to notice. And then there was that car that drove out of the place lickety-split!"

"What car? You didn't mention it before."

I told her about the car.

"Could you see anything of it at all?"

"Only its back fender; it disappeared just as I got to the window."

"Then what happened?"

"Then the phone in the library rang, which shook me, since the phone in the study was dead, and a woman asked for Hilary but wouldn't identify herself. Just kept saying she was a friend of his, and what was I doing there? She sounded definitely hostile, and she wouldn't let go until I told her how interested the police would be when I told them about her phone call. At that, she hung up."

"Did you tell her about the body? Well, you must have, if you were talking about telling the police."

"Yes. I forgot to mention that. When I told her about the dead body, she shrieked, 'Hilary?' in a way that made me think she must be terribly in love with him or something." I looked at Claire. "Do you know anything about his love life?"

She shook her head. "Nothing. That is, the assumption here has always been that he was so traumatized over his wife's infidelities that he's been living in monastic gloom ever since. I wonder if it was his wife who called?"

"Would she be that upset if something happened to him?"

Claire shook her head. "I don't know. People are strange, as you'd be the first to agree. Her goings-on may have been as casual and meaningless as erring husbands' are always supposed to have been. 'Darling, she didn't mean a thing, I swear to you . . .' that kind of thing. Only with the new liberation maybe women are beginning to share some of the sins of the fathers and the husbands. If it wasn't his wife or, rather, ex-wife, I don't know who it would be. If he does have a girlfriend, I don't know who would know about it."

"Would there be anyone here who would?"

Claire rubbed her finger up and down her nose. "Chris might. Chris Swade, one of the assistant rectors here. His brother knows, or knew, the van Reiders. Shall I ask him?"

"If it's okay with you and with the church. It would certainly help in my investigation."

Claire turned, picked up her receiver, and dialed three numbers. "Hi, Chris. It's Claire. Catherine Maitland is here—yes, the same one who found the body up at St. Cuthbert's—and was asking me something about Hilary van Reider. I said your brother knew the van Reiders and you might be able to answer —that is, if you don't mind. Okay, see you."

She turned back towards me. "Chris was much impressed with the fact that you were the person he'd been hearing about in the news. I'm surprised, in fact, that you hadn't been hounded yourself by the press this morning."

"I have an unlisted number, which may account for that. Not that an enterprising reporter couldn't find it without too much trouble. Thank Heaven I have an answering service."

At that moment, Claire's door opened and a portly man with a pleasant face came in. He looked to be somewhere in his thirties.

"Come in, Chris. This is Kit Maitland."

He reached forward a slightly pudgy hand. "How do you do. I've been hearing about you in the news."

"Yes. It feels odd to be a reporter who is now being reported on."

"Oh, so you're a reporter yourself. Were you on some story when you were up at St. Cuthbert's?"

"Yes. Ostensibly I was assigned to write a magazine piece about the house itself, Rivercrest, a.k.a. St. Cuthbert's. But my editor's real motive in sending me there was the death of another reporter, Crystal Mahoney."

He looked so blank that Claire filled in. "The girl who died in the motel in the nearby village." She turned to me. "Only the fact that a body was found in St. Cuthbert's, i.e., church property, would penetrate Chris's conviction that nothing since the early Anglican fathers is worth reading or listening to."

"Not fair, not fair. I do surface from time to time."

"And conducts *wonderful* retreats," Claire said.

He made a small bow in her direction, slightly impeded by his girth. There was something very endearing about him that reminded me strongly of Pooh Bear.

"What do you want to know about the van Reiders, and, of course, which van Reider? Although I suppose it must be

Hilary, since he's the only direct descendant of this generation still around."

"Not to put too delicate a point on it," Claire said, "does he have a loving girlfriend?" She paused, and then, "I can see, from your expression, that I'd better explain." With admirable succinctness, she gave a summary of what had happened up at St. Cuthbert's. "Have I left anything out?" she asked when she'd finished.

"Nothing," I said. "Aside from my reporter's instinct, there is the fact that at the moment I seem to be the chief suspect to urge me on. I told the police about the woman on the telephone, but since I didn't have a clue as to who she might be, I didn't get the impression that they believed me."

"They might have believed you, nevertheless," Chris said, "and may be now conducting their own investigation. However, Claire here has a good friend among the police, a Lieutenant O'Neill, dating from the time of our own troubles, and you could probably talk to him."

I turned to her. "Do you really? Do you think I could talk to him?"

"Of course. I'll be glad to call and introduce you, if that would be any help. I should have thought of it myself."

"In the meantime," Chris said, "the van Reiders, or rather Hilary van Reider and the state of his love life . . . The trouble is I don't really know. Gerald—my brother—went to school with Hilary and his brother, James, the one who was killed. He was exactly between them in age. I don't think he much liked James, but he quite liked Hilary, although I seem to remember his finding him difficult. He's supposed to have a very hot temper. And I do remember Gerald was here to lend Hilary aid and comfort during the dark days of the divorce."

"Then, he'd probably know if Hilary has a girlfriend. But would he say?"

"Probably not. But it's academic anyway. He's on a dig somewhere beyond the Hindu Kush."

"If I thought it was really vital I'm perfectly willing to track him down there," I said. "That is, if the police would let me."

"But, from what you tell me," Chris said, "the only reason you want to know is because this female called on the telephone, said she was a friend of Hilary's, but refused to say who she was."

"It's a little more than that," I said. "When I told her about the dead body, she shrieked, 'Hilary's?' in a distraught way that is usually associated with—er—close relationships."

"Ummm. Well, for what it's worth I did hear via some gossip or other that Hilary had taken up with an unlikely female. This was at some point after his divorce, but I didn't pursue the matter. However"—he paused—"according to my brother, Hilary has always been something of a dark horse where women are concerned. He doesn't look it, but he definitely goes for the glamour girls. One after the other."

"When you say, 'unlikely,' do you mean unlikely for him, or unlikely in the social sense, or unlikely in the sense that his girlfriends are all raving beauties who could have movie moguls, rock stars, royal princes and corporation heads?"

He looked unhappy. "I'm really sorry, but I don't know. It's not my word—I was quoting. And I didn't ask."

I stared at him. Not asking the question was almost beyond my power to understand. "When somebody says something like that, how could you *not* ask? I mean, just out of plain curiosity? Or is that just because I'm a reporter and curiosity is my stock-in-trade?"

"Probably that reason," Chris said, smiling.

"Added to which," Claire said, "is the fact that Chris is one of the few people who really practice all the moral prohibitions against gossip."

"That's admirable," I said. "But to me incomprehensible. Gossip is one of the most interesting things in life."

"True," Claire said. "I'm rather fond of it myself. But it can be destructive."

"Without it, nine tenths of the press wouldn't be able to function."

"Would that be a bad thing?" Chris asked. He asked it so amiably, I found it hard to be miffed.

"Are you among the several million people who appear to loathe the press?"

Chris gave a friendly grin. "A necessary evil, I agree."

"You have to remember our problems with it in the past," Claire said. "Sometimes we felt like we were being hunted."

"So you can't help me in trying to find the female who was being so concerned about Hilary. Well, it doesn't matter. My contacts in the magazine world can probably dig up the information for me."

"You know," Claire said, "it suddenly occurs to me that one explanation for the woman's behavior is that she's married. I think I saw a gossip item somewhere that coupled Hilary's name with that of some married socialite."

In my mind I heard again the cool, upper-crust voice. "That would fit," I said.

"Anything else?" Mr. Swade asked. "Sorry to rush, but I have someone coming to see me."

"No," Claire said with a smile. "Thanks for your help."

"Delighted." He waved at Claire and disappeared out the door.

"By the way," Claire said, "I'll be happy to introduce you to Lieutenant O'Neill if it will do you any good or be of any help."

"Yes. I think it would. Any friend at court will certainly help, though I doubt if there's any official connection between the police in Manhattan and those up in Dutchess County. Could you get in touch with him for me?"

"All right." She turned to her desk and consulted a roller card file. Then she lifted the receiver, dialed nine, and called another number. "Can I speak to Lieutenant O'Neill?" she asked. "This is Mrs. Claire Aldington." There was a pause. Then, "Could you please ask him to call me at this number when he comes in?" And she gave him the church's number. She turned to me. "As soon as he calls I'll tell him about you and then I'll be in touch to let you know. Sorry he wasn't there."

"Thanks anyway for calling. I'll hope to hear from you before too long. And if either of you hears anything that you think would help—about the van Reiders, about Crystal Mahoney, or about the house—please let me know." I hesitated for a moment, then said, "You told me that Mahoney was once a client of yours. I realize that this was a confidential relationship. But is there anything at all you *can* tell me that would help in getting some information about her?"

Claire gave me one of her level looks. "Are you asking as a reporter, or as somebody who may be in trouble herself with the police?"

I didn't say anything for a moment, then, "I don't really know the answer to that. I suppose I can't take too seriously my role as a suspect. And I've been a reporter for so long that it's second nature by now."

Claire sighed. "Actually, there's nothing I can tell you. And our relationship was one of client and therapist and therefore confidential. The fact that she was a successful graduate of our drug program was of public record. I guess that's about the only thing I can say."

"But there's no reason I can see why I can't go to your drug program and ask somebody there, is there?"

"No, because it is not wholly our drug program. It's part of a community outreach program in which we share. But I bet you won't get much more."

"I forgot to tell you," I said. "According to van Reider, the Krauses haven't been seen for a while. The house certainly looked empty when I arrived there."

"You mean, they've left—just quit the job and gone?"

"That's what he thinks. Says the house hasn't been cleaned or dusted—he's certainly right about that—and the Krauses haven't been visible for some time."

"Did he say how long?"

"No. We were too busy having a fight."

Claire stared at me. "Good heavens! I suppose none of us felt any need to keep up with them—it hasn't been anybody's particular responsibility. More's the pity." She paused. "Is the place really a mess?"

"Parts of it are under layers of dust and dirt."

"My God! The whole thing's been a disaster from the beginning, including the original wretched contract itself. And I wonder now where on earth the Krauses have left the keys; that is, if they left them."

"According to van Reider, he's been hearing noises and said

that for all he knew people could be taking pictures, silver, whatever—but it wasn't his business any more."

Claire sighed. "The rector will be furious. It's bad enough he's inherited all the rest of the muddle about St. Cuthbert's!"

"What muddle?" I was curious. The identity of the ownership of St. Cuthbert's was turning out to be more ambiguous than I'd realized.

Claire hesitated. "The whole St. Cuthbert's business is not one of our more glorious enterprises. The rector who bought it did so in such a burst of enthusiasm that he just rushed in and didn't read the small print in the contract. And when Norbert, our last rector, was equally gung ho about selling it to get money for what he thought were much more important things, he didn't read the small print either."

"But surely your vestry must have had a say. And I'd bet that some of them were lawyers."

"It's hard to explain. Both rectors, the one who bought and the one who wanted to sell, were highly emotional, charismatic men who carried others along with them. When in each case the rector was rallying them along to do what he thought was a great good, nobody sat around and asked awkward questions. So now we're stuck with an expensive white elephant, eating up money in taxes and upkeep, that we'd dearly love to sell. But whoever buys has to honor the clause that the van Reiders may live there."

"In perpetuity? That's what van Reider said to me."

"I think that's wishful thinking and hoping on van Reider's part. But there's no question but that he has a right to live there—or at least in a suite of rooms there—as long as he wants. And that's what's holding up the sale. The guru wants to take the place over in its entirety. In fact, I'm not sure he doesn't want to rebuild parts of it."

"And van Reider is sticking there like a bone in the throat of the whole thing."

"Exactly. And now that the Krauses have flown, the plot gets murkier." She got up. "Anyway, thanks for telling me. I'll have to go upstairs and confer with Sally Hepburn. She'll have a heart attack, I'm afraid. And it's not going to be easy to find another custodian, with van Reider generally cutting up in the background."

"I think he'd be happy to have the place kept up."

"Yes, but on his terms, not on ours."

"And in the meantime he's not going to move a finger to help me with my research. But I bet he knows a lot more about Crystal Mahoney and her death than he's about to say."

"Probably." She smiled. "Anyway, thanks for telling me."

"You might remind Ms. Hepburn that if I hadn't gone up there, the Krauses and the keys would still be missing, but you wouldn't know about it."

"If she starts making a fuss, I'll be sure to remind her."

I picked up my bag. "If you can think of something you can tell me that isn't under some seal of the sacred or therapeutic confessional, I hope you do so."

"I will. And I will talk to Lieutenant O'Neill about you and be in touch."

I stood outside the church for a moment, pondering my next step. Then I ducked into a nearby office building where there was a line of public telephones and called my answering service. I was told that Piers Somerville had called, a Detective Jensen had called, several newspapers had called and so had a few of the local television news stations. Also, two men and one woman who had not left their names but said they would call back.

I sat there in the phone booth thinking about the two men and a woman. There were two men with whom, from time to time, I had dinner or went to the theater or a movie. One was married and separated, one was a good friend who was gay. There was not, at the moment, anyone with whom I was now seriously involved, or as seriously as I allowed myself to be. My old trait of backing off when things between me and any interested and interesting man came to a certain unmarked point, still held. "It's like a bloody wall," one angry young English news correspondent had said, encountering my resistance. And I knew he spoke the truth. But there appeared to be nothing I could do about it.

I called Piers.

"Do you know the whole damn town is looking for you?" he asked. "I came in from LA this morning, read the paper, and have been trying to get you ever since."

"I've been out," I said. "So you know now what happened up at St. Cuthbert's."

"Yes, dear girl. Everyone now knows what happened, including your interest in Crystal's death. Why on earth didn't you call me?"

"I'm calling you now."

"Are you all right? Have the cops been hounding you?"

"Yes, I'm all right. And the cops only hounded me through yesterday. I don't know whether my saying I was going to call my lawyer got them to let me go, or whether they were going to anyway. But after mutterings about not leaving the New York area, they released me."

"What happened? And where the hell are you now?"

"I'm in a phone booth on Lexington Avenue."

"Meet me for lunch and tell me all about it."

"Piers, I have a lot of things I have to do. Besides being a leading suspect, I'm also supposed to be doing a story. Remember? So I'm going to grab a sandwich at the nearest coffee shop and get to work. Can you tell me anything at all, other than what you already have, about Crystal Mahoney?"

"Why are you bothering about her now? Did you see a connection between her and that body you found?"

"Somehow it seems reasonable that there should be a connection. And the more I can find out about her, the more likely I'll be to find what it is."

There was a pause. "I think I told you everything I knew, Kit. If you want the sordid details, I had a couple of one-night flings with her once. But beyond that I know nothing. It seems to me that finding out who the body is is much more of a story, and if you could do that, you'd scoop everybody."

There was something here that was not quite making sense —not if I remembered Piers's eagerness for me to find out how and why Crystal died.

"Why are you backing off from Crystal?" I asked. "All of a sudden you're much more interested in an anonymous body found at Rivercrest. Why?"

There was a pause.

"Come on, Piers," I said. "What gives?"

He sighed. "I told you we—the magazine—have an angel. Well, one night, not long before Crystal went up to Rivercrest, I took her to one of those wild loft parties in Soho, where most of the literary world was busy getting stoned or drunk—you know the kind of thing I mean. It was a publication bash for some long-haired photographer out to portray the sores of our society. I hesitated to take Crystal there, knowing the trouble she'd had, but she said that it wouldn't bother her. At the party she and I kind of got separated, and the next time I saw her, she was deep in conversation with—guess who? Our angel. Before I could fight my way over, they disappeared. Left the party. That was the last time I saw her.

"To be truthful, Kit, it wasn't only fondness for Crystal that made me wonder about what happened to her up at Rivercrest. I'm afraid my vanity was also involved. My nose was out of joint. Mr. Dan J. M. Troilais had walked off with her. Well," he said, after a slight pause, "now you know who the angel is. For God's sake keep it to yourself. I don't want him snatching his money away."

"Have you asked him about her?"

"Of course. He said he took her home and that was the end of that."

"Did you check with her doorman—if she had one?"

"She didn't have one. She was no longer making that kind of money. She lived in a walk-up in the east thirties."

"Who's Mr. Troilais? Where did he make his money?"

"I haven't the faintest idea. That's not entirely true. He's a Greek or of Greek extraction. Probably shipping. I suppose it's too much to ask you not to look him up. But, for heaven's sake, be careful, and don't tell anyone where you got the name."

"Okay. I'll be discreet." For a second or two I debated telling Piers my suspicion of who the man might be whose body I found and where I thought I'd last seen him. But I decided that that would just confuse things further. So instead I said, "Have to go now, Piers. I'm sorry. I'll stay in touch."

Then I sat on the little jump seat in the phone booth and considered my options. If I called the newspapers who had called me, or the TV reporters, then I would certainly find out whatever had happened since I left the police station the day before. On the other hand, I might find myself back there. I knew that reporters felt strongly about protecting their sources, but the fewer people who knew where I was at the moment, the better. On the other hand, sooner or later I would have to go home. I could, of course, take a room under a fictitious name in some dump of a hotel. But there was Topaz to consider. The only time I had ever sent him anywhere to board while I was on assignment, he returned cadaverous. The pet house I had boarded him in was almost tearfully apologetic and charged me, in the end, only half the price they'd quoted. He had simply refused to eat. After that, when I was away for more than a few days, I paid a cat-sitter to stay in my apartment to look after him. He didn't eat much when I was away, but he didn't go on a full hunger strike.

For a moment, I toyed with the idea of asking my regular cat-sitter to stay in my apartment now, so that I could really go to ground and pursue my own investigations. But the thought of reporters and police tramping into my apartment and maybe carelessly letting Topaz out (it had happened once before) decided me against that. Very well then, I'd get as much done as I could before I had to return this evening.

With that in mind, I went to a newsstand and bought the *Times,* the *News* and the *Post.* If anybody would have the most recent scuttlebutt it would be the afternoon paper. But careful scanning of the story produced nothing in the way of identification of the body. Which did not mean the police didn't know, I reminded myself. It meant that they weren't saying.

I needed some time to think for a moment, so I went into a depressed-looking hamburger place, ordered coffee and a tuna-fish sandwich, and read all the papers more carefully.

There was a gratifying amount about me, whom one of the papers described as a "well-known magazine writer," another as a "distinguished reporter" (I liked that, even if I wasn't crazy about the reporter whose byline was above the story or the paper he worked for) and another as a "prize-winning correspondent." (That was a gross exaggeration. I once received one of journalism's minor awards for a story I had done on a child who had run away from home.)

What was not gratifying was that I occupied far more newsprint space and attention than the body. This was probably by default, since they didn't know who the body was, or at least, the police weren't telling them.

I sat there staring at the folded papers, stirring my muddy coffee. What effect would my prominence in the news accounts have on the murderer—whoever he (or she) might be?

The murderer, X, would be delighted, I would think. The more attention on me and the less on him the better. And if I were X, wouldn't I do everything I could to encourage this?

None of the above thoughts did anything to cheer me. And suppose, my mind went on, I was right as to the identity of the body, that he was the man who had been staring at my window; why had he been doing it? If he had been acting under instructions, whose were they? And what did his death mean?

Exhaustion the night before, and the activity of going to the church this morning and talking to Claire, had kept me from confronting these possibilities. Now that I did, a sense of depression threatened to come over me. This had not often happened in my life, and when it did, my mother's unfailing prescription was, get up and do something. This did not make for a reflective life, but it made for a balanced one.

I had a list of things I wanted to do: get in touch with the drug rehabilitation group that Claire mentioned, find a lawyer, try to find out, somehow, who Hilary van Reider's girl was, check on this Dan J. M. Troilais, Greek shipping magnate, discover what, if any, connection there was between Crystal's death and the van Reider papers scattered around and (perhaps most important) find out whether her death was suicide or murder. I had absolutely nothing to go on as far as the latter was concerned. The police themselves seemed to accept the fact of her suicide. But I still wanted to make sure.

Feeling grubby, I glanced around for a ladies' room and saw a sign at the end of the restaurant. The room was small, but at least there was a mirror where I could powder my nose and comb my hair. The face that stared back was white and tired-looking. Like my mother, I have blueish-gray eyes, dark brown curly hair and wide cheekbones. I also have my mother's slightly aquiline nose. But I have my father's height and length of leg, which caused me endless agonies in my youth. Except for Joris and Simon, I was always taller than any of the boys I knew or went to parties with.

It was when I had paid my bill and was leaving the restaurant that something curious happened. I was walking towards the door to the street. In front of me was a wall covered with a mirror. I saw my tall body stride forward, and idly checked to see if my scarf was straight. What I saw in the mirror, behind my form, was a man sitting at a table at the back, watching me. And he was not watching in any way that led me to believe he was admiring me. For a moment our eyes met. Then he looked away.

Outside the coffee shop I paused, careful to stand away from the glass of the door and window front so that I would be out of sight from inside the shop. Then I crossed the street quickly, as the light was changing, and ducked into a shoe store with a large window display. Standing back from the window, and behind a display cabinet of shoes, I watched the door of the coffee shop. In less than a minute the man came out, stood on the sidewalk and looked in either direction, fastening his jacket. Fortunately, less than a second before he looked across the street I guessed he would and ducked down behind the display.

"There are no shoes on that side," a young woman's reproachful voice informed me.

"I just dropped something," I said, running my hand over the carpeted floor behind the stand.

"Oh, what? Maybe I can help you!"

Mentally I cursed her good nature.

"It's a contact lens," I lied. "I think it'd be better if you just let me see if I can feel it on the floor."

"Oh sure. My boyfriend wears them and he's always groping around on the floor. I'll be careful not to step there." Answering my silent prayers, she walked away. When she was safely on the other side of the store talking to a customer, I peered around the side of the display and then yanked my head back.

The man was standing on the sidewalk outside the shop, looking one way for a minute or two, and then the other.

He could, of course, simply be waiting for me to come out. But I didn't think so. If he knew I was in the store, he would have parked himself where he could keep an eye on the door.

"Found it?" My young friend was back.

"I'm afraid not. But I haven't quite covered the floor yet. I'm an old hand at this. Please don't let me keep you away from your customers."

"Take your time. It's only that . . ."

Something in her voice made me look up. "That what?"

She looked down at me, and for a moment I had a clear picture of her face. She was even younger than I'd thought.

"That if you're trying to avoid the man who's been hovering outside, I can let you out a side door."

I didn't dare get up. With my height I'd tower above the display, but I did change my ridiculous kneeling posture to at least a semi-squatting one.

"It's just as well I didn't decide to become a CIA agent, isn't it? I'd be a bust."

She grinned.

"What is my pursuer doing now?"

"He's looking one way and then another, but every now and then he comes up to the window and looks in here."

"I wonder if he's guessing, or if he's seen me."

"I think he's guessing. On one side of our store is a travel agent, and he could easily see if you were there. On the other side is a coffee shop with a counter. He could see you there, too. But our windows are curved inward a little and tinted, so he'd have a hard time being sure you were in here. I think he isn't sure."

"Have you taken early retirement from an intelligence outfit yourself?"

She smiled again. "No, but my sister's a cop and I've heard a lot from her. Besides, you're the reporter who found that body in that mansion up the Hudson, aren't you?"

The shock was like a douche of cold water. I started to get up and remembered just in time not to.

"If you can take me someplace where I can stand up without

being seen so that I won't get locked knees, then I'll be happy
to tell you."

"There's a partition about three feet away, if you can scurry
over there while I stand in front of you, you can stand up.
Better go now, he's still looking around."

Feeling absurd, aware that I looked like a waddling duck, I
ran, with knees bent, to the partition, where I was finally able
to stand. It felt wonderful. "Hoo!" I said. "Just not squatting
has been underappreciated. It should be classed with not
banging your head against a wall . . ."

"You *are* the reporter, aren't you?" my helper said.

"Yes. I guess they must have been running photographs of
me."

"In the morning news." She looked up at me carefully, her
eyes wide and dark. "You didn't kill that man, did you?"

"I did *not.*"

"I didn't think you did, but the news media and the police
are so male-dominated that it's just par for the course that
you'd be suspected."

I didn't say anything for a moment. I'd certainly had my
problems with sexism in a variety of manifestations: meatier
stories given to male reporters when I was on the staff of one of
New York's dailies, a rather patronizing attitude taken once by
an elderly police sergeant who felt that women should report
only fashion and who would not give the information unless
there were male reporters present, and the usual bevy of leers,
whistles and ill-conceived jokes. On the other hand, I did not
feel that the police were being particularly sexist. If I had been
a man caught in the vicinity of a still-warm body, I think I
would have rated just as high as suspect number one.

"Well," I said. "I hope you won't tell anyone I was in here, or
that I was being followed. I'm trying desperately to do my own
investigations."

"Of course I wouldn't. Do you think the man out there is
from the police, or is a reporter?"

Her question had an odd effect on me. It made me aware
that I didn't think he was either. This was one of those convic-
tions that seemed to rise from no rational area of my being. I
couldn't possibly justify it, yet I did not believe he was sent

either by the police or by some editor on a paper or television news show.

"I don't know," I said. "I haven't seen him before . . ." my voice faltered. Suddenly my not seeing him before was no longer a certainty.

"But you're not sure?" my friend said.

"No. I'm not. But I am sure that I'd like to take you up on your offer of a side door, before it occurs to him that that's what I'd be doing all this time."

"All right. Follow me."

We went down a dank and not very clean hall, past two doors marked "Women" and "Men" and another marked "Private." At the end of the hall was another door.

"Go through that door. You'll find yourself in the place we stack the shoes. There's a couple of inventory clerks there. Just say you've been sent out for lunch or something. The door leading out to the side street is to your left."

"I can't thank you enough," I said. "When all this is over and I'm not trying to hide myself, I'd like to take you out to lunch."

"Do you think you could advise me how to get a job on a newspaper?"

She was a little like a child wanting to know how to become a rock star.

"Have you thought of journalism school?"

Her cheerful expression faded. "Yes, but I couldn't get accepted. You have to have a college degree for that, and I'm a high school drop out."

I owed her something. On the other hand, the longer I stayed, the closer my shadow would come to realizing I had made an exit elsewhere. After that, it would only be a matter of minutes before he'd be on the side street examining shop exits.

"Look," I said, "when this is over I'll be back in touch, I promise you. If that man comes into the store, just hold him as long as you can."

I leaned forward and squeezed her shoulder. Then I went quickly through the stacks and out the side door. Providence was with me. A cab, going in the direction away from the avenue, was cruising by. I waved frantically. He screeched to a stop.

"Where to, lady?"

I thought for half a minute. Then told him to drop me at the corner of Perry Street and Seventh Avenue. I wanted to go home, where I could have peace and quiet to think. On the other hand, I wanted to get into my apartment as unobtrusively as possible, and I thought I knew how I could do it.

When I had come back to New York after my flight from Simon, I had had a stroke of rare luck in apartment hunting—never an easy task in Manhattan—unless, of course, one has unlimited funds. But I had been the happy recipient of a sublet from a fellow journalist who had been transferred to London. When the lease was up, I became the tenant of an apartment that would never in the ordinary course of events come my way. The brownstone in which my friend had had his apartment was one of eight, four on one street, four on the street back of it, that shared an entirely enclosed garden. Each house had a small back patio, and a few feet of dirt in which to grow flowers or vegetables. The rest was commonly held lawn, with two trees, benches and a small play area for children. Such gardens were not unique, but they were rare and the rents of the apartments and/or houses surrounding them soared accordingly. My writer friend had been in his apartment for a long time. The owner of his brownstone couldn't be bothered finding more affluent tenants, and preferred people in the arts, anyway. By law she could have yanked my rent up much more than she did. But she went away a lot and knew that her house would be kept in good order by me and the other five tenants.

I walked along Perry Street, turned at the end of the next block and found my way to the street back of my own. My gay friend, Paul Randley, a man of some private income which allowed him to pursue his greatest love, musical composition, lived back of me. If he would let me go through his garden apartment, and the tenant in my own house who owned the garden apartment was in, then I could get into my building without the busybodies in front knowing.

Holding my breath, I rang Paul's bell.

"Who is it?" his voice came down through the intercom.

"Kit," I said, as loud as I dared.

The buzzer sounded and I was in the front door. Paul's door at the end of his hall opened. "Do you know that you are being sought by the constabulary, to say nothing of your ill-bred friends in the public scandal sheets?" (Paul was no friend of the media, or, for that matter, the twentieth century.)

"I know. That's why I'm bothering you. If I could go across the garden to Letty's house, I could sneak into my own apartment without being found by them. I don't dare peer down my own street. That's one of the disadvantages of being tall. Are they outside my house?"

"Like a clutch of parasites. You're lucky to find me in. I just came home along your street. They're there with mikes and cameras, interviewing anybody who comes along who might know you."

"Ouch. I wonder if Letty's in?"

He waved a hand towards his phone. "Be my guest."

I dialed her number. When she answered, I told her my predicament and asked if I could use her garden and back door.

"Any time," she said. "When I think what those beasts might do to Topaz . . ." As always, her ready sympathy was not so much for me and my problems as to how they might devolve on the welfare of Topaz. Letty herself owned eleven cats. She would have been an ideal person to board Topaz with, except for the fact that Topaz terrorized her Petunia, a female of advanced years and timid temperament. So when I was away on a short assignment or holiday, she went up and fed and played with Topaz, as she did for every other cat owner in the apartment house.

Hoping that none of the neighbors whose windows looked out on the inner lawn were friends of the press and/or police, I ran across and into Letty's garden and living room, where Letty was waiting.

"I just thought you might need this for a while, so I'm giving you my extra key." And the seventy-five-year-old Letty produced a key from her apron pocket as though she were the turnkey for the Bastille.

"Thank you, Letty, a thousand times." And I aimed a kiss at

her white head about a foot below mine. Beneath the apron, she had on jeans, with running shoes on her feet and her white wavy hair in an urchin crop that mostly stood on end. The great single cause of her life was animal welfare, and she could be found in protest marches in front of the Pentagon, pharmaceutical companies and research hospitals. She had been arrested many times. Second only to her passion for animals was her ardent belief in parapsychology, astrology, spiritualism and the tarot.

Picking my way among Meadow, Tony, Tufty, Hefalump and Grazia, whose well-cared-for bodies were draped around Letty's living room, I reached her door.

"If you'll give me your key, I'll go out and get your mail from your box," Letty said. "They might be able to see you through the glass of the outer door."

"You are a friend and a wonder," I said, and handed over my mailbox key.

"By the way," she asked. "What is it they want you for?"

It was sometimes hard to remember that Letty had neither television nor radio, nor did she approve of newspapers. She took various animal-welfare magazines so that she could keep up with where she should march next and when the next cat show would be on. Other than that, she cast horoscope charts, threw the I Ching and meditated. She also fed every stray in the West Village.

I took a deep breath. "I was on assignment to go up to that great house on the Hudson, St. Cuthbert's, also known as Rivercrest, to do a story on it, that is, ostensibly, but really to find out why a female reporter committed suicide in a nearby motel with lots of the van Reider family papers around. Only, I stumbled over a body in the house itself, so it's not only the newspapers and television news who're after me. I bet it's the police."

"You're looking in the wrong place," she said, and disappeared out the door with my mailbox key.

"Here." She handed me my mail. "They're all out there. I don't *think* they could see it was your name on the mailbox I opened. But I can't be sure."

I took the mail without looking at it. "What did you mean when you said I was looking in the wrong place?"

"I don't know what I mean. I just meant what I said; whatever it is you're looking for, you're looking in the wrong place."

A little experience in the past with Letty had led me to be leery as to how much I questioned her about her psychic insights. She could suddenly get very cross and say, "You're trying to muddle me." She was always as nice as she could be the next time I saw her, and vaguely apologetic. "You see, things over there aren't the way we understand them over here."

Once when that happened before, she looked at me earnestly out of her English blue eyes. The reporter in me strained at the leash. I wanted to ask her what "over there" and "over here" meant, although I had a fairly clear idea. But I had bottled up my impulse. "Yes," I said, because I was fond of her. "I can see that."

I recall the occasion because she looked at me with great kindness. "No you can't. You think it's all a lot of nonsense. But you don't want to get me upset, because you're fond of me. But it's true, nevertheless, it's true."

I thought of this now. "Well," I said. "I'll try and look in the right place. And if you have any prayers, all help would be gratefully received."

"Prayers are all around you all the time, you silly girl. Didn't you know that?"

I thought of my severely Anglican, conservative, doctrinally oriented father. "I guess I don't."

I was about to close her front door when she said, "Be careful."

There was an odd, intense, uncharacteristic note to her voice.

"Of what?"

"Of an old love that isn't a love. Be careful."

I grinned to myself as I climbed the three flights of stairs. "Beware of the dark man riding a black horse." It sounded like the standard gypsy gibberish. Come on, Letty, I thought. You can do better than that.

I opened my door. Topaz was sitting in front of it in his classic pose. Seeing him like this, it was easy to understand why the Egyptians worshiped felines. They looked as though they contained the wisdom of the gods and of the sages. He stared at me out of his great yellow eyes, and then gave a gigantic yawn. After that he came toward me on his padded, tufted feet and rubbed backward and forward against my legs. "Mine, mine, mine . . ." I thought I heard him purr.

I sat down on the sofa, partly to let him have his immediate portion of TLC, which he received while sitting in my lap, and to check in with my answering service.

The messages were from all the people who had called before: representatives of various branches of the media, some known to me, some unknown, some of them leaving messages alluding to journalistic solidarity, now that I myself was the story. There were Detective Jensen, Piers, and one man and one woman who did not wish to leave their names. Putting down the receiver, I wondered what happened to the second man who refused to leave his name.

"All right, Topaz," I said, reaching around his solid form to get at my mail. There were three direct-mail solicitations and two letters. One of the letters was from a girl I went to school with. The other had a typed address and the name of a law firm in the upper left-hand corner.

Well, I thought, I was looking for a lawyer. Maybe this would be the one. Tearing the envelope, I took out two pages and did what I always do first: glanced at the signature. Then I felt a shock go through my system. The signature was "Simon."

5

"I've been sober now for almost a year," Simon wrote, "including the three months I spent in the most recent rehabilitation hospital. I say 'recent' because over the past several years, there have been five hospitals, quite a few jails for drunk driving, some drug rehab centers and a couple of bad accidents.

"I'm writing now because I want you to know how sorry I am for the way I treated you—not only the physical abuse, although that was unforgivable, but all the rest: the lies, the accusations, the irresponsibility. I hope you will someday be able to forgive me.

"I've finally landed a job at the bottom of the heap in this law firm and am trying, among other things, to repay the debts I managed to accumulate . . ."

I snatched up the envelope. The return address said, "Reiser, Bach, Gonzalez and Morton." The address was somewhere down in the Wall Street area. Then I looked at the top of the first page. There was no residence address there.

"The creep," I said aloud, my old rage ballooning in me like a red wave of fury. I stood up, unseating Topaz, who gave a loud squawk. "How dare he?" I stormed, walking back and forth in my living room. "How *dare* he write me after all he did!"

The memories, all too available, crowded into my mind: the stinging slaps, the backhanded blows across my mouth, cutting my upper lip with my teeth, the blows to the side of the head, the drunken insults, the vomit, the awful, degrading life of those last few months. "The nerve," I almost shouted. "The bloody nerve, writing me like that . . ."

I tore his letter into shreds, across and across and across. Then I set fire to the pieces in an ashtray, and flushed them down the toilet.

After that I went into my bedroom, took off my raincoat, lay on the bed, and cried. But they were tears of frustrated anger. I wanted to scream at the top of my voice, and wished for a moment that I had one of those large rubber things people have to punch when they want to relieve tension. Better still, I would like Simon to punch, again and again and again until he was nothing but a piece of bloody jelly. Then I cried again, this time out of exhausted emotion.

When I finally stopped, Topaz was on my stomach, kneading his claws in my jacket, purring loudly, and the telephone was ringing.

I let it ring, waiting for the answering service operator to pick it up, which she did on the fourth ring. A few minutes later, I leaned over and pushed the lever on the bottom so that the ring would be silent, then I lay back. What I had to do, when I could pull myself together and stop thinking about the enormity of Simon, was to make a plan of action. I must go to the place where Crystal Mahoney had managed to get off drugs, I had to call Claire Aldington to see if she had been able to get in touch with her friend in the police department and I had to think about the two men who had shadowed me, one now dead . . .

It was at that point that I dozed off.

It had been an exhausting day, and I slept heavily and longer than I would normally. When I awoke, I knew I had been awakened by something, although I didn't know what it was. And then I saw in the near-dark room, at the end of the bed, a ginger-red striped cat, its back arched, its tail straight up, giving its raucous miaow, a sound that brought back a flash of recollection: the ginger cat beside Hilary van Reider's son lying on the bed. It also brought back something else: an overwhelming sense of fear. My skin crawled.

"Topaz," I cried. Then I leaned over and turned on the light beside the bed. There was no cat. Topaz was nowhere to be seen.

"Topaz!" I yelled. My apartment is not big. It's an old building and I'm lucky to have a floor through including a kitchen with a window. But there is only a bedroom, a study and a living room.

"Topaz!" I cried again. I flung myself off the bed and onto the floor, and without bothering to put on my shoes, went looking for my cat. It took what seemed an endless time and was not made easier by realizing I had left my kitchen window open that morning and forgotten to close it. There was no fire escape to let someone use it as an entrance, but I had failed to put in the new screen I had bought when the old one tore. Topaz, in pursuit of a fly or a bird or a piece of fluff could and would leap out. Cats have no sense of depth. Filled with guilt, I peered down onto the courtyard. There was no sign of a fat marmalade-colored cat. Finally, a faint miaowing attracted my attention. Topaz's considerable girth was squeezed between the back of the stove and the wall. I could have killed him for sheer relief.

"You rotten, wicked cat!" I said loudly, shoving and pulling at the stove. "Don't you ever again give me a scare like that." I still couldn't reach him, so, when I had widened the passage enough for him to free himself, I took a box of dry food out of the cupboard and shook it. This was a treat usually reserved for a once-a-week sprinkle on his regular canned delicacy. He adored it and would have been more than willing to make it his entire cuisine. But I had been told by my vet to use such treats sparingly. I continued to shake the box. Making funny noises to himself, Topaz finally emerged, dirty and smudged. I picked him up, dirt and all, and hugged him.

"Rotten cat!" I repeated. The beginnings of a purr started deep in his well-covered ribs. I put him down and he pecked away at the few dry pieces I had put in his dish. Curiously,

though, when I started out of the kitchen to get the new screen
I had brought to put in the kitchen window, he left the dish and
came after me, still following when I went back into the kitchen
and put the screen in the window.

"If you had jumped out, it would have been my fault," I said.

Then I picked him up again and went back towards my
room. Just before I entered it, he pushed his strong back legs
against my arm and jumped to the floor.

"All right. If that's the way you feel, don't join me in bed."

I didn't really want to lie down again, but I seemed gripped
by a strange lassitude. So I stretched out, deciding to plan my
course of action. After a moment, I heard one of Topaz's
characteristic squawks. He was sitting, in his Egyptian-god
pose, at the threshold of my door, but he didn't come in.

I sat up in bed cross-legged and confronted the curious
sequence of events that had just occurred.

For some reason I could not imagine, Topaz had been at the
end of my bed, with his back arched and his tail up, making a
sound that had reminded me strongly of the cat at St. Cuthbert's. When I turned on the light, he had obviously taken off
and run behind the stove.

But why? He had never done such a thing before in his life.
He had his own squawk, but it was by no means even approxi-
mately the feral sound that had come from that strange red cat
at the end of my bed and on the bed beside young van Reider.
Besides, the red cat was lean, smooth and short-haired.

There was so much I had to do, phone calls to make, plans to
arrange. Why was I sitting here, surrounded by depression,
unable to function, with my cat refusing to enter my room?

The desire to sleep was becoming stronger. I was beginning
to lie down when Topaz gave one of his characteristic miaows,
which usually meant simply, "Dinner: where is it?"

"Oh, all right," I said. "Not that you deserve it." I made
myself stand up and walk across the room.

Then I went back to the kitchen, with Topaz loping ahead of
me. He ate a can of food a day; one half in the morning, one
half in the evening. But he did not like it cold, so I set the can in
some boiling water, while he paced back and forth beneath me,

rubbing against me from time to time. When the food was warm, I put it in his dish and gave him some fresh water.

Then I went back to my living room and checked with my answering service. There had been several calls since I had turned my bedroom phone off, one of them from Claire Aldington, and two from men who did not leave their names.

"What time did those calls come in?" I asked, surprised both that there had been so many and that I had not heard the living-room telephone.

"Well, they came in all the way from four-fifteen, when you must have gone out, to nine-thirty."

"*Nine-thirty?* It's nine-thirty?" I glanced at my watch as I spoke.

"Nine thirty-four to be exact. Why? You sound funny. Are you all right?"

I had used this service for a long time and was on friendly terms with most of these operators.

"Yes," I said slowly. "I'm all right. The thing is, I was here, but I was asleep."

"You sure must sleep soundly," the operator, a girl named Doreen, said. "I could use some of that talent when my children get going. Had you taken a sleeping pill?"

"No, of course not. I was just taking a nap . . . Sorry, Doreen, I didn't mean to snap like that. I think I'm a little ashamed of sleeping so soundly."

"It's okay." And she closed off the phone.

Slowly I put the receiver down. I realized the reason I had snapped was that it had occurred to me that I had slept with the leaden depth I remembered from the few times I had ever taken a sleeping pill. Nor had I even noticed, consciously, that day had become night . . .

I continued to sit there, with Topaz calmly washing himself on the carpet in front of me. There was something struggling to the surface of my mind that was bothering me. Topaz was a big, fuzzy, squushy marmalade cat. He was not ginger-striped. I had only once before to my knowledge seen a ginger-striped cat, and that had been at St. Cuthbert's. No, there was another time . . . Finding a memory that was lost, I decided, was like trying to catch air in a sieve.

I was wondering whether eating something would make me feel better or not when there was a knock on the door and a voice called, "It's me. Letty."

"All right. Just a minute."

I got up and opened the door. "Come in."

She came in and looked around. Then she looked down at Topaz, who was rubbing against her legs. A mild jealousy filled me. Topaz had never before done that to anyone but me.

"You should be flattered," I said, trying not to sound grudging.

"You all right?" she asked.

"Of course. Why?"

"Just asking."

Perhaps it was Letty's English accent, for which I always had a slight weakness. Whatever the reason, I found myself telling her about the ginger-red cat and Topaz behind the stove. "It just must have been one of those horribly vivid dreams. I was sleeping like one dead. My answering service said all kinds of calls came in, and while I had my bedroom phone turned off, I'm surprised I didn't hear the one in the living room. It's not that far away."

"Did you say you'd seen a ginger cat before?"

"Did I say that? I must really be going mad. Yes, beside a boy lying on the bed upstairs at the mansion. But that was obviously a real cat. This plainly was a distorted image of my own darling Topaz."

"But Topaz was behind the stove, you just told me. I brought up a prayer book. You wanted my prayers. Well, here I am. I'm going to say some."

I couldn't have been more astounded if Letty had said she was going to sing the national anthem. On the other hand, it's not the kind of things you can tell a person not to do.

"Of course," I said lamely.

So, feeling distinctly foolish, I stood there while Letty, her hands clasped around the book, gazed straight ahead with her incredible blue eyes. She didn't say anything, and yet I found there was absolutely no question in my mind that she was doing what she said she would be doing: praying.

"Now I shall go into your bedroom. That needs it far more."

I followed her in, and Topaz followed me. Topaz and I stood at the door while she walked around my room saying nothing, doing nothing outwardly, yet . . . I felt the drugged, sleepy feeling fall off of me as though it were a wet coat.

"Lock your windows when you leave the apartment," she said. "And I brought you some tofu."

"Thank you." I hated tofu. But I reached out and took the damp package.

"I know you don't like it, but give it a try." She glanced down. "Topaz might like some. He'll be all right now. By the way, your friend Paul brought me his key for you to use when eluding the Furies."

"The Furies?"

"The press. He said you could always come through his apartment. He tried to call you, but there wasn't an answer. I said I'd bring it upstairs. You can go into your bedroom now. It'll be all right. Try to remember about the ginger cat. It comes from somewhere in your life, but long ago. Good night."

I called Claire Aldington the next morning.

"Lieutenant O'Neill says you can come and talk to him, but wants you to call him first. He's not always at his desk. This is his number." And she gave it to me. Then she said, "I didn't hear any more about you or the mansion or the boy in last night's television news. You must have evaded your fellow journalists."

"I did." I hesitated for a moment. The fewer people who knew about my escape route the better. On the other hand, I was quite certain I could trust her. "Please don't tell anybody; I live in a house that backs up onto a garden shared by eight houses in all. And I was able to enlist the help of some neighbors about getting in."

"Lucky you. With all due respect to your profession, regard for others' privacy is not their leading concern."

"No. I wouldn't have admitted that a few weeks ago, but I can see how it is from the other side. Well, I'll call your lieutenant friend." And I hung up.

I dialed the number Claire had given me and asked for Lieutenant O'Neill.

"O'Neill," a male voice answered.

"My name is Kit Maitland. Claire Aldington gave me your number and—"

"I know who you are. And I'd like to talk to you."

This was a slight turn of the tables. "Oh," I said.

"Isn't that what you wanted too? To talk?"

"Yes. But the way you said it, it sounded as though the police were out hunting for me."

"If they were out hunting for you, Miss Maitland, they'd have found you."

I was finding this conversation less and less comforting. However, I had asked Claire to make this introduction. I could blame only myself.

"Let's start with you," the lieutenant said. "What is it you want to talk to me about?"

"About the feeling I had that the police up in Westchester were looking on me as a suspect."

"I think they are. I've just finished talking with them."

"But—" Except for keeping on saying that I had not killed the man, there wasn't much I could say.

"Why don't we meet?" Lieutenant O'Neill said. "Why don't you come down here?"

I didn't want to. I wanted to get started on trying to track down Crystal Mahoney's drug-rehabilitation place, so that I could talk to some of the people who knew her then. However, I also didn't want to tell the lieutenant this. "Okay," I said. "When and where?"

"How about right now down in my office here?" And he gave me an address in the financial district.

I jotted it down. "Okay. I'll be there in about an hour."

I checked all the windows, remembering suddenly Letty's statement, "Lock your windows." They were all locked.

Feeling somehow that I owed Topaz something, I left him a smattering of dry food in the bottom of his dish.

"Now try and stay out of trouble," I said and bent down and kissed him between his ears.

I rang Letty's doorbell. When it was obvious she wasn't at

home, I let myself in, went through her apartment to her back door, across her garden and through Paul's flat.

Forty minutes later I was facing a wiry man of about my own height, with very blue eyes and a guarded expression.

"Sit down," he said, indicating the chair in front of his desk. I glanced around the stained buff-colored walls, the incredibly high ceiling, the window looking out on another wall.

"Early Sweatshop," I said, indicating the decor.

"They don't want us to feel they have any money for frills. How come you know Mrs. Aldington?"

"Didn't she tell you?"

"Why don't you tell me too. Two perfectly honest people can give two different accounts of an accident or some other event."

I took a breath. "I went to get the church's permission to go up to St. Cuthbert's, the ci-devant Rivercrest—"

"The what?"

I felt ashamed. I was being sophisticated and literary and he was letting me know it.

"The mansion up the Hudson built by the van Reiders and called Rivercrest by them, but bought by St. Anselm's and renamed St. Cuthbert's."

He grunted. "Go on."

"The rector was away, so I was sent to Mrs. Aldington's office. She gave me written permission. The next morning I went up there . . ."

Doggedly I went through everything I could remember that happened from the moment I encountered the unpleasant van Reider and even more unpleasant Akela, to the time I finally returned home. The lieutenant sat, one hand fiddling with a pen, his eyes sometimes on me and sometimes on the pen.

"Was that your real reason for wanting to do the piece?"

I was fairly certain that Claire may have told him about Crystal Mahoney. "As I am sure you know from Mrs. Aldington, no. I went up to see if I could find any link between the apparent suicide of a newspaperwoman, Crystal Mahoney, who died in a motel room with van Reider papers on her bureau, and the house itself. Especially considering its queer history."

"Did you ask van Reider this when you talked to him?"

"I did. He was not only uncooperative, he was generally boorish and rude."

O'Neill was watching me carefully. "Did he give you any information at all that could be thought of as a link? What did he say about the fact that his family papers were there?"

"He implied . . . I don't think he actually said, but he certainly implied that Crystal, like all reporters, had no compunction about pawing through the furniture in the house."

"So he really didn't answer?"

I paused. Then, "No, he didn't. Piers, the man who assigned this story to me—"

"That'd be Piers Somerville, of *The Public Eye?*"

"You know him?"

"In a manner of speaking. So he assigned you the story. Why?"

The trouble was, I couldn't remember whether I had told Claire about Piers. If I had, then she might well have told O'Neill and he would be testing me, which I didn't care for. But since I couldn't be sure, then I would have to answer.

"Piers had heard about Crystal—how she had died, possibly committed suicide while on a story about the house. And that when the police came to her room in the motel where she died there were van Reider family papers scattered over the bureau. His real reason for sending me off to do a story on that ancient and ugly monument was to see if I could find out about Crystal."

"But he didn't tell you right away, I take it."

"No." The more that aspect of the whole thing was talked about, the more I felt a fool for not having seen it right away.

"Weren't you suspicious immediately?"

"No. Maybe—probably—I should have been. But I've done stories for Piers before, and he's always been very straight with me."

"Why do you suppose he wasn't being straight with you now?"

"Why all these questions, Lieutenant?"

"Look, you looked me up, not the other way around. Mrs.

Aldington led me to believe that you wanted to talk to me. Am I right?"

"Yes."

"Okay. Why do you think he wasn't being straight with you?"

"I think you'll have to ask him that yourself. He gave me a sort of reason recently, yesterday, in fact. But I think you should hear it from him, not me."

"Okay. Why did you want to meet me and talk to me?"

At that particular point I would have given much to deny that I had. But I couldn't. For one thing, it wouldn't be the truth. For another, it would be letting Claire down with a bang.

"I guess, because I was hoping to find . . . find a friend at court, so to speak."

"But you wanted a friend at court—so to speak—who wouldn't ask any questions of his own, who would just take everything you had to say without a word of query. Right?"

We stared at each other. "I suppose it's right that that's what I wanted. I see now it wasn't very . . . very feasible. I guess I wanted someone to believe what I said."

"I haven't said I don't. But before I get into something like this I like to know where I am."

"How did you get into it—that is, besides being Mrs. Aldington's friend? I mean, are the New York City police connected with the Dutchess County police?"

"No. We cooperate when necessary. Luckily for you, the guy in charge there is a buddy of mine. I talked to him early this morning."

"Has anything new come to light? I mean, do they know who the man is whose body I found?"

He didn't answer for a moment. Then, "You have no idea yourself?"

"What makes you think I might?" I knew, of course, I should tell him right away. But wouldn't my role as chief suspect then be marked in stone?

"Come on, Ms. Maitland. You know something, and you're not making our job easier."

"All right. I'll tell you. But please remember, *I did not kill him.*"

"I'll remember that you made that point. Now please go on."

"Beginning a couple of months ago, I noticed a guy standing on the corner opposite my apartment, staring up at my windows. At first I just thought he was watching somebody fix the roof or something—my apartment is at the top. But then I saw he was watching my windows." The sense of eeriness came back as I talked.

"I'm three floors up, so my view of him was out of perspective. I had an excellent sight of the top of his head. His eyes looked like dark slits, but then anybody's would at that distance and angle, and he had a bump on his nose. He was dressed in jeans and denim jacket with some kind of dark T-shirt or turtleneck sweater underneath.

"The first time I was really sure he was looking at my windows, I tore down the stairs—all three flights of them—to ask him what the hell he thought he was doing. But he'd gone by the time I flung open the front door. How he knew I was going to run downstairs—there isn't an elevator—I don't know. But it happened several times afterward. I always ran down when I saw him, and he had always disappeared. Maybe he's some kind of expert in ESP or something. I don't know. But the thing is, he'd be there for a while, and then I wouldn't see him for several days or a week, and then he'd be back . . ." I paused. "I can't be certain, because, as I said, seeing somebody from three floors up is not the same as seeing them lying on the floor. But the guy—the dead guy—looked slightly familiar. I told that—or at least implied it—to the police in Dutchess County when I called them. But I couldn't think where I'd seen him. It suddenly came to me when I was talking to Mrs. Aldington. Because the last time I thought I'd seen him was the morning I went to see her to get permission to go up to St. Cuthbert's."

"What I can't understand," Lieutenant O'Neill said, "is why, when this guy seemed to be harassing you, you didn't call the police. You could have called while he was watching you, and a couple of officers would have driven up and caught him at it. Why didn't you call then?"

"I don't know. Now it seems like the obvious thing to have

done. Probably if he'd done it every day, I would have. But he didn't. He was irregular and unpredictable."

"So you didn't run down every time you caught him looking up towards your apartment?"

"No, I couldn't. Sometimes I'd be undressed, or just out of the shower."

"Did you mention it to anyone?"

No. I hadn't. Only at this moment, being questioned by Lieutenant O'Neill, did it occur to me how strange that might seem. For whatever reason, I had never been a confiding person. I had many acquaintances, most of them connected with my work. But I did not make friends easily. And after the debacle of Simon, I had become something of a loner. The thought of Simon made me remember the letter I had just received. I shifted in my seat.

"Well?"

"Well what?" I glanced quickly at the officer's expressionless and implacable face. I remembered his question, but I didn't want to answer it because of the implications my answer might make to him.

"Did you mention the man watching your windows to anyone?" he asked patiently.

"No. I didn't. I'm not a gregarious person, Lieutenant, and I don't have girlish exchanges and confidences with other women over dinner and coffee."

"Too middle-class for somebody like you, I guess."

"That's a snide response."

"Sorry. I didn't intend you to take it that way. I was being literal. You're a professional woman, and I assumed you meant you had put a distance between yourself and kaffeeklatsches in the suburbs."

"Women can still confide in one another," I shot back, and saw that I had obediently fallen into the hole that he had dug in front of me.

He grinned. "But you don't. All right, all right. That wasn't fair. But don't you think it's odd, when a woman observes a man staring up at her apartment, a voyeur, whatever his motives, she a) doesn't call the police or b) tell some sympathetic friend about it?"

I knew then, of course, why I hadn't told anyone about the man, even though I was frightened by him and by his watching me. But I did not want to go into the matter with the lieutenant.

"No," I said now. "I don't think it's odd. I just think that I'm not a confiding person."

There was a short silence. Then the lieutenant said, "All right. I'll leave that for now. Since you remembered who the man might be, have you told the Dutchess County police?"

"No. I assume you will."

"Yes, I will, but I also think you should."

"Why?"

"I'm not your lawyer, Ms. Maitland. Nor am I a sort of liaison. I'm a police officer. I'll certainly pass this information on to my buddy, but I think it would look better coming from you. Be my guest." And he pushed forward the phone on his desk.

I got up. "I'm not going to be pressured by you, Lieutenant. As you just finished saying, you're not my lawyer. I think I'll find myself one before I take any further steps."

"As you wish. By the way, did you tell your boyfriend?"

"Which—" I stopped, furious at having almost answered an obviously fishing question. "And I don't like trick questions, either."

He grinned. "Let me know if I can be of any more help."

"I will," I said, refusing to smile back, even though the impulse was there. He was one smart cop.

I came out of the police station and walked towards the nearest subway station. I'd looked up the address of the community drug-rehabilitation place that Crystal had gone to, which turned out to be a few blocks from the Seventy-seventh Street subway stop. While I was waiting for the train, I reflected wryly on my insight as to why I had not confided to anyone about the man watching my apartment. Somewhere in the back of my mind I had associated him with either Simon or Joris. Why, I wasn't entirely sure, except that I was always on the alert for anyone who could tell me where Simon might be, so that I could complete my steps toward a divorce, and

Joris—? I had thought the old obsession had died, as surely Joris must have done by now. Yet obviously it hadn't. Behind everything else was still the hope that he would somehow, someday send me a message, and then I would find him again, and learn what had happened to him, and why he had left me.

But you know now where Simon is, my rational mind pointed out as I paced the platform. I was so surprised at the duplicity of my inner self, that I stopped pacing and stood where I was, a few inches from the platform's edge. On the one hand, I did not mention to the police a man's harassing me, because he might, remotely, reveal where my still undivorced husband might be. On the other, when a letter from the husband came, I went into such a fury over what he'd done to me, that I destroyed all evidence of the letter as though it had emanated from the KGB and I were a spy. I must be nuts, I thought. But did I destroy the envelope? I couldn't be sure. For a moment, I was tempted to go up out of the subway station and go over to another which would take me home, where I could look. In fact, I half turned—

"Look out, lady," somebody yelled.

Something struck me a glancing blow and then veered off. At the same moment, the train, its whistle shrieking, thundered a few inches past me.

I was too stunned to be frightened. "What—?" I started.

"Lady, don't you know better than to stand at the edge of the platform? Are you crazy or something, knowing the kooks that litter the subways these days?"

There was a small crowd around me. The man talking was a transit cop. "Don't ever do that," a woman said to me. "You could have been killed."

"What happened?" I said.

"Are you going to take this train?" the cop asked.

"Yes."

"Well, get in. I'll take it with you." He took my arm and we stepped into the train. The doors closed.

"Sit down, if you want to," he said.

There were plenty of seats. The people in the car were staring at me, whether because they knew what had happened from people coming into the car or because they thought I was being arrested, I didn't know.

I didn't sit down. Instead I said to the cop, "What happened? What went flying past me?"

"You didn't know?"

"No. I didn't. Or I wouldn't be asking you."

"You nearly got knocked off the platform in front of the train. That's what nearly happened. Didn't you see the guy shoot past you?"

I shook my head. "No. I didn't see him. I was busy trying to regain my balance." The full meaning of what the cop was saying then penetrated. Fear turned my insides into mush. "You mean . . . are you saying that somebody *tried* to push me off the platform in front of the train? I thought it was just some kind of an accident."

"It wasn't an accident. But you were lucky. Some other guy shoved the one who was trying to push you, and they both took off up the stairs. Do you know what all this is about?"

In my mind I saw again the man in the restaurant. I saw his face and his eyes, and the mole beside the right eye. But I had eluded him. I had gone out the side entrance, and then gone into my own apartment house by a different route, the same route I had used this morning to leave. How could he have found me?

"Do you have any idea who it could be?" the cop persisted.

"Yes, no."

"Well, which?"

"I'm not sure," I said.

"I think we'd better go down to the precinct and talk about it."

"I just came from the precinct. I don't have to go back."

"Which precinct?"

"Lieutenant O'Neill," and I gave the address.

"He ought to know about this."

"I'll tell him, but not right now. I'm feeling a little shaken."

"The sooner you tell him, the better."

"Okay," I said. "I'll call him when I get home."

"Where are you getting out?" the transit cop asked, getting out his notebook.

Suddenly I changed my mind about going to the drug rehabilitation center. "I'm going to the Church of St. Anselm. I
want to talk to the Reverend Claire Aldington. I'm sure you
know the church's address."

"Yeah, I guess we do. You a member?"

"Not . . . exactly. I was thinking of going there one Sunday maybe."

"Then why're you seeing the lady clergyman?"

"Because"—I glanced at him—"conversations with the
clergy are privileged, Officer."

He shrugged. "For somebody who almost got knocked in
front of a train you seem stitched pretty tight."

He was right. Which was the reason I was going to see
Claire. Loner that I was, I had to talk to somebody . . . there
had to be somebody who could make sense of what was happening.

"That's why I want to talk to Mrs. Aldington."

But she wasn't in.

Having steeled myself for this interview in which I would
hold nothing back, I felt bitterly let down, depressed. As
though the powers that be were punishing me for not having
talked to the police before.

All right, I thought then, I'd go over to the rehabilitation
center.

The Eastside Community Outreach Program consisted of a
row of former tenements attached to a building that had once
been a school. Part of this hodgepodge was the headquarters
of a drug rehabilitation subgroup, although the halfway house
where some of the patients were assigned was two blocks away.
About 80 percent of the people working there, I decided, were
volunteers.

When I finally got to the woman who appeared to be the
administrative head of the rehab group, I said I was interested
in the late Crystal Mahoney, and as much of her history as they
could give me.

"We don't give out histories of our patients," the woman
said curtly.

She appeared to be about in her forties, with an intelligent but unrevealing face. She was also neither welcoming nor friendly.

"I am trying to investigate why this young woman died in a motel up in Westchester after she had gone up apparently to do a story on a historic house up there."

"Are you a member of the police? In which case, show me your badge."

"I'm not a member of the police," I said patiently. "I'm a journalist, an investigative reporter."

"Something we really don't need up here. We do as good a job as we can with very limited funds. The government has cut down what little we had and private donations have fallen off. You're not the first news reporter to come poking and prying around here to find something discreditable about one of our successes, Crystal Mahoney, and I'm not going to make the same mistake with you as with him."

So somebody had been there before. "Did the story that appeared denigrate your establishment here?" I asked.

"Since you've undoubtedly read it, that question is superfluous and I see no reason to answer it."

"I haven't seen any story about this place, ma'am. I came here at the suggestion of the Reverend Claire Aldington."

I had dropped the right name. The woman's hard face softened a little. "I'm surprised at Claire. It's not as though we haven't had more than our share of media publicity."

"I know you don't believe me. But I truly have not read anything about Crystal Mahoney. Would you at least tell me where the story appeared?"

The hostile dark eyes stared at me for a moment. Then the woman leaned down, opened her bottom desk drawer and handed me some sheets stapled together.

I took them. This was the first time I had seen a photograph of Crystal Mahoney, albeit showing her in death. The body was lying on the bed of what was plainly a motel room. The face was turned away, so I couldn't see it too well, but the abundant bleached hair was highly visible, as was the woman's excellent figure. She had on a robe that had fallen open to reveal the cleavage of opulent breasts and excellent thighs. Yet there was something degraded and pathetic about her. Piers had said she had some journalistic talent. Here, she seemed to reflect more the profession she had fallen into to feed her drug habit.

Certainly the story underneath the photograph was written with sensation in mind.

"This pathetic young woman, former patient of a noted rehabilitation house, a drug addict, thought by her friends to be cured . . . who had been unable, once more, to resist the lure of drugs . . . Known for the parties and the discos she attended, often as the guest of some rich tycoon or chairman of a multinational concern, Crystal died in a country motel, undoubtedly on her way to another assignation . . . Perhaps it is lucky that she appears to have no family."

There was no mention of the papers supposedly strewn about her room, or the fact that she had gone up to investigate something about St. Cuthbert's. The story hinted, not too subtly, that she was on her way to a trick . . .

I wondered if that was the way Claire had seen her. I couldn't convince myself that this would be the case. Claire was no dummy. I also wondered if she had seen this particular news article.

"Do you know if Mrs. Aldington has seen this story?" I asked.

"I see no particular reason why she should." Was there a touch of hostility there? I wondered.

"Well, Mrs. Aldington did treat Miss Mahoney at some point."

"Then, she may very well have it. May I have it back?"

Quickly I glanced at the running head on the top of the first page of the story. It revealed the name of the same supermarket tabloid that Crystal had worked for. Curiouser and curiouser, as the immortal Alice had once said. If Crystal Mahoney had been hired by that paper to do a story—whatever kind of story, I still wasn't sure what it might have been—then why would they portray her now as a super party girl, a call girl, a prostitute?

"Can I have this just for a while?" I asked. "Only long enough to take it to the copy shop in the next block and have it copied."

"Why would you want to do that? And how do I know you'd bring it back?"

"You don't. But I don't think I've done anything to make you think I'm dishonest."

We glared at one another for a moment. Finally, grudgingly, "We have a copier here. I'll have a copy made for you." And before I could take in her intent, she had snatched the stapled sheets from me and disappeared from the room.

Since she seemed inclined to suspect me of a variety of crimes, I decided, in the interest of allaying her suspicions, I would remain nailed to my chair, my eyes straight ahead, so she could not accuse me of riffling through her files in her absence. Which was just as well, because she was not gone long.

"Here," she said, handing me some stapled sheets, and replacing the original in her bottom drawer. "And now, if you'll excuse me, I'm very busy."

I got up. "Thank you," I said as cordially as I could. And left. I didn't have a hope of getting anything more out of this woman until I came with far more powerful credentials than just myself and a mention of Claire's name.

Outside, I became aware that I hadn't eaten since seven and that it was now—I glanced at my watch—two. In the immediate vicinity there on First Avenue were a variety of eateries: the Asparagas Stalk, plainly a health-food place, Gino's, an Italian restaurant, the Levant, something Middle Eastern, Pietro's Pizza, and two burger places. I decided for pizza.

With a good segment of cheese and mushroom pizza on a plate in front of me, and sipping a soda, I scanned the copied story that the woman at the community project had given me. It ran about four pages—unusually long for tabloids of this type. Nevertheless, I decided, after going over it twice, it had been longer. The jump from the third to the fourth page could, if pushed, make sense, but not if one read down the paragraph.

Either by design or accident, one page had been omitted. And I was quite sure it was not by accident.

6

I sat there staring at the pages, trying to remember if I had seen any other than the front page with the photograph of the girl on the bed. But, of course, I hadn't. One page, or even more pages, were left out. I could, of course, go back and demand to see the full story. And just how far would that get me? I thought sardonically. It would get me back to the front door in double-quick time, and all I'd do would be to strengthen the resolve of the inimical administrator toward me.

I folded the sheets and put them back in my bag and stared at the half of the pizza segment I hadn't eaten. A series of depressing realities marched through my mind: in nothing I had gone to investigate had I succeeded in finding anything— that is, anything that mattered. I was watched by a man who turned up dead. I was watched and followed by another man who barely missed pushing me off a subway platform in front of a train. I . . .

And at that point the horror of it, the fact that I had missed a dreadful death by inches and through what seemed an accident hit me fully for the first time. The whole, awful scene

unrolled in my mind. I could feel myself losing balance, I could
see the oncoming train, I could hear my own scream, I could
even feel the disbelief, the feeling of slow motion that a remembered accident brings. And then the wheels coming
closer to my body lying across the tracks, my frantic effort to
escape, my failure . . .

"Are you all right, miss?"

The man, the pizza man, was looking at my face, only his was
on top and mine was underneath. There were other faces
staring down at me. I started to get up, and a wave of nausea
hit me. I put my hand up to my forehead, which was clammy.

"We'll call an ambulance, lady. You don't look so good."

"What happened?" I asked.

"You just fell off the chair and onto the floor," the pizza man
said. "You fainted."

"Maybe we should get a doctor," a third voice said.

"No." I sat up, waited for the wave of nausea to subside, and
then slowly, helped by several pairs of hands, stood up and sat
on the chair which somebody hastily righted for me.

"Put your head down," another voice suggested.

I was glad to do so.

"Maybe a doctor?"

"No." I sat up. "I'll be all right. No doctor, no ambulance.
But it would be nice if somebody could get me a taxi."

"You wait right here, lady. I'll get the taxi."

The Good Samaritan rushed out of the pizza parlor, and the
owner brought me some water.

"You take care, lady. No good letting your health go. Most
important thing you have."

Next to my life, I thought. The fearful fantasy of what had
almost happened at the subway platform threatened to replay
itself. I stood up. "Thanks very much. You've been very kind.
Do I owe you anything?"

"Not a thing. Now, you do like I say, like my old lady is
always saying to me."

"And what's that?"

"You take it easy!"

"I'll try."

I got out of the taxi at Perry Street and rang Paul's bell. If he were in, then I didn't want to use the key and tramp through his apartment without, so to speak, his expecting me. But he was not in, so I let myself into his house, and then into his apartment. I crossed his living room, went into the hall leading to the kitchen and opened the door leading to the garden. Then I crossed and went through the whole thing again with Letty's apartment. Letty, too, wasn't in. By the time I got to my own apartment I felt I had been on a safari.

Topaz was, as always, sitting in the front hall a few feet in front of the door.

"You heard me downstairs," I said.

He yawned, then came over and imprinted me all over again as his in case the old mark and/or smell had faded.

I went straight to the living-room wastebasket and emptied it onto the floor. Then I picked over every single paper and envelope twice to make sure I hadn't missed Simon's. When I knew beyond doubt that I had not thrown it into that wastebasket, I went into the bedroom and examined that with equal care. Plainly, I decided, putting all the stuff back into the basket, I had destroyed the envelope along with the letter.

And with that realization came another, this time in the form of a question. How did Simon know where to send his letter? I had an unlisted phone number, therefore was not in the directory. As a journalist, I knew there were other ways to get an unlisted address. Being a lawyer, he probably had even more resources. However, he had to make something of an effort, which somehow added weight to the sending of the letter. That brought me back to trying to remember the name of the law firm that appeared in the upper left corner of the envelope.

I might as well have tried to recall the first line of the Odyssey—if I had ever known it. The only name from the group of lawyers that stuck was Gonzalez . . . and how far would that get me?

I was sitting there trying to dredge my recollection, when the telephone rang.

"The receptionist said you'd tried to see me today," Claire's voice said. "I'm sorry I wasn't in. Is there anything I can do?"

By this time my overwhelming need to confide in somebody had passed. My basic, reserved nature had reasserted itself.

"Well . . . I guess not. It was just an impulse. There's no need to take up your time."

"By which I take it that you've lost your eagerness to talk. The receptionist said you sounded quite anxious."

The receptionist should mind her own business, I thought crossly.

"A couple of odd things have happened . . ." My voice trailed off.

"Such as?"

The "couple of things" trooped through my mind: a second man not only seemed to be following me, but was most likely the man who tried to push me off the platform . . . I just got a letter from my separated husband, a lawyer who might have had a hand in assigning all these watchers, and destroyed any chance I might have of remembering his address . . . the woman at the rehab center grudgingly gave me the story about Crystal Mahoney, and then left out at least one page . . .

"Are you still there?" Claire asked.

I took a deep breath. "Yes. Talking . . . confiding . . . has never been my leading virtue. I find it hard. When I called by the church today, I had just come fresh from nearly being killed . . ." I paused as the memory started again.

"That could certainly serve to loosen the tongue," Claire's voice was dry. "Are you packing it back down inside you again?"

"I guess so. The shock didn't hit me at first. It seems to be hitting now."

"Why don't you come on up now and talk about it?"

"I guess because I've just got home and I'm tired and there's the usual gaggle of people waiting at my gate to see if they can forestall me."

"Didn't you tell me you had some other way of getting out?"

I sighed. "Yes."

"It's up to you. You tell me you nearly got killed and are beginning to feel the shock. I think you ought to talk about it to somebody. I'm not trying to drum up customers. But don't bottle it down. It may give you trouble later on."

What she said was good sense. Why did I have this enormous reluctance to talk now that the scare was not as fresh?

"Okay," Claire said. "You know where to find me. Please feel free—"

"I'll get there as soon as I can find a taxi."

"I'll be here."

Sitting in Claire's pleasant study, I went backwards and forwards in time and events, beginning with the "accident" on the subway. She knew, of course, that I thought the man whose body I had found up at St. Cuthbert's was the same one who had been watching my apartment.

"Did you tell O'Neill that?" she asked with one of her steady, rather penetrating looks.

"Yes, I told him that. He wanted to know why I hadn't called in the police." I hesitated.

"Did you tell him?"

"I thought . . . I don't know why I thought, but I thought the watcher might have been sent by . . . well, either by my former husband— Actually, he's not former, we're only separated, but you know what I mean . . ."

"Or?" Claire asked after a moment.

"Or my half brother, Joris." There, I thought, it was out. I wondered if it would sound as crazy to her as it did to me. "You don't know about Joris, of course."

"Joris who?"

"Joris Maitland."

"I don't think so. Should I?"

"I don't know why, because what happened, happened twenty years ago. I was twelve. You couldn't have been much older. Joris, my half brother, was twenty-two. He was a student at Princeton, but he went to a party here in New York, and after he left the party was never seen again. Of course, at the time, the papers were full of it. It was written up in the newsmagazines. It was the greatest tragedy in my life . . ."

And at that, the flood burst. The tears came from a deep well that had never really emptied. "It's ridiculous," I said, groping for some tissues. "I was a child. My father and I . . . well, there was a wall between us a mile high. But Joris, his son by a previous marriage, was all that an older brother, or even a father, should be. And then he was just gone . . . And no one knew where or why . . . Except that I never believed he was dead. Everyone else did. But I didn't." After that I just cried for a while.

Claire sat quietly. It was rather curious. With anyone else I would have been embarrassed, or uncomfortable . . . But with her it was all right . . . I blew my nose. "Sorry about that," I said finally.

"It probably did you good."

We were quiet for more minutes. Then Claire said, "Were those tears all about Joris, or was there anyone else, or anything else in there?"

"Well," I said, "there's Simon."

"Simon?"

"My husband . . . my separated husband. He was Joris's cousin—no relation to me. 'Mr. Me-Too,' Joris and I used to call him. In a funny way, he looked like Joris, only everything was second-rate. He was tall, but Joris was taller. Joris was lean, whereas Simon was skinny. Joris had bright blue eyes, Simon's were a light gray . . ."

"That sounds very hard on Simon, to be compared constantly with his cousin and always to be found wanting."

"Yes. I suppose so. It's hard for me to have any sympathy at all for any part of him, considering the way he treated me after we were married."

"What happened in the marriage? No, maybe first of all, given what you've just said, why did you marry him?"

"I've asked myself that a dozen times. All I can say is that I met him after many, many years, and he seemed entirely different. I'd last seen an oafish, boring copy of Joris, who always hung around us when he could, and tried to copy everything Joris did, usually falling flat on his face. Then he went off to college—the University of Virginia—and out of my life. Two years after that, Joris graduated from Princeton, and walked into oblivion . . .

"I didn't see Simon for several years, then one day he called me and asked me out to dinner. Since I'd last seen him he'd graduated from Virginia, gotten a law degree, and joined a rather good law firm. He looked much better too. Not as much like Joris. Still, the resemblance was still strong. A lawyer who was trying to help me with my divorce once asked me the question you did: why did I marry him? And the only reason that makes any sense to me is, because he did remind me of Joris, of Joris who had gone, and because Simon seemed very different from the way I had remembered, funny and amusing, and because—back to Joris—Simon was a tie to him. Now all that sounds to me like the worst collection of reasons to marry anyone that I've ever heard of.

"What I didn't know was that he was a drunk. I probably should have known. Both of us drank a lot. In fact, our whole courtship—if you can call it that—floated on a sea of alcohol. But after a while I just stopped knocking back all that alcohol. I'd had enough. I didn't really like it that much. But Simon drank far more than I had realized when we were drinking together. It took me about a month to realize he was an alcoholic. And then . . ."

It was still hard, to accept the fact that I had let myself be beaten that way. Why I didn't walk out after the first episode, I couldn't now imagine . . .

"And then?" Claire reminded me gently.

"And then I saw that I had married not only a drunk, but a wife beater. He hit me and slapped me around. I had black eyes and a bloody nose and a swollen mouth more times than I like to admit."

"Why didn't you leave right away?"

"I don't know. That's what makes me ashamed. The fact that I didn't. I suppose, each time when he apologized and swore that he'd never do such a thing again, and begged my forgiveness, I wanted to believe it. But it happened again and again. After the last time, I got out of our apartment. I never went back, not even to get my clothes or the photos of my parents or anything. I just left. I found myself an assignment abroad and didn't come home for quite a while. When I did, I got another address and have an unlisted number. Finally, I tried to get a divorce. It can be done without the presence and cooperation of the other partner, but it's hard. My lawyer hired private eyes to see if they could run him down. We found out that he was finally fired from that law firm and from two or three after that. Then he just dropped out of sight. I suppose if I had been willing to spend more money, I could have tracked him further. But I didn't. I let everything slide and forgot about him. Then all this happened, and when I got home last night, lo and behold! there was a letter from my erring husband, saying he was sorry he had treated me the way he had, that he had been sober for almost a year, and that he was making . . . an amend . . . or something."

"Sounds like he might have joined Alcoholics Anonymous. They speak of amends, and one of their steps of recovery is to make amends to all those they have injured . . . Did he say anything about AA?"

"I don't know. When I started reading his letter, all I could think about were those blows he gave me. I guess I never really acknowledged to myself how angry I was, because this huge rage burst from me. I tore up the letter into small pieces, burned it in an ashtray and then flushed it down the john."

Claire grinned. "You really wanted to grind him to powder and flush him away, didn't you?"

"Yes. But the funny thing is, when I was thinking about needing a lawyer, I suddenly remembered that on the upper left hand of the envelope he'd sent, was the name of a law firm. Only, I couldn't remember the names—I'd certainly never heard of the firm before, it's probably tenth-rate. The only name that came anywhere near my memory was, I think, Gonzalez."

Claire was looking at me in an odd way. "Do I take it that after all he's done to you, you were considering using Simon as a lawyer?"

"It's hard to believe I could have, yet I must have, because when I got back to the house, I searched in every wastebasket to see if I had failed to destroy the envelope. But that must have gone the way of the rest of the letter, because I couldn't find it."

"So you were considering him as a lawyer who could help you out."

"At least he might know one. When he was not drinking—the brief time I knew him before his drinking got out of hand—

he was a good lawyer, and we used to know a lot of other lawyers. Maybe that was the reason I was trying to find the envelope, to see if he could remind me of somebody we'd known before. Of course, Piers will know a lawyer."

"It's a small irony, I suppose, that van Reider himself is a lawyer," Claire said thoughtfully, "in view of the fact that he himself is involved. But it could help him in any problem."

"He *is* mixed up in all this," I said. "I didn't kill that wretched man, but I'm not at all sure he didn't."

"Did the police up there give you any thought that they might suspect him?"

"On the contrary. But I have suspicions of my own about the police up there and Mr. van Reider. As I've said before, if they knew there was a connection between the van Reiders and Crystal Mahoney, why wasn't that fact published? It was Piers who told me about the papers, van Reider papers, strewn around her motel room after she was found dead. The van Reiders are still a powerful family. And he's no admirer of St. Anselm's, or at least he didn't sound so to me. He's determined to stop the sale of that house to what he described as an outfit of loonies."

She sighed. "The truth is, I'm inclined to agree with him in that. I'm not wild about the sale of St. Cuthbert's to Swami Gupta Nanda and his outfit."

"I thought the church felt it needed the money to help the poor and homeless and all that."

"That's certainly what the previous rector thought. But then, he had an obsession about it. I don't mind selling St. Cuthbert's. I just don't like this particular buyer."

"Why?"

"I don't know. Maybe it's prejudice. But nobody knows anything about him except that he has tons of money and has some kind of a community going in California—naturally. I mean naturally in California. Sometimes I think that anybody carrying a Bible or any other holy book and wearing a white sheet could start a brand-new religion out there in Orangeville."

"Tut! That's just New York prejudice. Also, maybe, Christian prejudice."

"I'll plead guilty to one but not the other. I believe that Christianity is true. But I also believe there are truths in other religions that we have somehow missed. And anyway, when you get to the heart of each, most of them say mostly the same thing. So I'm not being a nineteenth-century missionary. I've heard of some very admirable Hindu and Buddhist leaders and mystics. But nobody knows anything about Swami Gupta Nanda. I've tried to find out something and I can't. I've even thought of asking Lieutenant O'Neill if he has any information. How did you get along with him, by the way?—O'Neill, I mean."

"Very well, if one bears in mind that the interview was conducted by him and not by me. I really wanted a police friend at court, and he turned me inside out instead—or tried to."

Claire smiled. "I strongly suspect that if he thought you were responsible for the death of that man up in St. Cuthbert's he'd have you behind bars by now. Or at least the Westchester police would. Does he know about this latest adventure on the subway platform?"

"No. I haven't told him."

Claire picked up her phone and pushed it towards me. "Do it now. I don't like the sound of that man at all. And I'm not happy about people who seem to be following you."

I stared at the telephone for a moment. My trust in Lieutenant O'Neill was not as great as Claire's. On the other hand, I never again wanted to go through that moment on the subway platform if I didn't have to.

"You know," I said, picking up the receiver, "you remind me of your buddy O'Neill a little. He tried to bully me into calling the Westchester police from his office and telling them who I thought that body belonged to. I told him I'd do it when I got home."

"He was probably telling you to do that for your own good."

"Yes, that dreary thought did occur to me afterwards."

"O'Neill," his voice snapped at the other end of the phone.

"This is Kit Maitland, Lieutenant. I'm in Mrs. Aldington's office. She thought I ought to tell you about something that happened to me on a subway platform an hour or so ago."

"You mean the time somebody damn near pushed you under the train, I take it."

"How on earth did you know?"

"Well, of course it would have been nice, not to say helpful, if you had thought to call me up and tell me. But I got it through the transit cop who, luckily for you, happened to be there."

"Oh."

"So fill me in now. Who was this guy and why does he want you dead?"

"I'm not sure it's the same guy, but there was another man following me yesterday." And I told him about the man I had noticed apparently watching me in the hamburger place and then saw loitering outside the shoe store. "I got away from him through a side entrance, thanks to the girl in the store. I thought he might be the man I saw tearing up the subway steps with somebody right after him."

"Why in God's name didn't you come straight to the precinct so we could talk about it? Doesn't it occur to you that somebody, we don't know who, is arranging to have you watched, we don't know why. And that somebody else, whose identity we also don't know, managed to have man number one murdered in such a way and at such a time that you could easily be held as the suspect? I mean, Miss Maitland, I know you're a gung-ho reporter, out there on the front lines with ships going down and planes taking off, but don't you have any sense of survival at all? You're after a story, well, so are we, and you seem to be involved in it up to your charming eyes."

Oddly, I'd never put the whole thing together in just such a way. But when the lieutenant did, the whole sequence sounded deadly.

"Did you hang up on me?" he asked.

"No. I was just taking in what you said. Funnily enough, my housemate, a slightly scatty lady who's into the psychic, has been telling me to be careful. I guess she had her reasons."

"A psychic, huh? I used to laugh at those."

"But you don't any more?"

"Not since one helped me with a case. I still don't understand it, mind. And I'm not at all sure the Holy Mother Church is happy about my—er, tolerance—but there it is. Now back to you. Is there anybody who, for any reason, would want to have you watched? Is there anybody you're a threat to?"

"Who on earth would I be a threat to?" I asked. "Only possibly my estranged husband; and he just sent me a very friendly letter. That is, the part I read was friendly."

"And what about the other part?"

Feeling a lot more foolish than when I talked to Claire, I told him about the letter I'd received from Simon and what I'd done with it.

"No harm in talking to him," O'Neill said.

"But I destroyed the envelope, too, so I don't know what firm he's with."

"Was there the name of the firm on the envelope?"

"Yes. There were a lot of names. But the only one I can recall is Gonzalez."

"What's your husband's name?"

"Simon Warfield. Even though we're not, technically, divorced, I took back my maiden name."

"Well, we'll work on it. I'll let you know. I'd like to suggest that you be careful, and when possible, not go around alone. Is that too much to ask?"

"Yes. I'm afraid it is. I'm not going to just sit in the house. But I will try to be careful."

As I hung up, Claire asked, "Why would Simon, your separated husband, consider you a threat to him?"

"Well, I just said he'd sent me a friendly letter."

"But before that, when I gather from your side of the conversation that O'Neill asked you if there was anybody you'd be a threat to, you mentioned Simon. How would you be a threat?"

Now that she asked me, I couldn't really produce an answer. "I don't know. Maybe just that I know things about him."

"Or maybe you feel *he's* a threat to *you* and you transposed it in your mind." As I stared at her, she said dryly, "It sometimes happens. In the meantime," she went on, "are you really and truly going to be reasonably careful?"

"I do not now nor have I ever had a death wish," I said. "I shall be careful."

She sighed. "What would be perfect would be to have a companion of some kind. Somebody whose sole job is to see you're safe at all times."

I got up. "What a wonderful idea! Got any suggestions?"

"Unfortunately, no."

We both laughed.

"Is there anything else you want to talk about?" Claire asked. "Anything that's been acting up in your life?"

"Only my cat, Topaz, who gave me the scare of all time." And I told her about the red cat in my dream and about Topaz's bolt to behind the stove. "Before I found him, I could have killed him out of sheer rage, and when I did finally locate him, I could have killed him again from relief."

"That's odd. Did you say something about a red cat being beside the boy, Bart van Reider, when you saw him there?"

"Yes. There was."

"You seem to be haunted by cats. I assume Topaz is ginger too."

"He's more a sort of marmalade. He's a big, squushy cat that looks like an overweight pot of English marmalade."

"In other words, ginger."

"No. He really isn't. At least, not what I mean by ginger. I know that sounds like a distinction without a difference. But the cat beside Bart and the one I dreamed about were almost red with darker stripes as markings."

"So he's really not like the cat you dreamed about."

"No," I said slowly, "he's not. He's not like any of the other three."

"Three?" Claire cocked her head to one side. "I feel like I'm in the middle of that book *Millions of Cats*. I thought there were two others, the one you dreamed about, the one you saw on the bed by young van Reider, and then Topaz, who you now tell me is different."

It was no more than a flash, like the still frame of a motion picture shown and then blacked out—nothing before or after.

"You okay?" Claire asked.

I shook my head. "Weird," I said. "If not queer." I rubbed my eyes.

"What? What's weird and/or queer?"

"The third cat," I said slowly. And then, "Do you mind if I sit down?"

"Of course not. Here." She got up and pushed the chair I'd been sitting in against the back of my knees. "Now sit."

I sat down.

"What are you feeling, this minute?"

"Awful. Like I was going to faint. But I'm not."

"What else?"

"I don't know."

"Come on, now. What are you feeling this minute? Happy, tired, sick, angry, paralyzed . . . ?"

I took a deep breath and forced myself to answer her question. "All of the above, except maybe happy."

"In other words, depressed."

I nodded. "But I've never had depressions."

"Maybe not. But something kicked one off right now. I don't mean you're sinking into a lengthy state, but something one of us said, or you thought, changed you from a robust woman coping with a lot of difficulties, including almost being knocked off the subway platform, into somebody who looked like she was going into what the Victorians called a decline. What was it?"

"You're going to think I *am* crazy," I said after a minute. "But what were we talking about?"

"Cats. As in two ginger and one marmalade, or three ginger and one marmalade."

Suddenly I shivered. "There was a flash through my mind," I said. "And I think it involved a cat. But I can't get it back."

"Whatever it was," Claire said, "it frightened you."

"Yes."

Trying to catch something that wings through the mind without stopping is, I'd learned, impossible. If it returned, it would return at its own time and pace. I shook my head. "I can't get it now, and it's no use trying. Anyway, I feel better." I got up. I stood there for a moment, vaguely turning over in my mind what I would tackle next. Then I remembered something I hadn't mentioned to Claire that would certainly concern her. . . .

"There's something I forgot to tell you. I went to that rehab

place to do some research on Crystal Mahoney. The woman
there was, to put it mildly, hostile. Mention of your name
softened her a bit, but not much. To prove how terribly the
press had treated Crystal, one of their successful graduates,
she showed me some sheets from the same yellow rag that
Crystal was presumably working for. When I asked her for a
copy, she grudgingly took the pages off to copy, and it was only
in the restaurant later that I realized she'd left out at least one
page. Possibly more. I'd say accidentally or deliberately, except that I really don't think it was accidental."

"Do you have the copy?"

I dug in my handbag. "Here. One of the things I find odd is
that Crystal was up at St. Cuthbert's to do some kind of story
on the house and the van Reiders for this same sheet. But the
way they write her story here, she sounds like a hustler killed
before she can get to her next trick. And there is, of course, no
mention of the van Reider papers found there."

Claire took it. "You'd better sit down again. I'd like to look at
this."

I sat down on the sofa under her window and let my head
rest on the pillow on the back. Then I closed my eyes. I knew
what I ought to be doing was putting together the various facts
that had cropped up since I'd gone up to St. Cuthbert's—no,
before that, since the man started watching my apartment, the
man whose body I found when I went up to St. Cuthbert's . . .
I would try to put the questions, the ambiguities, in some sort
of order, I thought:

Who was the man who was watching me?

Why was he killed?

Why was he killed so I would find him immediately afterwards and probably be blamed for it?

Who killed him?

Who was the man who now appeared to be following me?

Was it a coincidence? (Of course not, my Rational Mind
said.)

There has to be a reason why these men are/were watching
me. What is it?

It's pretty obvious, isn't it, that there's some kind of link
here? (Yes, R.M. said.)

Now, I thought lazily, if I just went over the whole thing again, up through my conversation with Piers about Crystal . . .

Back to questions. Where does Crystal come in all this?

Never mind, on with the chronology . . . I went to St. Cuthbert's, found the body, found the boy, Bart van Reider, because—

"What on earth was that?" I sat up suddenly.

Claire, who was still looking at the news pages, said, "Probably one of the neighbor's cats. It's an enclosed garden down there, and they prowl around the back . . . You look odd again. What's the matter?"

"Are you sure?" I got up. "I mean, about the neighbors having cats down there?"

"Look for yourself."

I went around the back of the sofa to the window, which curved a little. Sure enough, two cats, one gray, one black and white, were facing one another. A third, a black and gray tiger, was slinking off.

"You're right," I said. "They are down there." The relief was overwhelming, completely out of proportion simply to the sight of three cats. Claire was staring at me in a thoughtful way.

"Were you asleep?"

"I must have been. Or at least half asleep." I sat down on the sofa again. "I was trying to put all the things that have happened that seem so unrelated and crazy into some kind of sequence: questions to be answered. And then there was this terrible sound . . ."

"What terrible sound?"

"A cat."

"They were just having the ordinary cat fights that happen any time you get a bunch of them together. I grew up with cats, so I know. Didn't you ever know any as a child? You told me once you lived in the country in Virginia? Didn't you—"

"That was it," I cried. "That was the sound. I must have dreamed it, maybe I heard the cats outside, but what I dreamed was a cat's scream of pain. It was horrible."

"Then, you must have heard it at some time in the past for

you to react that way. What you heard outside was not horrible
—just noisy."

My knees were shaking, and so were my hands.

"What did you see in your dream when you heard what you
thought you heard?"

I closed my eyes. There was something, but I couldn't see
what it was. All I could see was a small light swinging backwards and forwards, backwards and forwards . . .

"There's nothing," I said. "At least I can't remember it."

"Nothing at all? Absolutely nothing?"

"Just a light, like a . . . well, I don't know what it's like, but
it's swinging back and forth."

"Interesting," Claire said.

I got up. "I think I'd better start finding the answers to some
of those questions. By the way, what did you think of that story
on Crystal?"

"You're right. It has been bowdlerized. If I run off yet another copy of this, I'd like to call up the woman who gave it to
you and who seemed so hostile. I don't suppose you know
what her name is."

"No. I never asked. Which is stupid. As a reporter I nearly
always remember to ask first thing. She was about forty or so,
good-looking, upper-crusty. Her mouth was thin, but that may
have been her extreme displeasure at my asking questions."

"I'll find out. Something tells me she was a volunteer. Let
me get this copied."

While Claire was away, I stared down into the garden behind
the church. The church and the school attached to it took up
three sides of the square, but there were four town houses and
an apartment house occupying the remaining side. The back
quarters of the apartment house were separate, walled off with
a high fence even a cat couldn't climb. But the divisions among
the gardens of the town houses were low, if not nonexistent. At
least two of them shared a garden with no wall in between. The
tiger cat was now sitting on one of the low walls, slowly and
methodically washing. The gray was asleep under a bush, and
the black-and-white was stalking a bird, which, I was glad to
see, took off.

Topaz had been an accident in my life. I found him dirty,

starving and with an abscessed ear one winter evening on Hudson Street. He was leaning against a warehouse building. I passed him. Something forced me to look back. He opened his mouth and the faintest miaow came out.

"What's the matter?" I said, standing my distance. Somehow I had never been tempted to make friends with cats.

The bedraggled creature slowly got up, wobbled, sat down, got up, wobbled and started towards me. When I leaned over and touched him, he uttered a cry of pain and ducked his head. It was then I saw the pus in his ear. But he still managed to rub his emaciated form against my leg. Then he wobbled and sat down on my foot.

I was late for my assignment, but I somehow picked him up, avoiding touching his ear, and looked around. The God of All Living, including cats, was on the alert. There, staring at me across a small square, was a sign: ANIMAL CLINIC.

I had to wait, of course, and spent the time composing a letter to the person whom I was standing up. When I got to the vet and showed him the ear, the vet looked at it, then started feeling the scrawny, dirty marmalade body.

"The ear is only one of the things wrong. How long have you had this cat?"

"About twenty-five minutes, including the time I've been sitting here waiting for you."

"Oh. Then he's a stray."

"He was sitting against the wall of that warehouse over there."

"What are you going to do with him when we've got him well?"

"Why are you being so bloody-minded? I'm not the enemy. I see a sick cat and bring it here and all I get from you is a snotty manner."

There was a pause while we regrouped.

"Sorry," he finally said. "We get a lot of neglected or abused animals in here and it makes me angry."

"I understand. But don't take it out on people who are not guilty."

"Are you going to keep the cat?"

Curiously, that had not occurred to me. "Well, I—"

At that moment the cat raised himself onto his feet and rubbed against me.

"Yes," I said, and wondered why it felt as though I were pushing against some deep objection within me.

"All right. Call us tomorrow, I'll let you know what has to be done and how much it'll cost."

It cost quite a lot, but it didn't matter. I took him home and called him Topaz, because that was the color of his eyes, and he had been a major part of my life since.

"Here you are," Claire said, coming back into the room. She handed me my copy of the news story. "I keep wondering if there's a common theme that runs in all this—Crystal, the dead man at St. Cuthbert's, you being nearly pushed under a subway train . . ." She paused and then said, "I don't suppose you'd want another investigative assignment; do you?"

"I'm not doing very well on what I already have, but what did you have in mind?"

"Well, it's not unrelated to your original assignment—to find out what's going on at St. Cuthbert's." She looked at me for a moment. "I'd do it myself, but I'm known to be connected with the church here, so I don't believe I'd get very far . . ."

"Well?" I said finally. "You've got me curious."

"That was the idea. I wish you'd find out what you could about the people who're trying to buy the place: Swami Gupta Nanda and his folk."

"I shouldn't think that'd be hard at all. I mean, there are so many groups that one would think they'd all know about each other."

"One would, wouldn't one!"

I looked at Claire. "I take it to mean that you've tried and come up with nothing."

"You're exactly right. It isn't that I'm against the sale of the place, as I told you. If I thought it were going to some outfit that was involved in *pro bono publico* work, then I'd be delighted. We could use the money right here, with people who don't have homes or jobs or food. But every time I try to find out what the swami wants to do with the place, other than buy it, the answers are all vague." She paused. "And as I reminded you before, this is not an anti-Eastern religious bias."

"I'm surprised this wasn't gone into before the church decided to sell."

"First of all, it tore the congregation apart. Second, the rector had such an obsession about getting money for our outreach, that I honestly think he would have sold it to the mafia."

"What about your present rector?"

"He hasn't been here very long, and found an awful lot on his plate when he arrived, what with the old scandal and so on. As a matter of fact, when the representatives of the swami started to push him, he was just going off on his present trip and asked me to find out what I could—which turned out not to be much. I think you'd have a much better chance."

"Okay. I'll see what I can do. Can you tell me anything about it at all?"

"The representatives say that the group started in India a few years ago, that the swami is a very holy man who feels that he has been deputized by the spiritual forces he's in touch with to bring his mission over here, and wants to have an eastern foothold. He already has one somewhere in California, as I told you."

"I take it their financial credentials are okay; that when they say they want to buy, they give proof of having the X millions they're going to produce."

"Absolutely. Even our most conservative vestryman, a banker himself, said everything was financially kosher. The money's there. So all I have to go on is just a gut feeling. I've asked around among my friends and nobody who's into that Eastern stuff has heard of Swami Gupta Nanda, or, if they have, they've heard he's okay, but no particulars."

"So what makes you think he might not be?"

"I don't know. Maybe because I feel it shoudn't be so hard to find out something."

"Who are his representatives?"

"His representative is a Mr. Martin Joliad, Mr. Martin S. Joliad, to be accurate."

"Have you met him?"

"No. Nor has anyone here. Norbert, the previous rector, did all the negotiating."

"What about the conservative banker? Didn't he have to deal with him?"

"No, he's tried to reach him, but Mr. Joliad's been abroad. The banker's information comes from the banking network, which says that the money is there. Nobody is trying to pull a fast one."

"Can you give me an address?"

"No. I'm afraid I can't. The rector has all that information."

"But obviously the negotiator came here when he made the sale."

"He hasn't quite made it yet. I know you didn't get a very good impression of Hilary van Reider, and he certainly behaved badly toward you. But his insistence about having an apartment there in perpetuity is the one thing that's holding everything up. And the feeling around the church here is that that's a good thing, until we can get some line on this guru. Capish?"

"Capish," I said. "Okay. Maybe it isn't too farfetched to think that there's a tie-in between all this and Crystal and the men who've been following me. I'll let you know." I surprised myself then. "Say a prayer and all that."

"Don't worry. I will! By the way," Claire said as I reached the door. "There's one question that occurred to me to ask you. Have you ever been hypnotized?"

"No," I said firmly. "I don't believe in all that. And I would *not* like the idea of handing over control to somebody else."

"I just asked."

I grinned. And I answered, "Bye. When and if I know something I'll report back."

7

When I got home it was dark, and I was so tired I could hardly think. So therefore I forgot entirely about my circuitous route through Paul's and Letty's apartment, and walked straight into a covey of three newshawks. Suddenly brilliant light was directed at my face, and I knew that I'd probably see myself on the late news. The questions came like thrown rice.

"What's the status now between you and the police?"

"Ask them," I replied.

"Who was the man you found?"

"I still don't know."

"What's your connection with the murder?"

"None. Will you please let me through?" Numb as I was, I found that my capacity for being annoyed was undamaged. "Come on, now," and I gave a huge push.

I heard the shouts as I raced up the front steps. I knew, of course, that by the time I got my key out, there'd be more of the same, so when Letty flung open the door she looked like an angel of light.

"Thanks, Letty," I said. "Thank you a million times."

"In the early days they'd be considered public nuisances and arrested accordingly."

"How do you know?" I asked. "And what early days, where?"

"Sixteenth century. Quite a lot of places. And I know because . . . well, just because." And she threw me a defiant look. That meant that she was referring to her clairvoyance or mediumship or knowledge of regressed lives. Sometimes I teased her. But tonight I was too grateful.

"I'm a great believer in freedom of the press," I said, making an obligatory bow in the direction of the First Amendment. "But right at the moment, I wish they'd all go to jail."

"Not all of them out there were news people," Letty said. She sounded worried. "But I'm not sure who . . . anyway, I did not feel anything evil or of ill intent coming from him."

"What are you talking about?"

She threw a look at me. "You've had a poorish day, I think. Though necessary. You will see things now that were hidden from you before."

I bit back a snappy comment about loony occultism. I was grateful to her about a lot of things, and however crazy she might be, the least I could do was be polite.

"Yes, dear," she said cheerfully. "I know how you feel. You just go upstairs and get into bed. I have some peppermint tea I'm going to bring up, with a bun. It'll do you a lot of good."

I opened my mouth and closed it. Peppermint tea and a bun sounded wonderful, and perhaps the most wonderful thing about them was that I didn't have to fix them.

"Thank you, Letty," I said meekly.

Topaz was his usual self, I was glad to see, his bizarre behavior in taking shelter behind the stove entirely forgotten.

"Purr, purr, mine, mine," he muttered, moving back and forth across my legs as I walked into my apartment.

After I fed Topaz his evening delicacy and before I got into bed, I called the answering service. This time there were no people who wouldn't leave their names. The assortment who did were some news types, Piers, Lieutenant O'Neill and Simon.

"Simon who?" I inquired, my heart beginning to race with the fear and loathing his name always brought.

"Didn't say. He had a nice voice."

"Then, it couldn't have been the one I've known."

"He left a number."

"Don't bother." I hung up.

I let Letty in, and then, with her instructing me every step of the way, got into bed. She then placed on my knees a tray on which was a pot of simmering tea and what turned out to be an English muffin, open and buttered, on a plate. There was also a small jar of marmalade.

"Just the color of Topaz," I said. "Thank you, Letty. You're an angel."

"You were quite relaxed when you came home—that is, after you got in. Now you're all upset," Letty said with her usual lack of beating around the bush. "What happened?"

"My former husband called me."

"I didn't know you were divorced, dear." She frowned. "Are you sure you're right about that?"

"No. I'm not divorced. Yet. But we've been separated for about six years. I haven't seen him. And I don't want to see him. He's a drunk. And he beat me."

"Yes, but I don't think he is now."

"You know, Letty, I try to be as open-minded as I can be about your . . . your . . ."

"Idiotic theories?" she finished helpfully.

"Yes. But you've just gone too far. Simon *beat* me. He gave me black eyes and bloody noses and swollen lips."

"What you need is a good sleep. Come along, Topaz."

"Topaz sleeps with me," I said angrily.

"Of course, dear. Now get a good night's sleep."

The next morning, I was sitting in my living room, drinking my third cup of coffee, more or less reading the paper, with Topaz on my lap, when the bell to my apartment rang.

I put down the paper and stared. Whoever it was had gotten into the building without buzzing me first, a phenomenon that gives any seasoned New Yorker sound cause for fright. Well-intentioned people buzz the bell in the lobby between the outer and inner front doors. Neighbors within the house yell their names through the door. The bell rang again.

"Who is it?" I called out.

There was no answer, but the bell rang a third time.

I got up, went nearer to the door, where my hand was in reach of my telephone, and asked again, "Who is it?"

"Simon," the voice said.

There was a pause while I recovered from the combined relief and rage that washed over me.

"How *dare* you come and ring my doorbell?" I asked furiously.

"Did you get my letter?"

"Yes, but what has that got to do with it?"

"Quite a lot. For one thing I've been sober now for nine months. And—"

"So you said. But since you told lies without drawing a breath between them during our delightful marriage, I don't see why I should believe you."

"Do I sound drunk?"

"No. Not at the moment. But I don't want to see you."

"I thought you moved heaven and earth and employed lawyers to find me so you could get a divorce."

"I did. But now that I know where you are, I can go ahead without seeing you."

"First we have to meet, Kit. Come on. I'm not going to hurt you. Open the door. It's important."

So, finally, I did.

I suppose I expected Simon to look more or less the same as he had when I last saw him: puffy, red-faced and bleary-eyed. But he didn't. The man who stood in the doorway was lean, with thin cheeks and clear, deeply set gray eyes. He gave a half smile. "Hello, Kit."

Reluctantly I stepped back. "All right. Come in. Now," I said when he was inside, "what do you want with me? And by the way, how did you know my address and telephone number? I'm unlisted."

"One of the partners knows a guy in the police department. He got them for me."

"That's supposed to be against the law."

"It is. Everybody gives a little." He paused. "I wanted them so I could tell you how sorry I am for having abused you so terribly."

"You did that in the letter."

"And then to say that for a while I was in a rehab place with Crystal Mahoney."

That certainly got my attention. "You were? When?"

"About two years ago. It wasn't, then, a success for either of us. But we crossed paths for about a month."

"Where?"

"A place in the Midwest. I can give you the name and address if you want, but I don't think there's anything they can tell you beyond what I'm saying now."

I stood and stared at him for a moment. My back was to the window, and the morning light fell full on his face. He was standing there with his hands in his pockets, apparently relaxed, but for the first time I noticed the lines of strain around his mouth and eyes. And there were scars—one on his chin, and one slanting off the side of one eye—that I hadn't noticed before. For a second I saw him without the two shadows, the one of Joris that for me he'd always had, and the other of memory—my own memory of what that face looked like as he struck me. He'd not had an easy time, I found myself thinking, and then the memory washed back.

"What do you mean, 'It wasn't a success for either of us'?"

"Fairly obviously, that neither of us stayed clean." He hesitated. "But I think for different reasons."

"Meaning?"

"She didn't really stay long enough. She left before I did, and the general feeling was that she hadn't had long enough at the rehab to recover. My own reason was that I only took to drugs when I was trying to stop drinking. When I left, I didn't fool with coke, pot or pills, or even heroin—I went back to my drug of choice—alcohol."

It was hard to get my mind off Simon and onto what he was saying, off the fact that he was here, off our past, off my anger. But I decided I had to. He might be able to give me answers to questions for which I hadn't been able to receive any answers.

"Do you want any coffee?" I asked.

"Yes, I could use a cup."

"Still take cream and sugar?"

"Yes." The half smile came back. "You remembered."

I looked at him carefully. "I remember all of it, Simon."

For a moment he met my gaze, then he looked down. "You can hardly be blamed for that."

I went into the kitchen and poured a second cup of coffee, put in cream and sugar and brought it out.

"I take it you read the papers and/or saw the television news."

"They would have been hard to miss."

"Well," I said, sitting down and drinking my own, now luke-warm, coffee, "what were you going to tell me about Crystal other than the fact that you shared the same academy for a while?"

"Just that I have a feeling that during her years being an expensive call girl, when she got hooked on drugs, she also got to know more about them, about their sale and source of supply, than was good for her."

"What makes you think that?"

"She told me once. As is often the case when you're coming off any kind of narcotic, you can get terrible downs. She was in the middle of one when she said that to me, and also said she was afraid somebody might put out a contract on her."

"Why haven't you told the police?"

"I have. I told your friend Lieutenant O'Neill when he called me."

"He's no friend of mine. He's Claire Aldington's friend." I stared down at my coffee for a moment. "What did he say when you told him?"

"He asked me a bunch of questions, seeing if he could get more information out of me about who she was talking about. But he couldn't, because I didn't know any more."

"Then, why are you telling me now?"

"I gather from O'Neill and the papers that you seemed to be assigned to Crystal's story. I couldn't be sure that O'Neill would help you, so I decided to tell you myself."

"If that's really all you know, then you could have written it."

"Did you read all my letter?"

"No. I didn't. I got to about two thirds of the way down the first page. The rest went into . . . into the garbage."

"I thought that might be the case."

"Then, why did you write?"

He got up. "Because, as I think I've told you now several times, I wanted to . . . to make an amend to you for what I did. An amend you plainly don't want to accept. Well, I can't help that. I did my part. But it's a pity you tore up or burned or flushed the rest of the letter, because I told you something that I think would interest you."

"And what is that?"

He stared at me for a moment, the lines around his mouth much more noticeable. Then he said, "Let's let my apology come in the form of telling you this piece of news, and not doing what I am sorely tempted to do—walk out and make you come to me for it."

"I can't think of anything that would make me come to you."

"Can't you? Try this. I have become fairly sure that Joris is still alive. So long," he said as I stared at him, still in shock. "Nice to have seen you."

The front door was open when I was suddenly galvanized into action. Flying across the room, I slammed the door before he could get out. "Don't you dare leave on that. What the blazes do you mean about Joris? Or is this one of your tricks?"

He leaned back against the table near the front door.

"No, it is not one of my tricks, and I do not know where Joris is or what he's doing. But the last night before Crystal left the rehab, she and I were sitting and talking on the front-porch steps. I was talking about my home and background. Somewhere in the course of that I must have mentioned Joris.

"She said, 'Joris Maitland? I knew him once,' and then added, 'but not under that name.' There was something else, which I've forgotten. Then she said, 'Funny thing, you look like him. Who did you say he was, your brother?' I told her, no, he was my cousin, and if she knew him under another name, how did she know it was Joris? She said she didn't, at first, but she had this vague but growing feeling she recognized him, and then one day she remembered where she had seen his face.

"It was when she was a child. Her father was a cop and he'd sometimes bring home pictures of missing persons and tape them to the refrigerator door so he'd be sure to recognize them. After she recalled that, she remembered the rest about Joris. I asked her if she told him she recognized him. She said no and then added, not very believably, that she didn't think it was important. I think what happened was that in our relaxed conversation she mentioned Joris without thinking—people in rehabs are inclined to talk freely to one another. And then she was sorry. I tried to get more information out of her, but I had the feeling she regretted saying what she had, and she finally told me to get off the subject, she was sorry she'd brought it up.

"The next morning, she was gone. Nobody at that place would give me Crystal's address. I tried to find her after I came out, but started drinking almost immediately, so that absorbed most of my time and attention. I never saw her again, but I knew then that it was at least possible that Joris was alive. When I saw the small announcement of her suicide in the paper, there was nothing to do, but when I read of your adventures up at that place and learned from the lieutenant that you had gone up to investigate Crystal's death, I decided to tell you what she'd said. That's why I came. Now I've told you and I'm going to go. I think you were right. It would have been better to have spared us both this unpleasantness."

"Are you sure there's nothing more?" I asked. "Nothing more you can tell me about Joris being alive, or what Crystal meant?"

"Yes, I am sure, Catherine. My God! You are as obsessed now—at what age? Thirty-two or -three?—as you were when you were twelve. This means, of course, that you will start looking for him, won't you? Well, good luck. I hope I never lay eyes on him again!"

I shouldn't have said it, of course. I should have been big enough not to. But I said, "You always did pale in his shadow, didn't you?"

He was at the head of the stairs by this time. But he paused. "Mr. Me-Too. Wasn't that what you both called me? I think I can live without that now."

I sat in my apartment a long time, my head in my hands. The astonishing thing was that I wasn't astonished that Joris might still be alive. With the years, the child in me had died, or so I had thought. And when the child went, my belief in Joris's immortality went too. I had believed that he wasn't dead, because he had told me that he had a special thing he had to do, something that no one knew about. And then, finally, I grew up and learned that that belonged with other fairy stories and had come to think that Joris had probably died as the victim of a crime and was buried where nobody could find him, or disposed of in some other fashion.

And now?

And now, I thought, the one person who might have told me about Joris—Crystal Mahoney—was dead. So Joris was out there somewhere and I had no idea of where even to begin to find him . . . although there was no question but that I must. The urge, the yearning, was almost physical. Once, I would have dropped everything, abandoned every obligation, and taken off after him. But I was not twelve, or even twenty-two. Common sense told me that if he had wanted to find any of his family, he would have done so within the past twenty years. So either he had his reasons for not doing so, or something had changed him completely—such, for example, as amnesia—so that he was no longer the same person. All of which meant that finding him would be a long, arduous and probably expensive task.

In the meantime, I had to finish the job at hand and get on with my investigations, which seemed to be going nowhere. I pushed myself away from the table. I could start with returning some of the calls I had ignored the night before.

I began with Piers.

"How are things?" he asked with noticeable sarcasm. "I send you out on assignment, you come up with a dead body, and then you don't answer my calls."

"Sorry, Piers. I've been having my ups and downs, mostly downs—in fact, almost as far down as under the subway train." And I told him about my adventure of the day before.

"I'm getting sorrier and sorrier that I got you into this. Would you pay attention if I told you I'd pay you the fee I promised, but asked you please to forget about the whole thing?"

"No. And anyway, why would you do that?"

"Because, bizarre as it may seem, I don't want to have your own murder on my hands."

I shivered suddenly and reproached myself for being a superstitious dolt. "It wouldn't do you any good to take me off the story, whether for my own good or not. I'm already in it and on it, and a herd of rhinos couldn't make me budge."

"Have you listened to the morning news? The police have apparently identified the body you found up there at St. Cuthbert's. His name was Ahmed Ramedos. He was illegally in this country, although there seems to be some doubt as to where he came from. Nobody's eager to claim the honor."

"Does anybody seem to know *why* he was murdered? Even more to the point, why he was murdered there?"

"No, or if they do, they aren't going to tell the media."

There was a short silence. I snatched up the paper, which I hadn't had time to read properly, and glanced over the index. There was nothing unexpected there.

"Has anybody said, indicated or implied that there was a connection with Crystal Mahoney?"

"I'm glad to say, no. I was rather hoping the press and the police would stay off that. But I suppose you told the police that that was the real reason for your going up there?"

"Considering that I had just stumbled over a dead body, I felt the least I could do was be honest. Why should it have been such a big secret?"

"I'm not implying it should have been. But since everybody seems now to know that that was what you were after—information about Crystal Mahoney—then your chances of getting an inside story were limited. You know what I mean: somebody might spill some beans to you about Crystal if they didn't think there was any big deal about it. But it's now one of the hot topics."

He seemed, I thought, more annoyed than the whole subject warranted.

"Piers," I said. "Does the name Joris Maitland mean anything to you?"

"No. Should it? I have a vague feeling I heard it somewhere. But nothing I can put a finger on. With the same name as you, I take it he's a relative. Or is Maitland your married name?"

"No, maiden. I took it back. Joris is my half brother, and my —er—separated husband was his cousin. That's another long, boring story."

"I'm sure it's not boring. In fact, it sounds like one of those southern gothic tales filled with incest and madness."

"You've been reading too much Tennessee Williams. Anyway, about Joris: nearly twenty-one years ago he walked out of a party one night after graduation and was never seen again. As a child, I was convinced that he was alive and one day would return trailing clouds of glory. When I got older I realized he'd probably fallen prey to some mugger or other criminal and been killed . . ."

"Why are you concerned about it now?"

"Because Simon, my . . . my husband, told me this morning that Crystal Mahoney had recognized Joris's name. He had mentioned it in passing when they were both at the drug rehab. She said she thought she had known Joris, but under another name."

Predictably, Piers asked my question, "Then, how did she know it was this guy if she knew him under another name?"

I told him about her father the cop and the posters. Then I said, "Apparently it just grew on her. When Simon tried to get more details then, she just clammed up."

"Hmm. By the way, I thought your husband was long gone. Aren't you divorced?"

"I'll tell you the whole sordid tale someday. I didn't get divorced, because I couldn't find my loving mate. He was busy drinking himself onto skid row. He now seems to have sobered up and read all about me in the newspapers. So he came to see me to tell me that."

"You mean after all these years, all of a sudden, your husband turns up? Like that—out of the blue?"

I sighed and suppressed the temptation to tell Piers that Simon and my marriage were none of his business. "I got a letter from him a couple of days ago, telling me he wanted to . . . to say he was sorry for his behavior when we were married, and that he had gotten sober. Apparently, he put the news about Joris in the letter, but I flew into such a rage over his writing to me . . . and over the things he did when we were married, that I tore his letter up before I had finished the first page. Then I burned it. Then I flushed it down the john . . ." I couldn't help it, I laughed. "I sound like Lady Macbeth, don't I?"

"More like Medea or one of the Furies. What on earth did he do to you?"

I really didn't want to go into detail. Why, I wasn't sure. I had never suffered attacks of such delicacy before. "He behaved the way all chronic alcoholics behave: got drunk, stayed out, lied about his drinking—"

"And beat you up, I would suppose."

"You supposed right. I'm trying to accept his amend and forget the past, or something."

"I find that quite noble. I now know that if I take it into my head to give you a black eye, you won't hold it against me."

"You're not—as far as I know—an alcoholic."

"Oh, I dunno—and besides does that diminish the responsibility?"

"Why are you being so sarcastic? Why should you care about my perils-of-Pauline marriage?"

"Possibly a touch of jealousy."

"Come on, Piers. You're always being written up in gossip columns as out with yet another cover-girl model. You're famous for your stable of beauties . . ." I wasn't entirely sure this was true or not, but I had a feeling it might be. I had seen such items in some of the local scandal sheets listing Piers and whoever his current girlfriend might be at a new, trendy restaurant or the latest disco.

"That doesn't preclude a certain weakness for you, does it?"

"No." I was flattered, but confused. As always, I took a step backwards. "What did you call me about, Piers? Just to reproach me for not calling you?"

"Mostly. After reading all those accounts of your derring-do, I felt somewhat responsible. Are you getting anywhere?"

"Not really. Every time I try and run down a channel I get bopped, as I was on the subway, or I find myself running down some other path, like bumping into a dead body. I went to the local rehab place here to ask about Crystal. But all I got was a copy of a sensational but well-censored story about her death, published in the same yellow sheet she worked for, plus outrage that I should be prying into the affairs of one of their more successful graduates."

"Where are you going to go from here?"

"I don't know. I guess I might try to get something about Crystal from the rehab place Simon said she was at. They may very well have the same rules of confidentiality that the local outreach place has. But I can at least try. Then I'm going to get in touch with Lieutenant O'Neill to see if he can tell me more about Mr. Ramedos."

"I take it you've made a pal in the police force."

"He's really Mrs. Aldington's friend. And for a while there I had the feeling that he could hardly wait to put me in handcuffs, but I daresay that was persecution mania."

"For God's sake, Kit. Everyone else in the world is either suffering from paranoia or an identity crisis. Don't you go neurotic on me."

"I'll see what I can do to maintain my image of Ms. Mental Health."

"Are you going to try and run down this Joris?"

For a moment, I had forgotten about him. "Of course, sooner or later. If he is alive, then something strange must have happened to keep him from getting in touch with me or somebody in the family."

"Try running an ad?"

"Thanks a bunch!"

"We're still not too sure where Ramedos began his short and misdirected life, but for the last ten or fifteen years he's been connected with the drug world," O'Neill said when I got him on the phone.

"You mean as an addict or a pusher?"

"A pusher, and a cut or two above the street type. He was one of those who got a supply from the local headman and then doled it out, probably mixed with something else, to the street pusher."

"I wonder why on earth he was watching me," I said.

"So do we."

There was a silence on the telephone. "Look," he said. "I'd like to talk to you. Do you think you could come down here?"

"Why do I feel that doors will slam on me and I'll never get out?" I said, trying to sound light about it. The truth was, it wasn't entirely a joke.

"Guilty conscience?"

"Not about drugs. If you're so fired up to talk to me, why don't you come here?"

"I'll do that if you're sure you don't mind the watchers at your gate, your colleagues in the press, seeing me arrive."

It was a good point. On principle, I didn't like to give in, but I did. "Okay. I'll come there. But I think I'll take a taxi."

"Scared of the subway?"

"Yes. Maybe I should be working on the principle of getting back on the horse that threw me, but until I know a little more about these people on my tail, I'll use other transportation."

I got there in half an hour and went straight to his office.

"Just for the record," I said, walking in. "I do not now nor have I ever had anything whatsoever to do with drugs. I've not taken them—if you discount the occasional drunk, well, more than occasional at one time, I have not sold them or passed them on or let people know where they could be obtained. I've been at parties where I've strongly suspected that people who kept going in and coming out of another room might be having snorts there, but I didn't pursue the matter."

He waved me to the chair opposite his desk and tipped his own chair back. "Have you ever done a story on drugs—research, that kind of thing?"

"No, I've thought of that, too. I've done stories on a lot of things, but not drugs."

"How do you feel about them?"

"What do you mean?"

"Some people are very libertarian about them—if people want to use them, okay. Do you mind being around people who use coke or acid or pot?"

I thought for a moment. It struck me for the first time that I had pretty much stayed away from people who were drug users of one kind or another, even when I knew or thought they were social users, as opposed to the really addicted. But whenever I felt a party was about to take out the drugs, I left.

"Yes, when I think about it, I do mind. Whenever people start to sniff or smoke around me, I usually find a reason to go. I hadn't seen it before as a pattern, but I do now. Maybe it's because of Simon. Alcohol is a drug as much as anything else. The fact that it's legal and socially acceptable doesn't alter that. I guess it *is* because of Simon. I had enough of people fooling around with another consciousness."

O'Neill put his hands behind his head and stared at the ceiling for a moment. "All right. I accept that. But in that case, can you think of any reason on earth why a man mostly involved in drugs would be watching your apartment? I mean, did you have any boyfriends who were into drugs, or girlfriends, for that matter, or neighbors?"

"No, no, and no. After what I said about the way I defected from druggy parties, you could imagine I wouldn't have a boyfriend who took drugs—at least not that I knew. And surely I'd know."

"If he were an addict, probably. But not if he was an occasional user. What about the people in your house? Anybody there who would fiddle around with drugs?"

I shook my head. "I only know one of them—Letty—well. She's into the occult and the supernatural, but she lives an unselfish, blameless life taking care of cats and dogs and feeding the strays of the neighborhood."

"Well, I must admit, I don't think it's your neighbors either. Why would Ramedos be watching your apartment if it was somebody on the floor below looking out a different side?"

I got up. "And I suppose you still don't know why he was killed, up at St. Cuthbert's."

"Nope. We don't." He looked at me. "Are you still on your assignment about Crystal Mahoney?"

"Oh yes." Suddenly I remembered what Simon had told me. "By the way, Simon, my ex-husband"—I'd decided to call him ex; it required less explanation to other people—"came to see me and told me something that Crystal had told him when they were both at a rehab place somewhere in the Middle West."

"I didn't realize that he had been there with her. Go on."

"He said that the night before Crystal left—I gather it was while he was still new there—they were talking about his family and home, and he mentioned the name of his cousin, and my half brother, Joris Maitland. He said she casually admitted to having met him. Apparently she had known him under another name, although she recognized him as Joris Maitland. But she wouldn't say when or where or what name he was using, and refused to go on when he kept asking her. Anyway, his head was still pretty groggy, so it wasn't until after she left that he figured out that she must have known Joris after he had disappeared and was long assumed to be dead." I looked at O'Neill. "Have you ever heard of him?"

"Joris Maitland," O'Neill said. "About twenty, twenty-one years ago. He walked out of a party and was never seen again."

"You remember him," I said, pleased that he should.

"I was a rookie then, just out of the police academy. A lot of men and time were put on that." He stared at me. "So you're his half sister. How old would that make him now?"

"Forty-three."

"So how old were you when he disappeared?"

"Twelve."

"Were you close to him?"

"Yes and no. I adored him. We had the same father, whom I couldn't stand, and Joris partly stood in for him. But ten years is a huge difference at that time. So let's say I knew him as well as a child of ten or eleven would know a young man of twenty or twenty-one. I've always supposed," I said more slowly, "that if anything more about him came to light, the police or whoever conducted the case would inform us. I went to the police when I first came to New York ten years ago. But the case was closed and I got nowhere."

"When you say, 'inform us,' who do you mean by 'us'? Yourself? Your parents?"

"No. Not now. They're both dead. I guess there'd be only me and Simon, and Simon hated him."

"Why?" The word rapped out.

"Because Joris and I used to make fun of him—not very kind, I'm afraid. Joris looked like a magnificent version of Simon—taller, more muscular, fairer hair, brilliant blue eyes. Simon is paler on all those counts—except for his hair, which is darker. We—Joris and I—used to call Simon 'Mr. Me-Too,' because he trailed around after us and tried to horn in on our conversations and modeled himself after Joris."

"And Crystal Mahoney told Simon Maitland that she had known Joris?"

"Yes."

"Did she say anything about him at all?"

"Not according to Simon. When he tried to question her, she told him to cut it out, as I understand it."

"And she didn't say what name he was using when she met him?"

"He didn't tell me if she did."

O'Neill stared at me for a moment. Then he said, "My God! What a long shot it would be if—" Suddenly he stood up and pushed the telephone toward me. "Call him, will you? Ask him if Crystal used any other name of any kind when she said she knew Joris Maitland."

I stood up too. "What are you thinking?" I said. Oddly, I felt terribly alarmed, as though something close to me were threatened. "I don't understand all this about another name."

"Just call him, Kit. Please, and ask him in as simple a way as you can. It's important."

I took the receiver off the hook.

"Dial 9," O'Neill said. "And then his number."

I hung up. "What am I thinking of? I don't know his number."

"Here." O'Neill checked in a file box on his desk. "This is the number. Now dial nine and then this number."

I did as he asked. A girl answered with the name of the law firm.

"Simon Maitland," I said.

"Who shall I say is calling?"

I glanced at O'Neill. "Tell him Lieutenant O'Neill wants to talk to him."

In a moment Simon's voice asked crisply, "Yes, Lieutenant? Anything wrong about Kit?"

"This *is* Kit," I said, "but I gave O'Neill's name because he has ordered me to call you."

There was a short pause. Then, "Okay, shoot."

I took a breath. "You told me that when you were at the rehab with Crystal Mahoney, the last night she was there the two of you talked on the front porch. You said you mentioned Joris's name, and she said something like 'Oh, I know him' but that he was using another name."

"That's right," Simon said.

"Did she tell you the name?"

"No, she didn't." He paused. "Certainly not what you could call a real name."

I turned and repeated the conversation to O'Neill.

"Ask him if she used any kind of a nickname." O'Neill said.

Obediently, I repeated the question to Simon.

"Nickname . . ." Simon said slowly. "As a matter of fact, she did. A queer one. I'd forgotten that."

"Well, what?" O'Neill asked impatiently.

Simon must have been able to hear that, because he said, "Just a minute. I have to get it out of whatever memory closet it's in. Hold on . . ."

"He's trying to remember," I said to O'Neill.

O'Neill turned and looked out the window, his hands in his pockets. The silence went on. I could almost feel Simon trying to force his memory to produce.

Finally Simon said, "I know that I'll remember it. But I can't seem to get it now." .

I looked over at O'Neill. "He says he knows he'll remember it, but he can't seem to at this moment."

"Ask him," O'Neill said in a louder than normal voice, "ask him if by any chance she said, 'The Archangel.' "

"My God, yes," Simon's voice said in my ear. Obviously he had heard O'Neill. "That was what it was. I mentioned Joris's name. She said something like 'Joris Maitland, I knew him once, but not under that name.' And then she said, 'We used to call him the Archangel.' That was what I'd forgotten."

I was still holding the phone, but I looked across at O'Neill.

"You were right. Simon says she said, right after saying she once knew a guy named Joris Maitland, 'We used to call him the Archangel.' What does that mean?"

"It means," O'Neill said, "that that confirms something we were beginning to put together but could never nail down. The Archangel is the name for one of the major drug distributors in this area."

8

"The archangel loved heights . . ."

I could see the words on the page. They were the first line of the book Joris was reading. He was in the hammock strung between two trees on the lawn outside Percy's Walk. I had been riding Buttercup and had been headed toward the house. But when I saw Joris lying there, apparently snoozing, his book open, face down on his stomach, I changed direction and went to him as a steel filing to a magnet.

"Hi," I said.

"I'm asleep," Joris said without opening his eyes. "Didn't you notice?"

"Pooh." I looked down at the book. "What's the book?" I picked it up and read aloud the title: *"Mont-Saint-Michel and Chartres.* Sounds boring." Then I flopped open the cover and front pages to the first page. That's where I read aloud, "The archangel loved heights . . ." "Is it about archangels?" I asked. We sang about angels and archangels in hymns in church. I hummed the verse, and then sang aloud,

Cry out, dominions, princedoms, powers,
Virtues, archangels, angels' choirs . . .

"That kind of archangel?" I asked.

"I'm asleep," Joris said, and snored. Then he opened one blue eye. "Archangels are not pretty things you hang on Christmas trees, Kit, they're great forces."

"What do you mean?" I was thinking of the stained-glass picture of St. Michael in church and imagined him, sword aloft, on his perch above Mont-Saint-Michel. What a marvelous figure he was, a towering archangel, fierce, beautiful, mysterious —like Joris. "I shall call you the Archangel," I said.

He laughed and then sat up and pulled my hair. "All right. It'll be my secret name between us."

"No," I said now. "It must be somebody else. It can't be Joris."

"Why not?"

"Because . . ." And then I remembered how I had thought that if he were still alive, he would have to be changed beyond recognition; otherwise he would let us know he was still living. But a drug dealer?

"It's impossible," I finally said, and realized I was near tears.

O'Neill didn't reply for a moment, just leaned back against the windowsill, his hands in his pockets, watching me. After a moment he said, "I'd like to know everything about him that you can tell me."

I made a gesture with my hands. "What can I tell you? He was magnificent. He paid attention to me in a way that even Mother didn't. Poor Mother was too busy trying to keep the farm together, and Father . . . well, Mother sometimes, in her more sardonic moments, called him a disappointed bishop. He was a rector of an Episcopal church in a nearby town, and his first wife was the daughter of an immensely wealthy, rather parvenue family that had moved into Virginia and built a magnificent estate. That was Joris's mother. But she died when Joris was about eight, and Father married Mother, who had no money, but an old name and an old, pre-Revolutionary family house.

"I followed Joris around like a pet sheep. He'd tease me, talk to me, confide in me, and I hung on every word. Once, I wrote a book of things he'd said to me, but that made him angry. He took it away from me."

I took a breath. "I also never believed that he had died; at least, I didn't believe it until I was grown and finally looked at all the evidence." I paused. "It seems now I might have been right, doesn't it?" I stopped, abruptly. I had not felt the feelings I was having for a long time, an overwhelming sadness and sense of loss.

"Here," O'Neill said, and handed me some tissues from his top drawer. "Why did you believe Joris wasn't dead?" he asked.

"Because Joris had told me that he had been given a special mission in life and that he had to go away to fulfill it. So, when he vanished, I assumed he was doing what he told me he would be doing . . ."

"You didn't mention it to anyone?"

"No. He made me promise that I would never tell anyone about things he told me in secret."

"What kind of mission?"

"He didn't exactly say, except he must have said something to make me believe it was . . . well, sort of high-minded and spiritual."

"If he's what I think he is, that's a laugh. It really is. Drugs have been flooding this whole area in increasing amounts over the past few years. If it's your Joris, his mission seems to have been to poison half the young population."

"Then it *can't* be."

"But you yourself said that he had to be changed to be still alive and not have let you know."

At that point, Simon walked into the room. "I had to come here," he said, and then turned to me and said rather formally, "I hope you don't object."

"No," I said. And was surprised to find I was faintly glad he was there.

"What's this about Joris' being mixed up in drugs?"

"We don't have anything like proof," O'Neill said. "It's only a wild theory that somebody put together. We've known for some time a local drug king is called the Archangel. That came out a few years ago. As a matter of fact, it was in one of the dailies back then, and somebody on the local television news picked it up. But we couldn't pin any definite identification on whoever it was. For a while we thought he was a prominent drug connection up in Harlem. But then the man we thought it was got caught and put in the slammer, and the stuff—good stuff from Indonesia—kept getting in. So we started all over again.

"Then one of the middle-rank distributors got into a fight one night with some of the competition and was left with a bullet in his gizzard. Our guys showed up in time to take him to the hospital. He was dying and we knew it, and after a while he knew it. The one thing he hung on for was revenge. No President of the U.S. has been more closely watched than this guy was. He knew his own side would do anything to get at him again, so he talked. He had nothing to lose. He came out with a lot of names. Some we knew, some we didn't. We kept asking him who the Archangel was—what his name was. He said he didn't know. Then one of us asked—almost in passing—if he'd ever seen him. He said he had seen him once, and then added, 'a big guy, white.'

"Finally we sent in an artist to keep drawing and showing the result to the dying guy, who kept saying no, until finally, shortly before he expired, he surprised us all by saying, 'Yeah, sorta like that.'

"We didn't have much hope, but we started comparing the drawing to mug shots. He could have been one or two of those, but circumstances ruled them out. Finally, one of the older officers, after staring at the drawing for two or three days, went to some old files and came back with a poster that had been circulated nearly twenty-one years ago. It was of one Joris Maitland, Princeton graduate, missing person.

"Of course, it wasn't by a long shot a definite identification —one was a photograph and one was a stylized drawing. And at the time he disappeared, the whole department had spent months trying to find him and came up with nothing. We couldn't afford to put that kind of manpower on it now. I made a few inquiries and followed it up as well as I could and got nowhere"—O'Neill paused—"until now."

"You mean you think the Archangel, your drug connection, is Joris?"

"It's the best possibility we have so far."

I was silent, trying to sort my thoughts out. I seemed to be having trouble taking in what O'Neill was saying. "You mean you think it could be Joris—our Joris?"

"Yes."

"Then that would mean he's alive," I said. "Do you have any idea where?"

"No, Kit, and I can't tell you how many false leads there've been. But we always land back where we started."

"Well, well," Simon said, and sat down on the edge of the desk. "I'll be damned."

My pleasure at his presence vanished before a far more familiar feeling. "I suppose it pleases you that Joris might turn out to be . . . well, not your 24-karat hero."

"You're quite right. It does. I'd be a liar if I said anything else. You're not the only person who considered me mere dust beneath his chariot wheels. I got that from the whole family."

I stared at him, ready to take offense as I always had, but I didn't. Over his perfectly pleasant, even good-looking face slid my memory of Joris's beauty. " *'I beheld Lucifer as lightning fall from heaven,'* " I said.

"Not 'Lucifer', 'Satan'," Simon responded. "Same person, but you might as well get it right."

"Who said it?"

"Christ, according to Luke."

"Why on earth am I thinking about that?"

"As the daughter of a rector, your unconscious made the connection that Satan/Lucifer was an archangel."

"What was the thing Joris told you that he was commissioned to do?" O'Neill asked. "I think you can part with that information now."

I sighed. "Father, of course, wanted him to go into the church. As a matter of fact, Joris used sometimes to act as crucifer, leading the procession, carrying the cross, and looking incredibly handsome in his vestments."

"And didn't he just know it!" Simon said.

"All right," O'Neill put in hastily. "Go on, Kit."

I glared at Simon, then said reluctantly, "I suppose so. He always had an interest in what he called the spiritual, but when he talked to me about what he felt he was meant to do, he said he'd decided that churches were worn out, finished. That real spirituality, knowledge of the other consciousness, et cetera, came from the East, and he was going to find it there. So I've always imagined him somewhere in India or Tibet, searching until he found the final truth about everything . . ."

"That's a nice picture," Simon said. "A little pie-in-the-sky, but it makes sense of some of the trouble he got into at Princeton. They were within an ace of kicking him out, but didn't because he was almost ready to graduate, and anyway, his father had gone there."

"I didn't know that," I said. "Nobody told me. Even you didn't tell me when we were married."

"I didn't see any point. Anyway, I probably thought you knew. He was caught with some hallucinogens, following the trail led by the Harvard professor who was always telling the kids to turn on, tune in and drop out."

"Why didn't I hear about it?" I asked. "Not one word was said about that at home, although his disappearance lay like a shadow over everything. Father withdrew into himself totally. He hardly ever spoke to me. But Mother—" I paused, realizing the answer to my own question even as Simon spoke.

"Your mother, I think, was protecting your father, or perhaps protecting him from having other people—including you, his second child—know about Joris."

As Simon spoke, something else rose to the top of my memory: Joris's voice saying, *"There are quicker ways of finding the path than sitting in meditation for thirty years."*

"What path?" I had said. I think I had a vague idea of a path through a forest.

"The Path, the Way—the road to God."

"But I thought you didn't like church. You said it was bunk."

That was when he said his piece about the church and how it was worn out and that the truth lay in the East.

"Well," O'Neill said, watching me. "Don't keep whatever it is to yourself."

So I told them what I remembered.

We all sat there silent for a moment, O'Neill perched on the windowsill, Simon on the table, and me in the one chair, as though we were waiting for something.

Then, without even thinking, I said, " *'How art thou fallen from heaven, O Lucifer, son of the morning!'* "I shook my head. "Where did all that come from? What's the matter with me this morning?"

"It's somewhere in Isaiah," Simon said.

I looked at him. "You seem to know a lot about the Bible. You weren't the son of a priest."

"I've been doing some reading of it in the last year or so. In one of the rehab places I went to, it and AA literature were about the only things available to read. When you can't sleep, you read what's there."

"Yeah, it's out of Isaiah, even I know that," O'Neill said. "We had it in Catholic school."

"But why is this running in my mind? Just because of the Joris-Archangel link—not that I am totally convinced of it?"

"Oh yes," O'Neill said, "you're convinced. You just don't want to admit it."

Simon added, "And for you, it would indeed be like the fall of the Morning Star—another name for the archangel who was called Lucifer or Satan or the Light Bearer."

I didn't say anything, because O'Neill was right: to say something would be to admit something. And already I was struggling with the desolation of loss. I got up.

"I'd better get on with what I was doing," I said. I looked at Simon. "You told me that you and Crystal were in some rehab together. I'm going to go there and see if I can get any further line on Crystal. The agency here seems to have taken a vow of silence about her. She was one of their successful graduates, and they're not about to tarnish her memory. So I'm going to your drying-out place. I think she went back to drugs after that, or maybe I want to think so. I'm just hoping that they won't be as closemouthed there."

"You can try," Simon said. He stood up. "It's called Brentwood, and it's in Ohio, just outside Cleveland. The man to see —the only one who'd really be able to give you any information—is Dr. Britton. I'll give you the address and phone number."

He took a small address book out of his breast pocket, looked inside, then scribbled on a piece of paper and handed it to me. "If you want me to, I'll call him. I, too, went back to drinking after I left there the first time, but I liked him and I think he liked me."

"Why not call him now?" O'Neill asked.

"All right."

Simon reached for the phone and dialed. "May I speak to Dr. Britton?" he asked. Then, "When do you expect him back? Thanks." He put the phone down. "Bob's away. He'll be back day after tomorrow. No point your going there till then."

"Thanks," I said. It was a struggle for me to be civil to Simon.

"Don't mention it." There was a snap to his voice.

"I don't know what you have to be snotty about, I was the one who got beaten up, remember?"

"Indeed I do. And if I should, for a day, forget, I can depend on you to remind me." He turned to O'Neill. "If you need me for anything, you know where to get me." Then he walked out.

"He beat you up?" O'Neill asked.

"He was drinking," I felt compelled to say.

"Good thing he's sober now."

"Yes."

"When are you going out to this place?"

"I guess tomorrow night. Simon said Dr. Britton would be back day after tomorrow."

"Who's paying for it?"

I debated telling the policeman that it was none of his business. But I said, "I hope the magazine. I'm going out there as part of my assignment to do the piece on Crystal Mahoney."

"Even though your main reason for going out is to see if you can track down someone else she talked to about Joris Maitland." He grinned, showing crooked teeth. "There's the credit-card, expense-account world for you! While we public servants have to account for every stick of gum."

I looked at him. "Yeah, I bet. And absolutely no bribes, no tips, nobody on the take."

"I've never taken a bribe or been on the take in my life."

"I believe you. And I hope you believe me when I say that I have never cheated on a business trip. It's true I'll ask around to see if anyone has any memory of what Crystal might have said about Joris. But I'm also going to see how she got back into the drug world, who she knew there, and who might have been her contacts. If this had nothing to do with the article, I'd take a big breath and pay for it myself."

"Okay, I believe you. And I hope you'll share any knowledge you have with us. I'll tell the people in Westchester that you're going."

That, I thought as I left, was to let me know that they were still interested in me. As though I had any doubt!

That afternoon, I called Claire and asked her if I could come and see her the next day.

There was a pause. "Can you come between one and two? It's technically my lunch hour, but I'll order something in."

"I can bring sandwiches for us both. I need to talk to you—both for me and the article. What kind of sandwich do you want, and how do you take your coffee?"

"Now," Claire said the next day at one, after we'd opened the sandwiches and coffee and put everything on a small table in her office. "What's on your mind?"

I told her what Simon had told me about Crystal and her revelation about Joris.

"And the unnerving thing was that that was my nickname for him: the Archangel. I think I thought he looked a little like the stained-glass portrait of St. Michael in the church. And of course my hero worship was boundless." I looked at the intelligent young woman in the clerical collar. "I know this comes under the heading of professional confidentiality, but I have to ask. Did Crystal, while you were treating her, say anything about Joris Maitland or somebody called the Archangel?"

Claire didn't say anything for a moment. "No, neither one. And I certainly would have remembered someone named the Archangel. But then, she didn't want to talk about her drug life much. I'd try to get her back to the subject from time to time, because I felt that by denying that, she was also denying other aspects of her life—her family, her work to become a reporter, the parties she went to, the men she knew. That's one reason why I didn't consider her therapy a success. She wasn't really interested in turning over any of those rocks." We ate in silence for a while. Then Claire asked, "How are you feeling about Simon these days?"

"Confused, I suppose. Every time I open my mouth something nasty comes out. I seem to forget that he has tried to make his amends."

"Ummm."

"What does 'ummm' mean, Madame Therapist?"

"Nothing much—I suppose that you aren't ready to let your resentment go yet. You keep feeding and watering it. Maybe it's because you could never get hold of him to tell him what you thought of him, and before you could do that, he writes you an apologetic letter and robs you, you think, of your chance."

"You sound just like a therapist," I said crossly. "Let it all hang out, and if it knocks down a few people, that's okay too."

"I didn't suggest that you shoot him or beat him over the head. I just suggested that you tell him how rotten he made you feel when he beat you up."

"I feel like a louse myself doing that, when he's made his handsome amend."

"You think he robbed you of the right to kick him in the shins."

I was about to take offense when it occurred to me that that was exactly the way I felt. "Yes."

"Well, tell him that. I'm sure he'd rather cope with that than snide reminders for the rest of his life."

"He did say that if he ever forgot how he behaved when he was drinking, he could count on me to remind him."

"That's what I mean."

"Why are you sticking up for him so much?"

"I'm not. I'm sticking up for you. I'm not sure that shoving a needle in him is your road to happiness."

"Thanks a lot." I glanced at her and then laughed. "I guess

you're right. I'll do something about it when I get back from Brentwood."

"By the way," Claire asked, "have you seen that man again, the one who nearly pushed you under the train?"

"All I saw was his back. If it was the man in the restaurant, then I would recognize him. In which case, I'd tell Lieutenant O'Neill. But no, I haven't seen him." I put the last of my sandwich in my mouth and chewed. "Why?"

"Because . . . look, I don't want to make you walk in some kind of fear all the time. But watch out. There's something about this case you're on that I find scary. And the fact that it started out so mildly, merely a story on an ancient mansion, makes it worse. You discover that the mansion story is really a cover for investigating why a girl committed suicide in a motel room. Then you find the body of the man who watched your apartment. Then somebody tries to push you under a train— What I mean is, be careful. Keep an eye on people around you. Don't . . . well, don't start being the brave investigative reporter and do something stupid . . . You know what I mean. I wish you'd leave the whole thing to Lieutenant O'Neill."

"But O'Neill hasn't been offered a couple of thousand to do a story. Although—" It was at that moment that I remembered Piers's offer to pay the fee anyway, so I could stop running into danger.

"Although what?"

I told her about Piers's offer.

"And of course you refused," she said dryly. "Now that the bit was thoroughly between your teeth."

"Yes. I did. I still do. I'm not Mother Courage. But I can't leave this here, particularly . . . particularly when it seems to concern Joris." We were silent for a moment. Then, "By the way, as soon as I can get this tied up, I'll start looking up the thing you asked me about. You know—the people who're trying to buy St. Cuthbert's."

"All right. When are you leaving for Brentwood, and anyway, where is it?"

"Just outside Cleveland. I think I'll go there tonight, if I can get home, pack a bag, and get a flight. Also, I have to arrange

for Topaz to be taken care of. I'll ask Letty to do it, or if she's
not in, leave a note for her."

"Letty being a neighbor or a professional cat-sitter, I take
it."

"She's both, in a way. She's a psychic and a complete animal
nut—they often go together . . . She's said some odd things
to me." I glanced at Claire. "Before anybody else, she told me
to be careful, and I thought she was crazy. Also she said that
what I was looking for was not where I thought it was, or
something like that."

"She sounds very practical in her psychic gifts."

I glanced at her. "Even the lieutenant seemed to have some
respect for psychics. He said they used them sometimes."

"There are more things in heaven and on earth, et cetera, et
cetera . . . I mean there are a lot of aspects about the links
among the mind, body and spirit that we've ignored for several
centuries. Our unconscious and the spiritual world are closer
than we've ever been willing to believe."

"O'Neill said he didn't know how much Holy Mother
Church would approve of psychic help . . ." I paused. "I
know that my father was adamantly against anything like that.
He was for doctrine and dogma and faith. The rest for him was
superstition, witchcraft and other heathen leftovers among the
peons."

"You didn't like him much, did you?"

"No. And I extended my dislike to his church." I grinned at
her. "This one."

"Give us another chance. We're not all tyrannical clerics."
She got up and brushed the crumbs from her skirt.

I got up too. "I didn't mean that to sound like a criticism. I'm
sorry—"

She looked up at me and smiled. "I wasn't offended. But I do
have a client coming in about twenty minutes. But before she
comes, I want to mention something else. I had a talk with
Chris here—you remember, the assistant rector whose brother
knew the van Reiders. Chris says—in fact he hinted before—
that Hilary van Reider, who looks the soul of puritan rectitude,
nevertheless is one for the ladies. There's always a girlfriend
somewhere in the offing. So the female who called up and

panicked when she thought it was van Reider's body you stumbled over was probably just his current flame. However, because of the ongoing custody war over his son, van Reider is obsessed on the subject of publicity of any kind. He's convinced it's all grist going to the mills of his ex-wife's lawyers."

" 'Obsessed' is right. Well, thanks for telling me. That makes one puzzlement less puzzling."

"Also, as far as censored news accounts of Crystal's death and the van Reider letters thrown around are concerned, you have to remember that the van Reider family owns the two local newspapers."

"Ah so! Well, that does explain things a bit." I glanced at my watch. As I did, a buzzer sounded. Claire leaned forward and pressed a button on her phone. Then she lifted the receiver. "Yes?" She paused. "Oh. Well, you'd better send him up, but please make sure he understands I have a client coming in a few minutes."

She hung up. "Your favorite person, Hilary van Reider, is here and insists on seeing me. He wanted to see the rector, I gathered, but would make do with me."

"Sounds just like him. Do you want me to go?"

"You can if you want. But since our only connection with van Reider is St. Cuthbert's, and my intuition tells me he has come to complain about that in some way or other, then you might as well stay. This has become part of your turf too."

There was a brief knock on her door, then the door opened. Van Reider stood in the doorway. He had put a foot in when he saw me. "Oh, I didn't know you still had someone here." His eyebrows drew together. "Miss Maitland, I believe."

"That's right," Claire said. "We were talking when you were announced. Since I thought you would probably want to talk about St. Cuthbert's, and Ms. Maitland has an interest in the subject too, I told her she could stay, unless, of course, you would prefer that she didn't. By the way, won't you sit down?"

"No thanks. I won't be long and I'd sooner stand." He glanced at me. It was fairly plain from his chilly expression that he didn't want me there, but he didn't say so. Instead, he gave a slight shrug and said, "It doesn't matter to me. Ms. Maitland's aware of the subject I've come to discuss. It's the lack of any caretaker for Rivercrest. The Krauses are gone, no one has taken their place and the house is showing the results of neglect more every day. I'm not there during the week, and I think that fact has become known. I see what I am quite sure are signs of vandalism—the occasional cigarette ground out on the floor, a paper cup and some paper, scraping on the wooden floor. Rivercrest is now your property, but according to our contract, it is also my home. And I resent its poor upkeep and lack of care. From the most self-interested point of view, you should do something about appointing another caretaker. The house will bring much more money on the market if it's in reasonably good condition."

"You're absolutely right," Claire said. "I had no idea about the vandals, and I'm grateful for your mentioning it."

"It's no use your being grateful. Hiring somebody to take Krause's place would show your appreciation far better."

"I entirely agree, and I will set about finding someone immediately. Technically, the only person who would have the right to hire a caretaker is the rector, but I will talk to him in England this afternoon and ask him to give me the go-ahead to hire a new caretaker as soon as possible. Do you have any suggestions? You've lived up there. You know the people."

"No. I haven't lived there full time for a long time, and I don't know the people there as well as I used to. Surely a church would have far more resources for finding a good person than I would."

"We'll certainly give it a try," Claire said dryly.

"How's your son?" I asked.

"He's better, thank you," van Reider snapped.

"Does he live with you in New York?" I asked, partly out of curiosity, partly because van Reider seemed so much on the point of biting my head off; I found it irresistible to see if a small nudge would make him explode. It did.

"No thanks to you, *Ms.* Maitland"—he emphasized the Ms. as though flinging his gauntlet at the women's movement in the person of me—"his mother thinks he is unsafe in my custody, so has insisted on taking him back."

"I'm very sorry about your son," I said reasonably and a

little penitently—he had such a short fuse, I shouldn't have teased him—"but I didn't whack him on the head."

"No, but if the press had just let my home alone, instead of sending reporters to poke into things that weren't their business, none of this would have happened."

"Do you mean that you associate your son's injury with Ms. Maitland being there?" Claire asked. "Why?"

"I don't know why. If I knew every step in the chain of circumstance and logic, I would go to the police. But I don't. I do know that since that wretched reporter Crystal Mahoney came snooping up, followed by you, Ms. Maitland, the house has been vandalized, the caretaker's left, somebody attacked my son and my dog has been poisoned."

"The dog that attacked me?"

"He only did so because he was trained to guard and you were trespassing. He was a good dog. I was very fond of him. We—but it doesn't matter. He's gone now!"

"I'm sorry." It was, I thought, the most human thing van Reider had said. Curiously, he seemed more likable in his sorrow for his dog than he did in his angry anxiety over his son. "I'm sorry," I said again, and meant it. And then, "Is your cat still around and well?" I saw Claire glance at me. "The one I saw on your son's bed."

"What?" van Reider asked testily, returning to his usual manner.

"The ginger red cat I saw beside your son. Is he all right?"

"I suppose so. He's really a stray. He used to belong to a farm nearby, but the people moved away. Bart became attached to him. So he usually comes around when Bart's there."

"I should have thought your dog . . ." I hesitated, remembering what had happened. "Your guard dog might not have liked that."

"Naturally, we kept them apart."

"Yes, of course."

I stopped, as the ginger cat I dreamed about flashed in and out of my mind. What was Claire's curious question to me? "Have you ever been hypnotised?"

"Well, if that's all—" van Reider started.

"No, it isn't," I said. "Sorry. According to Lieutenant

O'Neill, whom I saw yesterday, the man whose body I found, and who probably hit Bart on the head, was a drug type named Ramedos. What he was doing there, I don't know. But . . ." I paused.

"But what?"

"But he was also watching my apartment. I thought I recognized him when I found his body, but wasn't sure. Later I became sure. I'd seen him outside my apartment on Charles Street, his eyes glued to my windows."

"I *said* there was a connection between you and him," van Reider said almost triumphantly, sounding much more like his old self. "Now you show me where it is."

"What I'm showing you, Mr. van Reider, is that I, too, am a victim to some degree. And I am not responsible for your son's accident. For a lawyer, you seem strangely unbound by the rules of evidence. You don't like journalists, so you decide that any misfortune that befalls your family has to be the journalists' fault."

He stared at me for a moment. "What you're saying is quite true. But there is a connection. I'm sure of it." He turned back to Claire. "Please let me know as soon as you have found a caretaker."

"I will certainly do that." Claire sighed. "I don't suppose you've thought of relinquishing your lifetime right to live there. If you did, the place would be bought immediately by this guru and our problems would be over."

"Your problems would be over. Mine wouldn't. You don't care about the place. I do. Good-bye." He gave a small, abrupt nod to each of us and walked out.

I looked at Claire. "I thought it was in perpetuity—I mean the family's right to live there forever."

"The wording is a little vague. It could easily be taken as that, and of course he states that it's so every time he opens his mouth. But, a day or so ago, I got our lawyer to have another look at the contract, and while Hilary van Reider's right to be there for his lifetime is perfectly clear, it's not terribly obvious that the right goes down to his son, et cetera. But I didn't want to tangle with him on that until we'd checked our lawyers again and the rector is back."

Her buzzer rang again. "That'll be my client. Have a good trip and call me when you get back. Oh—by the way." She came from behind the desk. "I have discovered that the reason you got a censored version of Crystal's story from the outreach program is because the part they left out is not very flattering to their clinic."

"I see. Okay, I'll be on my way. Talk to you soon."

I decided not to go the long way around into my house. "No comment," I yelled at the two or three people still hanging around our front entrance. Then I pushed Letty's bell, since I hadn't had the forethought to get out my key. There was a pause, then she pushed the buzzer to let me in. But when I got in and looked toward her apartment, her door was closed. Usually when she buzzed me in, she at least came to the door to pass the time of day.

"I'm up here," Letty called down.

I looked up the stairwell. Letty was coming down the steps of the third flight. "I knew it was you, so I buzzed you in from your apartment."

Letty was welcome to go into my apartment and had my keys for the times when she looked after Topaz. But something made me ask sharply, "What's the matter?"

She came down some more steps. "Kit, I'm so sorry."

I ran up the remaining stairs two at a time. "Topaz?" I said.

"Kit dear. Someone was in your apartment. Topaz must have got out. I'm so sorry."

I forgot about Brentwood and my flight to Cleveland and walked the streets looking for Topaz. I checked the big garden at the back before anything else. But nobody had seen him, he didn't seem to be in anybody's apartment, and while windows were open in apartments whose owners were at work, I somehow felt that Topaz wouldn't be there. He might have run into a strange apartment, but if he could get out again, he would.

Letty walked in one direction, and I walked in another. I asked all the people in the surrounding little stores, especially grocery stores. People in the Village were very animal-minded. Everyone I spoke to said he or she would certainly keep an eye out for a large, slightly obese marmalade cat, with a big head and rather small ears. When I thought of Topaz frightened or mistreated, it was all I could do not to burst into tears.

Finally I stopped at a stationer's and bought cards and some tape. On the cards I wrote a description of Topaz and gave my address and telephone number. Then I gave the cards to people I had talked to in the stores and anybody who showed interest or concern, and I taped some to neighboring trees and lampposts.

When I got back, I called Lieutenant O'Neill and told him about what happened.

"What did they take?"

"My cat. Or at least they let him out, and I can't find him."

"I mean, what property? Have you looked around?"

"No."

"When did this happen?"

"Sometime this morning when I was out to see Claire Aldington."

"It's five o'clock now. What have you been doing?"

"I've been looking for Topaz." I felt my voice waver and paused. "Lieutenant, is there any way you could ask some of your patrolmen to look out for a marmalade-colored, rather fat cat? I'm going to call the ASPCA to see if anyone picked him up and put him there . . ." Then the thought of animals given to laboratories for experiment made me feel sick. "People pick up animals, don't they, and sell them to labs . . ."

"Kit. Listen to me. I'm truly sorry about your cat. And I'll get word to the patrol car around there to keep a lookout for him. But is anything missing from your apartment—besides your cat, I mean?"

"I haven't looked. I'll look now and call you back."

"I'll hold on."

I put the receiver down and looked around the apartment, trying to get past the terrible gap left by Topaz's sturdy form. That was when I noticed drawers open in my desk in the living room. I went over. My basic tidiness was revolted by the mixup of everything in the drawers. Then I went into the bedroom. My overpowering concern for Topaz was demonstrated by the fact that not until this moment had I noticed that all the drawers of my bureau were emptied on the bed and then piled up on a chair.

I stared down at them. I'd inherited a little family jewelry from my mother, but it was in its usual box.

I looked in my closet. No clothes were missing, but everything on the shelves above had been turned upside down.

I went back to the living room and saw then, or took in for the first time, how many books had been taken from the bookshelves and piled up on the floor. Those left on the shelves were lying every which way, with no regard to title, author or previous order.

"Damn it to hell," I cried. Then I remembered the lieutenant, still (presumably) on the telephone. I snatched up the receiver. "They've turned the place upside down—books are on the floor, the drawers in the bedroom have been emptied on the bed, the drawers in here in my desk have been all mixed up."

"What's missing?"

"Topaz! I keep telling you."

"I mean besides your cat."

"Nothing, as far as I can find out. Mother's jewelry is still here." I glanced over at my desk. "My checkbook is here."

"What about your credit cards?"

"They're in my handbag, which I had with me."

There was a silence at the end of the phone. Then, "Does anybody know about this?"

"Just Letty."

"Letty? Who's—oh, she's the woman downstairs who's psychic. Did she know about it psychically or in the more usual way—because you told her?"

"I didn't tell her," I said slowly, beginning to think about it for the first time. "When I got home, I went straight through the front door instead of going around through the garden and Paul's and Letty's apartments. And I didn't have my key out, so I buzzed her. When I got in she was upstairs in my apartment, but she came halfway down to tell me that somebody had been in my apartment and that Topaz was missing."

"How did she know? Did she hear somebody?"

"I didn't ask her. All I heard was that Topaz was missing, and I've been looking for him ever since."

There was a slight pause. Then, "I'm coming over. Please ask Letty how she knew somebody was in your apartment. I'll be there in ten minutes." And he hung up before I could tell him that I fully intended to go out again to continue looking for Topaz.

"Damn!" I said, slamming the receiver down.

There was a knock on the door.

"Who is it?" I yelled.

"Me, Letty."

I went over to the door and opened it. "The lieutenant wants me to ask you how you knew that somebody was in my apartment."

"I was coming to tell you that. I was feeding the Pendletons' Jasmine, on the second floor, and I thought I heard noises above, though not immediately above. So I came out in the hall and listened. Then I heard a cry and I knew it was Topaz—I'm sorry, my dear," and she reached out and clasped my hand in her firm one. "So I raced downstairs to get your keys, and then up again. By the time I got there, there was nobody there and Topaz had gone. He must have slipped out when I was getting your keys. Also, your place was turned upside down, but I knew that that wouldn't even begin to upset you when you knew about Topaz."

She let go my hand and we both went into my apartment. I stood looking around vaguely, as though Topaz would materialize somewhere.

"You've checked behind the stove, I assume?" Letty said almost timidly.

"That was the first place I looked. Letty, Lieutenant O'Neill is coming over to talk to us. I don't know how much I've told you about the various investigations I've been on. You know about my being nearly pushed under the subway train . . . I'll try to fill you in." And I did, about St. Cuthbert's and the church and Claire Aldington and Crystal Mahoney. Letty sat there and listened. Along with Claire, she listened better than anyone I knew, although her method was different. Claire looked you straight in the eyes. Letty cocked her head on one side or she gazed into the air. When I first knew her I thought she wasn't paying attention and was slightly miffed. But I discovered that she could repeat, word for word, what I'd been saying for the previous ten minutes.

"There's something else," she said now, when I'd finished. "Something you haven't mentioned." If I'd felt less beaten down, I would have asked her how she knew, if only to tease her. Because she would simply say, "I know." This time I took it on trust.

So I told her about Joris and the Archangel and how Crystal had told Simon about him out in Ohio at the rehabilitation place. "Before I came home, I was going to leave on the first flight to Cleveland to see if the headman there knew anything about Crystal's tie with Joris and/or the Archangel."

Letty didn't say anything for a while.

"Can't you use your clairvoyance or something to give me these answers, so I don't have to leave when I'm frantic about Topaz? Better still, you're a psychic, can't you tell me where Topaz is? Why haven't I thought about that before? Of course! Oh, Letty, *concentrate!*"

"I have been my dear, ever since he went. But I can't see anything but a sort of swirling gray fog. Nothing's coming through." She glanced at me. "You know, you can't just summon answers when you want them. They come when they feel like it . . . However, I thought I might ask you to give me something belonging to Topaz, maybe a toy, or a blanket, or something, and I'd see if that would help."

I looked around. There was no use thinking about Topaz's blanket. It was the same as my blanket. In summer he slept in the small of my back on top of the bedclothes. In the coldest nights of winter, he slept in the same place, but under the bedclothes. Also, he was a great disappointment to anyone who brought him a present. Frequently he would go mad about a large paper clip and ignore the toy. However, there was one toy he liked, and I went around looking over the floor for it. It was a cloth mouse, and why he loved that and ignored the others I never knew. But periodically he would play hockey with it as the puck, or toss it into the air, or pounce at it from behind a chair.

"Here," I said, backing out from under my desk. "Here's his pet toy." And then I had to stop talking and get hold of myself, because it was still slightly damp from the last time he'd chewed it.

I was giving it to Letty when my buzzer rang.

"Who is it?" I called down the intercom.

"O'Neill."

I buzzed him in.

"Do you want to talk to him alone?" Letty asked, getting up. "I think I'll just go downstairs and concentrate on this toy. And—" She stepped back as I opened the door.

"Come in, Lieutenant," I said.

O'Neill was a slight man and only of medium height, but he somehow filled the room. "Sorry about your cat," he said, his eyes on Letty. "Is this the lady who found he was missing?"

"Yes. This is Letty . . . er . . ." I fumbled because I had forgotten her last name. "I'm sorry, Letty."

"It's all right. Letitia Dalrymple, Lieutenant."

"Did you do some psychic work with the Twenty-third Precinct once?"

"Yes, I did. I was glad to be of help."

"Good heavens, Letty," I said. "You never told me you worked with the police."

"You never asked. And I've always felt—until dear Topaz's disappearance—that you didn't really approve of my psychic goings-on."

I could feel myself blushing. "My apologies."

"It's quite all right. I'd never hold that against you. People are at different stages of development."

"Quite so," O'Neill said. "There's a question I'd like to ask you, Mrs. Dalrymple—"

"Miss Dalrymple, please."

"All right. Miss Dalrymple. I—"

"You want to know how I knew that there'd been intruders in Kit's apartment. Well, I heard them." And she filled him in on what she had told me, finishing with the lament: "If I'd just gone straight up, Topaz would still be there."

"And you might be dead," O'Neill said.

"I just didn't *think*. I don't think I thought of people at all. I just heard this cry from Topaz, and knew I couldn't get in without the keys, so went straight down for them."

"Lieutenant, what is it you want to ask me or tell me? I'm about to go out again to see if I can find Topaz."

"I came to ask you to go to Ohio anyway, although I suspected, given the way you feel about your cat, you'd want to postpone it."

"You suspected right. I'm not going anywhere until I get Topaz back."

"What Simon told you about his conversation with Crystal Mahoney has given us the first connection we've had between the drug king of this area and somebody's name. I'd like to talk to the people there as much as you do. But I think that if the police went out to that rehab place, the authorities—and any patients who might be repeats and have known Crystal— would be much leerier of answering, than if you went there and asked the questions. We're very anxious for you to go."

"Topaz—"

"And to speed matters on, I've talked to one of the people I know at the ASPCA. He's going to search around this area for you on his own time while you're away—"

"I won't go until I get Topaz. I'd like your friend in the ASPCA to help me. The sooner I find Topaz, the sooner I'll go to Cleveland."

"Kit, we have information that drugs are about to flood the streets, that a drug war is about to begin, and rival groups are getting their poisons and thugs out to knock off the competition. Do I have to talk to you about the number of young people who can get permanently hooked and corrupted?"

"Go, dear," Letty said unexpectedly. "I am getting the strong feeling that Topaz is all right and that we will find him."

"Oh, all of a sudden your psychic gifts are coming into play and you're sure Topaz is okay and will be found. Why now?"

I was irritated that Letty should seem to be going over to the side of the enemy. But as I had asked the question, I saw her fingers stroking and kneading Topaz's mouse.

"Because I simply had the feeling as you were talking. I am sure we'll find Topaz and that he'll be all right. I don't think he's far from here. But I do feel that it's important you go to

Ohio. Something bad may happen, but if you go, maybe it won't happen . . ." Her voice trailed off.

"I'm sorry, Letty, I don't mean to hurt your feelings, but I find myself less and less inclined to believe this witch of Endor stuff."

"I don't think you should confuse me with the witch of Endor, although she was undoubtedly misunderstood by a primitive people. I'm surprised at you, Kit. You never struck me as being a blind materialist. But I'll overlook it, because I know how worried you are about Topaz."

At that moment my buzzer rang. We all looked at one another. "Find out who it is," the lieutenant said.

I went over to the intercom. "Who is it?"

"Ms. Maitland, this is Gino over at the grocery. I think I've got your cat."

I buzzed, then flung open my door and started down the steps. Slowly plodding up toward me was the stout, friendly grocer who, with his wife, ran a Ma and Pa store at the corner. Then I gave a cry. Under his arm, looking furious at the indignity, was Topaz.

"Topaz," I said, then clutched him to me and hugged him.

"Come up, Gino," I said, trying not to sound as tearful as I felt.

"Where did you find him?" I asked, closing my front door behind us.

"He just walked in, bold as a lion. You should excuse me, I was about to throw him out when my wife said, 'Hold on, isn't that like the cat Ms. Maitland told us about? Let me get her card.' So I brought him over."

Gino refused all reward and left immediately. I put Topaz down. He looked a little less than his regal self, and his fur was dirty in spots. As though aware of my noticing this, he started washing.

"So that's the great Topaz," Lieutenant O'Neill said. "He's a little overweight, isn't he?"

"You wouldn't have dared to say that to Louis XIV, the Sun King."

"I guess you're right. My apologies. That sure was a wonderful piece of luck."

"Not entirely luck," Letty said. "I've been sending out messages and praying."

I looked at her for a minute, then went over and hugged her. "I'm sorry about all the things I said. I believe you."

"Yes, dear. It's nice to have a successful manifestation. But trying to believe when nobody else is—that's the real test."

O'Neill stood up. "And now will you go to Cleveland? There's a flight this evening. I'll arrange for a car to pick you up and will reserve a room for you."

"Yes, dear. You must go. I'm sure that's why Topaz was sent back."

"All right. I'll go pack a bag."

"I'll drive you to the airport," O'Neill said.

The strong arm of the police force must have cleared the way. The ticket was waiting at the reservation counter when we arrived at the airport. O'Neill sat with me until boarding time. I would have been flattered, except that it was so obvious that he didn't feel able to let me out of his sight. Finally the boarding was announced. I waved to O'Neill from the bend in the ramp. Then I got into the plane and slid into my window seat.

I was relieved that I seemed not to have a seat partner and would have a restful, quiet flight to Cleveland. But I was wrong. Just after the pilot turned off the seat-belt sign, I looked up. A tall man was pushing his bag into the locker over the seats.

"What are you doing here?" I said to Simon.

9

"O'Neill didn't want you to take this trip alone."

"The least he could have done was to let me know ahead of time."

"I think he thought you would have balked and refused to come."

"I would have."

"Then, that's why he didn't." Simon stood looking down at me for a moment, that half smile on his face. "You don't have to talk to me." Then he sat down.

"Where on earth were you? Sitting in the back, I suppose. Figuring that if you sat down before the plane took off, I might not take off too."

"You're very perceptive," Simon said and picked up his newspaper.

"I suppose O'Neill told you this," I grumbled.

"Yes."

When pressed, Simon admitted that O'Neill was having grave doubts about my safety and had enlisted Simon to watch over me. "He thinks that traveling with your husband would not be considered as unusual to anyone who was watching, as traveling with a police escort would be."

"A police escort!"

"Well, you know what I mean. He doesn't feel you're safe, and neither do I. Remember the subway incident? Somebody being with you could have forestalled that."

"Well, whoever is quote watching unquote would have to be somebody who didn't know we hadn't lived together for the past five years. Otherwise he/she would know how unusual this is."

Simon picked up his paper again. "Better than nothing."

"And anyway. I don't think it's so much that O'Neill's worried about me. I think he doesn't trust me."

Simon didn't say anything. As the silence stretched, and I reflected that I had forgotten to get a newspaper, I also realized that I wouldn't have been entirely averse to conversing with Simon. But I certainly wasn't going to give him the satisfaction of knowing that. Reaching up, I pushed the bell for a flight attendant. "I'd like a magazine," I said coldly when she turned up and directed a dazzling smile at Simon.

"Certainly. And you, sir?"

"No thanks." When the attendant had gone to get the magazine rack, he said, "I'd be happy to share the paper with you."

"I've already read it," I lied.

"Then you must have been interested in this note about St. Cuthbert's."

"What note? Where? Show me."

Simon grinned.

If the plane window were open, I thought, I'd push him out.

The attendant brought me an array of magazines, none of which I wanted to read. "Thank you," I said.

She smiled tenderly at Simon. "Changed your mind?"

He looked up and smiled back at her. "Not for the moment."

Her dimples quivered. "I'll check later."

Simon went back to his paper.

I went back to grumbling. "I don't understand how you can get so much time off, that is, if you really are a member of a law firm."

"I really am. But they're very sympathetic about family problems."

"You don't *have* a family."

"Not at the moment. But hope springs eternal."

Thanks to O'Neill, a rental car was waiting at the Cleveland airport, and reservations had been made in a nearby motel. Our rooms at the motel were next door to each other, but not connecting.

"Good night," Simon said at his door, which came first as we walked down the hall. "Sleep well."

"Same to you," I said.

I thought I would lie awake for hours, something I often do in hotel beds. But, to my pleasant surprise, I felt drowsy and drifted off to sleep almost immediately . . .

I was back on the streets of Greenwich Village looking for Topaz and calling him frantically—frantically because, in my dream, I knew that if I didn't find him soon he would be killed. So I ran down one deserted street after another. There were no lights. Everything was shut up. I knew Topaz was in terrible danger and thought I could hear him crying. I raced down the next street, calling after him. Finally I turned a corner. There, lying under the front paws of another huge cat, was Topaz. I started after him, but the great ginger-red monster bared its bloody teeth, I saw then the blood at Topaz's throat, and I screamed and screamed . . .

The pounding on the door finally made me stop. I came out of my nightmare and heard it for what it was.

"Kit, let me in. Let me in!"

Getting out of bed I fumbled my way in the dark to the door and opened it.

Simon pushed his way in, switching on the light beside the door.

I felt so groggy my head swam, and I sat down suddenly on the bed.

"Has anybody been in here?" Simon asked.

"No. At least, I've been asleep, I don't think so. What happened?"

"You've been screaming."

At that I remembered the dream. "The ginger cat," I said. "I saw it again."

"What ginger cat? Your cat? The one O'Neill told me about?"

"Topaz is not ginger, he's marmalade. The one in my dreams is huge, but much leaner than dear, fat Topaz, and he's a dark ginger, really red, with even darker reddish stripes around him."

"He sounds like Lucifer."

"Lucifer? Lucifer! What are you talking about?" Oddly, with a detached portion of my mind, I realized I was shaking. I could feel my hands, completely beyond my control, shaking, as was the rest of my body. "What are you talking about?" I repeated.

"Surely you remember the cat Lucifer at Percy's Walk. He was your mother's cat. He disappeared suddenly. No one knew what had happened to him. What's the matter, Kit?"

I could feel the sweat on my forehead. And then the wave of nausea hit me. I barely made it to the bathroom, and stayed there, heaving long past the time there was anything left to come up.

Simon came in. I was about to tell him to get out when another attack seized me, so I was occupied for a few minutes and then felt an ice-cold cloth slipping around my forehead.

"Here," he said as soon as I was able to straighten. "Put this in your mouth and suck it." And he slipped an ice cube between my teeth.

I felt so terrible that I allowed Simon to support me with his arm back into my room. He lowered me to the bed and went back into the bathroom.

"Hold this around your forehead," he said, coming back in. It was the washrag again, this time folded over some crushed ice cubes.

"Where'd you get the ice?" I mumbled, pressing the cold cloth against my temples.

"While you were heaving, I went out into the hall to the ice machine. It's right next door to you."

I sat there for a while, still holding the ice at my forehead, when I suddenly started to shiver.

"Cold?" Simon asked, getting up and moving toward the window.

"No." I didn't want him to shut the window. Closed windows at night give me claustrophobia. "I just feel—funny."

"Funny how?"

"Like a goose walked over my grave."

He came back and we sat there for a while longer in silence. Finally he got up. "You seem all right. I guess I'd better get back to my room."

I didn't say anything. Then, as he opened the door, I burst out, "Don't go."

He turned, looked at me for a moment, then came back. He sat down in the chair he pulled up beside the bed. "What's the matter?" he asked.

"I don't know. I wish . . . but I can't get hold of it." I waited for a moment and fought back another wave of nausea. After all, there was nothing left to get rid of. "Simon, what did you say about a cat named Lucifer?"

"Don't you remember? You were about ten. Your mother had this almost-red cat. Actually it was a sort of red ginger, with circles of even a deeper red-ginger going around its middle. You were always very fond of it. Then, one day, it disappeared. After that, you didn't like cats. Somebody gave you a kitten for a birthday or something and you refused to have anything to do with it. That's why I was so surprised to hear about your devotion to your cat in New York. I couldn't believe you'd have one in the house. How did you come to adopt him?"

I told him of finding Topaz leaning against the building and then taking him to the vet.

"Then, you must have recovered from your ailurophobia."

I took my hand away from my head. "My *what?*"

He grinned. "Your catophobia."

"I never—" I started. And then I remembered he was right. I had forgotten about the kitten that had been given to me by one of our neighbors. Mother also tried to interest me in another cat. Finally, because she missed Lucifer, she adopted one herself. I suddenly recalled her bewilderment, even hurt, when I wouldn't go near him . . . So what happened to me between then and the day I saw Topaz, half starved, wobbling over to rub against me . . . this ginger kitten?

"Not ginger," I heard myself saying. "Marmalade."

But he *was* ginger as a kitten, though he didn't have stripes. His reddish hue grew more orange as he grew older . . . And then, suddenly, there flashed through my mind the savage, feral red cat of my dreams, and I started to feel sick again.

"Tell me," Simon said, getting up and walking around. "Something is bothering the hell out of you. You were looking better there for a minute, and then that blanched, frightened look came back. What is it, Kit?"

The trouble was, I didn't know. And not knowing seemed worse than knowing. "I don't know," I finally burst out. "There's something, and it has to do with a huge ginger cat I keep dreaming about . . ."

"Lucifer," Simon said slowly. "And you were quoting quite a lot about Lucifer, Satan and so on today at O'Neill's. What's the connection?"

"I don't know. Maybe it was the cat I saw beside van Reider's son, who was lying out cold on the bed up at St. Cuthbert's."

"You didn't tell me about that," Simon said.

So I told him.

There was a long silence. "How does this St. Cuthbert's figure in the picture? I gather from the papers that it was once the van Reider mansion, that it now belongs to that church St. Anselm's and that they renamed it St. Cuthbert's."

"That's right; only the whole thing is complicated by the fact that, according to the original sales agreement, van Reider can occupy a suite there for his lifetime. The church is eager to sell it, but anybody who buys will have to accept van Reider's right to live in a suite there."

"Did anyone ever find out whose cat it was?"

"It seems to have been a stray. The people who had owned it had moved away. Anyway, it became attached to Bart van Reider and hangs around when he's there."

There was another silence. Then, musingly, Simon said, "Do you remember Joris once saying that he thought Lucifer was his familiar?"

It was like a giant monkey wrench closing on my head. "No," I said. "You're mistaken. He didn't say that."

Simon stood looking down at me. "Yes he did. I was there. So were you. He was in his warlock phase or something."

"It's not true!" I was almost crying.

"Why are you reacting this way? What difference does it make?"

"I don't know," I said and, deeply ashamed of myself, started to cry.

Simon watched me for a while. Then sat down on the bed beside me and put his arm around me. After a while he was holding me. Finally I stopped crying, but he was still holding me.

He said, "What happened to Lucifer?"

"I don't know," I said and could feel the sick sensation coming back.

"I think you do. I think Joris did something to Lucifer."

"No," I said. "He wouldn't do anything bad."

"Wouldn't he? I saw a lot more of him at school than you ever did. He once killed a mouse, slice by slice."

"No! No! I don't believe it! You're only saying that because—"

"I'm a rotten, wife-beating drunk," Simon finished.

"If he was like that, then why did you try so hard to copy him, hang around us while we used to make fun of you, Mr. Me-Too?"

"Because I was a stupid, spineless kid who'd do anything to gain the approval not only of Joris but of your whole family. Remember? Mother may have been genteel, but she made her money altering clothes—what money she had. I was only in Joris's school because I got a partial scholarship and because your father paid the rest of the tuition."

"I thought Joris's mother's side of the family was all filthy rich."

"Not all of the family. We were the poor relations, and the best my poor parents could think of for me was to cultivate my rich, brilliant cousin, Joris Maitland. Whenever I expressed doubts—and I expressed quite a few of them—I was told it was because I was jealous that I couldn't ever attain what he had, et cetera, et cetera . . . Oh, I don't blame them. Who could resist Joris? He'd descend on Mother with flowers and gifts and charm her straight out of her chair. Then he'd turn his back and give me a wink . . . I should have knocked his front teeth in. But I didn't."

"I never saw you express doubts. I just saw you trotting after us."

"And if by any chance you missed the sight, Joris reminded you, didn't he?"

I was about to deny it when I suddenly remembered Joris's voice saying, "Guess who's following us" or "Heard the latest about Mr. Me-Too?"

Simon went on, "I'm not trying to say I wasn't a copycat, trailing the two of you around, hoping for approval. What I am saying is that Joris did everything he could to encourage me. And I was ass enough to fall for it . . ."

I thought for a while. "When did you discover all this?"

"Getting sober is, among other things, enlightening and humbling."

We sat there in silence. "I've heard it—alcoholism—is a disease."

"Yes. So have I, obviously. You're a good example of the disease aspect of it. You drank knee to knee with me for a while, but it didn't seem to have the effect on you it did on me, and after a while you got fed up and stopped. Alcoholism is progressive. If you had been an alcoholic, you'd have gone on and gotten worse—as I did. Before our marriage and immediately afterward you got as drunk—and sometimes as nasty—as I did."

"What do you mean? I didn't whack you around."

"No, but you used your most powerful weapon, your tongue. You were extremely fond of quoting some of the sainted Joris's more withering statements, added to and adorned by some of your own. It didn't justify my laying a finger on you, but it was usually the occasion for it. I should, of course, have walked out the first time you told me you married me as a poor substitute but you had no idea how poor . . . any man who wasn't a chronic, self-hating drunk would have done so. Unfortunately for both of us, I was one."

He got up and stretched and looked at his watch. "You're going to get about five hours' sleep before you have to get up.

We have to be at Brentwood around nine-thirty. Good night. I
think you'll be able to sleep now."

After he left, I lay looking at the blowing muslin curtain at
the window. Jutting from the window was a small porch. After
a while, restless and unhappy, I got up, pulled the sliding
doors even farther apart and stepped out onto the little terrace. The moon was high and pale. The motel was on a little
rise, and much of the city lay before me, its streets lighted, a
network of golden beads. After a while I turned to go back into
the room. But I never made it. The cloth that was flung around
my mouth pulled me back.

I had on only my nightgown and bedroom slippers. The
latter kept sliding as whoever he was kept thrusting his knees
into the backs of my own knees.

I twisted and turned, my heart pounding with fear and
shock. The gag was cutting the sides of my mouth and I was
beginning to choke. My attacker was powerful and smelled of
sweat. Once, he gave me a savage thrust in the back with his
knee. I prayed. I prayed simply to get the gag off my mouth for
a moment. But the attacker, no fool, was holding that with all
his strength. He also kept pulling me towards the window.
Then I saw him reach one arm towards the railing that ran
along the top of the terrace railing. There wasn't much moon,
but the metal of the syringe flashed in what little light there
was.

I remembered then a trick I had read about or seen in some
movie. Suddenly I stopped fighting and yielded, taking the
man off guard. The hand holding the gag slacked. I twisted my
head and screamed, "Simon, Simon!" as loudly as I could,
praying that he would have opened his own window. How
Simon was going to get to me I had no idea.

The next moment, I saw Simon's pajamaed form standing
on the railing, one hand and one leg reaching around the wall
between our terraces. My attacker loosed me to turn on him. I
gave a mighty tug on the scarf he was still holding and lunged
towards the syringe. His attention divided, he turned back
towards me, at which point Simon sprang down onto the terrace beside me.

By this time there were voices from the terrace on the other side.

"Is everything all right?" a male voice said.

"No," Simon shouted, breathing rather hard. "Call the police and call the management and get somebody up here."

The attacker now aimed a blow at my head that would have been curtains for me if it had landed. Fortunately, Simon pushed me aside and took some kind of armhold on the man's arm. There was pounding on our door.

"Use a passkey," Simon yelled.

In a second, three men rushed in and there was the sound of sirens.

Evidently that sound galvanized my attacker. Simon had slackened his hold for a moment. The man broke loose, ran to the terrace railing, jumped up on it for a moment and then leaped to the ground two floors below. He tried to get up, but sank back. Two policemen rushed into our room.

"Down there," Simon said, pointing at the man still trying to drag himself away.

One of the police talked into his walkie-talkie for a moment, and two other policemen ran out of the motel and put a pair of handcuffs on the attacker.

Out of the corner of my eye I saw Simon slide the syringe into his pocket.

"Now," the first policeman said, "what happened?"

An hour later we had managed to convince the cops that I had been the victim of a casual thief. When they discovered we were husband and wife occupying different rooms, they gave us a funny look. Simon explained I had been ill and that he was a famously restless sleeper. I didn't for one moment think they believed him. But they left nevertheless.

"I don't think they bought my story," Simon said, rubbing his arm. "But I think I will do the husbandly thing and stay in your room for the rest of the night. I can sleep in the chair here."

About an hour later, when I was still awake I said, "Isn't the chair uncomfortable?"

"Yes," he said.

"Then why don't you come here. It's quite a big bed."

"Thanks for the invitation, but I think I'll stay here. It's almost daylight, anyway."

"Suit yourself," I said coldly.

I told myself as Simon drove us out to Brentwood that my impulse of the night before had simply been misplaced gratitude and that I was more than delighted that he refused. Then I took out my compact and looked at my face in the mirror. Had my looks deteriorated since I had left Simon? Of course not, I reassured myself. If anything, they had improved. For one thing, I was about ten pounds thinner—not because of dieting, but because when on assignment I often forgot to eat. As for Simon, I'd heard that men in the last stage of alcoholism frequently become impotent. Perhaps Simon had not regained his sexual powers, which would account for his brusque refusal to share my bed the night before. No man would wish to have that known about himself . . . There was certainly one thing I was not going to do, which was to mention it in any way or give Simon the slightest hint that I even thought of it.

"What was the matter with you last night?" I said. "Lose your taste for sex or just for me?"

"No, I have not lost my taste for sex, but for a variety of reasons, I've lost my fondness for game-playing, something you were always very good at. When I was a good boy you rewarded me. When I was a bad boy you locked the bedroom door. Perhaps you don't remember."

"I remember a great deal better than I expect you do," I said. "After all, I am not an alcoholic."

"No, but you got just as drunk as I did in the early stages of our happy association, and that's when you used your seductiveness as a pass/fail system for me. It drove me crazy."

"I suppose you're now going to say that that's the reason you drank."

"No, I drank because I drank. I drank because I'm an alcoholic and I would have been, regardless of what you did. But it still nearly drove me crazy. And I resented the hell out of it."

"So I suppose you had a wonderful time turning the tables on me last night."

"I'm not going to answer that. We have a job to do, and you seem to forget you were nearly killed last night, which would indicate that someone else is still very interested in your activities. I don't think a fight would do anything but divert our energies and attention, and if we go on with this conversation, we'll have a fight. This is the second time somebody has tried to do you harm, and I think we ought to concentrate on that."

I didn't say anything. He was right, and I knew it, and I was also badly shaken up. Two attempts to kill me were more than I had bargained for. I was not Ms. Brave. I was Ms. Scared-as-Hell.

"Yes," I said and left it at that.

"Don't worry too much. That's why I'm here, and we're on our way to find information that will (we hope) dig out the opposition and bring it to light."

"You're right," I said and stored away all of the really mean and evil things I wanted to say to him. It was humiliating to be saved by someone who didn't even want to go to bed with you.

Brentwood turned out to be a sprawling village with a long, low central building and several cottages nearby built in the same style.

"I take it this is a good place," I said, attempting to sound as normal as possible. Simon and I had a big battle due us, but that had to wait, and I wanted him to be fooled into believing that I had forgiven and forgotten.

"The best. There are a couple of very good others: one out on the West Coast and one in Minnesota, but this ranks with them."

"How long were you here?" I asked, curious.

"The first time, about six weeks. Then I left and drank again. Bob tried to talk me into staying, but I wouldn't. The second time, about three months."

"Did you like it? Hate it?"

"Both. I hated it when I first came here. I'd been sober and off drugs two or three times before and it never took. I was fully aware that the second time around they were in two minds about letting me in. There are plenty of applicants for the first time, and they don't want any two- or three-time losers to take up the places of people who'd get sober and stay that way. But they let me stay. And after I'd been here for a while, on my second visit—and thanks to Bob Britton, who runs the place—I began to like it, my head began to clear up, and I finally got sober and stayed sober—one day at a time."

"It doesn't look cheap," I said. "How did you pay for it?"

"I borrowed the money from a guy I'd once done a favor for. I think he was convinced he'd never see it again. But I've paid him back."

"I wonder how Crystal paid it."

"I don't know. But I do know that there are, so to speak, scholarships that are contributed by rich well-wishers or churches. Maybe St. Anselm's helped her. Even so, you're supposed to work off some of it as soon as you're physically well enough. Not because they're being cheap, but because it's important to feel that you're earning at least part of your recovery. Here we are."

We'd driven through the gates along the drive under the porte cochere. "You get out here, I'll park the car."

I strolled in the front entrance and over to the information desk.

"May I help you?"

"Is Dr. Britton in?" I asked, aware that I should be waiting for Simon.

"Yes. Who shall I say is asking?"

"My name is Catherine Maitland. I don't think he knows me, but there is something I would like to discuss with him."

"May I tell him what it's about?"

"I'd rather not discuss it here. I'm a writer, and need some information that only he can give me."

"I see." Her gray eyes were not hostile, but neither were they welcoming. And I knew that if I were alone, without Simon, my attitude would be conciliatory, not haughty and demanding. Why am I being this way? I asked myself.

The answer occurred to me, but I didn't like it, so I pushed it away. At that moment, Simon came in the front door.

"Jessica," he said, coming toward the desk. "How nice to see you. You're looking wonderful."

The formal mask unfroze. "Simon, you're looking marvelous, too. I take it you're doing everything you should be doing and it's agreeing with you."

"I wouldn't dare do anything else and come here. Is Bob in?"

The woman gave me a hasty glance. "Well this lady here—"

"My wife," Simon interrupted.

"But her name—"

"She's a modern woman and continues to use her own."

The woman looked at me. "Why didn't you say so?"

"She's a little shy," Simon said, perjuring his soul. "Don't tell me Bob's still away."

"No, no. I'll get him for you."

Bob was Dr. Robert Britton, who, according to some research I'd hastily done, was one of the country's better experts on alcoholic rehabilitation. He was a tall, chubby man with pink cheeks and gray curly hair.

"Well, son of a gun," he said, coming towards us with his hand outstretched when we went into his office. "And, I gather, Simon, this is your Mrs."

"Well," Simon said, "was, if we wish to be accurate. It's a long story, Bob, and not why we're here. Kit, my—er—wife, would like to ask you a question about Crystal Mahoney."

I saw the round blue eyes switch to me. My first impression —that they were as clear and guileless as a ten-year-old boy's —was hastily amended. Underneath their Santa Claus jollity, I sensed a shrewd, observant gaze.

"What is it you'd like to know about Crystal? I was very sorry, by the way, to hear of her death. Is it anything to do with that?"

"In a way," I said, temporizing, and then realized it was the truth. "I was assigned to do a piece on St. Cuthbert's—the van Reider mansion up the Hudson, now called St. Cuthbert's and the property of St. Anselm's Church. I thought it sounded like the world's dullest subject when my editor, Piers Somerville, of *The Public Eye*, allowed as how the real reason was to see if I could find out why Crystal Mahoney had committed suicide in a motel near St. Cuthbert's. He knew that she had gone up to look at something, though he didn't know what, and that some of the van Reider family papers were scattered over her room when the police found her. Anyway, he wanted me to find out as much about her death as possible. He was furious that the local paper, which had printed the obituary, carefully left out any mention of the St. Cuthbert/van Reider connection and said nothing about the papers in her motel room."

"So how can I help you?" Those guileless eyes seemed bluer and more placid than ever, but I could feel his watchfulness underneath.

I took a breath. "Simon, would you like to add your bit, about what Crystal told you?" I surprised myself by doing this. For one thing, it seemed to my rather feminist viewpoint that I was letting down the side: when the questions got really difficult, I turned to a man. But whether I was male or female, it was perfectly obvious that I was not going to get from Dr. Britton anything he didn't want to give me, and it was equally plain that he liked Simon.

So Simon repeated what he had told me, about Crystal's casual comment that she knew Joris and then linked his name with the nickname Archangel.

When Simon mentioned Joris's name I saw the doctor make a slight gesture.

"Yes?" Simon said. "Do you know Joris?"

"I've heard the name."

"From Crystal?"

"No. It was much longer ago than that. If I had had any idea she knew him—if he's the one I think he is . . ." He glanced at Simon. "How did she come to mention him to you?"

Simon explained the circumstances. Then, "Did she speak of him to you?"

Britton shook his head. "She did indeed mention her drug connection as the Archangel. But not the name Joris. I wish she had. She might still be alive. What do you know about this Joris?"

"It's a long story, Bob, but we—Kit and I—are both related to Joris Maitland, who walked out of a party one night twenty-one years ago and was never seen again."

"Did he go to Princeton?" the doctor put in abruptly.

"Yes, he did. He disappeared right before graduation." Simon paused for a moment.

"Go on," the doctor said.

"Well, as I say, he was never seen again. After a while the family reluctantly assumed he was dead. Even Kit here, his adoring half sister, who believed him alive longer than anyone else, finally gave up and accepted that he was dead. Then I repeated to her what Crystal said no more than a year and a half ago, which would make him appear not only alive, but connected with the drug world. Lieutenant O'Neill, of the New York police, was anxious for us to come out here and run this information down. He said that there was—or at least the police and other authorities believed there was—a drug czar of some kind about to go into a drug war with another big connection, which will mean, among other things, drugs hitting the streets at competitive prices."

"Let me get this straight," the doctor said. He turned to me. "This Joris, Joris Maitland, Simon says, is your half brother?"

"Yes. We had the same father. His mother died, and our father married my mother and had me. I was ten years younger."

"But Simon says he was related to this Joris too. And he's your husband?"

Simon smiled a little. "It's not as complicated as it sounds. Joris was my cousin on his mother's side. Kit and I aren't related."

"I see," the doctor said. "But you all three knew each other as children?"

"More or less. As Kit says, Joris was ten years older than her and one year older than me." He paused. "Where did you run into Joris?"

"I didn't, but I ran into his name. About seventeen years ago, before this place was built, I was in training under a Dr. Ralph Judson, who was one of the earlier ones to see the coming plague of drugs and try to do something about it. He had a small place in California, where he tried out various treatments, borrowing eclectically from whoever had a method that worked—notably AA.

"One of the worst cases we ever saw was a kid, a boy of about eighteen, who had gotten himself involved in some cult or other. Anyway, the cult used hallucinogens in their ritual, and he went from there to heroin. Ralph and I were outraged at what he had told us, and we informed the police. They raided the shacks up in the hills where the cult held its ceremonies. There they found a few unpleasant bits of evidence. But all the people had gone.

"Three days later, when one of the attendants went into this boy's room to wake him up, he found the boy had hanged himself—or so we thought. After the police had examined the room and its contents, and then done their autopsy, they said they couldn't be sure it was suicide. There were aspects of it—they told me, but I can't remember all the details—that made them think somebody had killed him. But it was a long shot, and by no means provable. It wouldn't stand up in court.

"But after the police were finished, the boy's older brother came to claim the body and collect his things. He was flipping through one of his brother's books when he came across the beginning of a letter the boy had been writing to him. In the letter the boy had told him that the head of the cult was somebody the older brother had gone to Princeton with. The boy remembered seeing them together when he visited his brother at the college, and at Princeton the future head of the cult, or guru, had been called Joris."

"What was the boy's name?" Simon asked.

"Chris Taylor."

"I suppose that was the surname of the older brother."

"No, I don't think so. As with you"—he nodded to me—"and Joris Maitland, they were half siblings."

"Is there anywhere we could look it up?"

"I'm afraid not. One result of the boy's death was that it ruined Judson's clinic. It closed down the following year."

"And I don't suppose you'd have any idea where the records are."

"They must have been destroyed. Judson died almost immediately, and who would want them?"

10

We had caught an early flight and arrived in New York at twelve-thirty. The headline faced us as we entered LaGuardia terminal:

SCION OF OLD NEW YORK FAMILY BEATEN AND KILLED BY INTRUDER.

I somehow knew even before I bought the paper and read the first two lines of the story that it was Hilary van Reider. According to the police, he had evidently walked in on a robbery in action in his apartment on Fifth Avenue. The place was turned upside down, and his wallet, watch and signet ring were missing. Also missing, on further inspection, were a radio and a valuable painting.

"The burglar or burglars were obviously intercepted," the newspaper story went on, quoting the police, "because the safe wasn't open, and other valuables—old jewelry, gold coins, and bearer bonds—were still inside." There was some doubt as to how the intruders got out, until they realized van Reider's apartment was next to the top of the old building and that the exit to the roof, which should have been locked, was not.

"Well," Simon said, reading over my shoulder, "that means

that the church will be able to sell the property now, I should think. Convenient for them."

"I trust you're not implying that they hired somebody to do this," I said coldly, turning to face him.

"Of course not. But didn't you tell me that anybody who bought the place would have to put up with van Reider living there?"

"Yes, I did. And there's no doubt, awful as this is, it gets them out of a sticky situation. But it *is* terrible. I thought van Reider was an irascible man with poor manners and a couple of obsessions: his son and the family mansion. But I certainly wouldn't have wished this on him."

Simon had taken the paper and was staring down at it.

"Well?" I said.

"Kit, you don't have to be a lawyer to think that within a few days a lot of screwy things have happened in and about that house and the people connected with it: your apartment has been watched, you've fallen over a dead body in the house up there, this guy's son is hit on the head, you almost get pushed off a platform, and now van Reider, who's stood between the house and whoever wants it, suddenly gets killed."

That fatal summing up of recent events had occurred to me also. "Yes, I know," I said. "I've thought about all that too." But to voice my suspicions seemed almost to bring them about, which made me realize that I was frightened. "You don't think this is just an incredible coincidence."

"Incredible would be the operative word—if it were a coincidence."

We stood there for a moment. Then I said, "That poor little boy. Well, at least his mother will have him now, for good. I hope she deserves it. Where do we go from here?"

"Well—" Simon started.

And then, before he could go on, I said, "I'm going to call Claire to see if she knows anything. After all, this happened last night. There's a bank of phones over there."

I left Simon leaning against one of the walls, his suitcase and mine lying at his feet. I dialed the number, which I now knew by heart.

"Mrs. Aldington," I said.

"She hasn't been in today."

"Can you give me her home phone?"

"I'm sorry, I can't do that."

I considered asking for someone else, the rector's secretary, or the tubby clergyman who knew the van Reiders—who was he?

"There's another assistant rector there. I met him with Ms. Aldington. A Mr. . . ."

"Swade?"

"Yes. That's it. May I speak to him?"

"Let me see if he's in."

There were a couple of clicks. Then someone answered. "Chris Swade," he said.

"Mr. Swade, this is Kit Maitland. I met you when I was in Mrs. Aldington's office and you came in to tell us what you knew about the van Reiders."

"Yes, I remember. Have you called about Hilary's death?"

"We—I have been in Cleveland, trying to run something down about Crystal Mahoney. She's the woman who—"

"Yes, I know. Claire's told me."

"I only learned about Hilary's death when I got off the plane. Do you know anything else, at all? Do they have any idea who did it?"

"I really don't know. Claire knows Lieutenant O'Neill and she might have talked to him. She isn't in today. I think she had an appointment of some kind outside the church. Is there anything I can do?"

"No. Thanks anyway. Unless you could give me Claire's home phone number."

"Sure. Just a sec. Here it is." And he reeled it off.

"Thank you."

I glanced over at Simon, who seemed to be reading the rest of the paper. But he looked up at me, so I realized he'd been watching me out of the corner of his eye. Picking up the two bags, he came strolling over. "Any progress?"

"Not much." I told him about my two conversations. "I think I'm going to call Claire now."

"Go ahead."

There was something, a tinge of impatience about his voice

or manner, that irritated me, perhaps because I was still stinging from the night before. "And have *you* come to any brilliant
conclusions?" I could hear the sarcasm in my tone.

"Not brilliant," he said coldly. "In fact, not even very coher-
ent at this point. But I'm bothered by this sequence of events.
Or at least by the relationship they seem to imply."

"Relationship to one another?"

"Yes. Aren't you? Why would a petty drug dealer be watching your house? Why should he be killed? Why should van
Reider, part owner of the house and chief obstacle to its sale,
be beaten to death? What's it all got to do with you? Where
does our great and good friend Joris come into all this? We
know from Britton that he was most likely the head of that cult
the patient at Britton's old clinic had been at. He also seems to
be the Archangel that Crystal knew, which would make him
something of a major drug connection. *But what's it got to do
with you?*"

"Maybe they thought I'd found out something."

"By going up to that Mad Hatter's castle—St. Whatever's?
But according to what O'Neill told me when he called me, you
were being watched before you went up there. So somebody
must have known you were going. Who?"

I stood staring at him for a moment. Then I said, "Piers. The
guy who assigned me. Maybe he told somebody."

"Like who? And why would whoever it was put somebody to
following you?"

There was something chugging at the back of my mind, but I
couldn't reach it.

"Look," Simon said. "Why don't we go over to that coffee
shop and have some coffee. The airline's idea of breakfast isn't
mine."

I was not hungry and I'd been planning to go home. But the
idea of coffee was welcome. "Fine."

When we were seated behind two watery cups of coffee,
Simon said, "Okay, let's begin back at the beginning. Your
editor, Piers, assigned you to go up there to look into Crystal's
death."

"Actually he didn't—not at first. He told me it was going to
be a sort of historic piece on St. Cuthbert's—its background

and so on. It was only after I expressed skepticism that this was a *Public Eye* kind of a story that he came clean about his real reason."

"What was Crystal to him?"

"He had some kind of a fling with her."

"So had large numbers of the Beautiful People on the East Coast."

"Also, she was a friend of the magazine's angel, which seemed to arouse Piers's jealousy as well as his interest."

"Hmm. Who was the angel?"

"A Mr. Dan Troilais. A Greek of some kind. Ever heard of him?"

Simon shook his head. "Can't say I have."

We were sitting next to a window looking out into the terminal lobby. A few feet away I could see more pay phones.

"I think I'll call Claire at home," I said. "Now that I have her number." And I went off to the phone.

I didn't have much hope of finding her at one o'clock on a fine afternoon, and indeed I didn't talk to her. I talked to a boy who said he was Jamie Aldington and was Claire's son. "I have a code," he said through thickened sinuses, and he sounded it.

"I'm a friend of your mother's, and I was hoping to talk to her. My name is Kit Maitland."

"Yeah, the writer." He paused to blow his nose. "Mom told me she'd met you. You did a piece on the kids who broke into the computer bank at NASA, didn't you?"

All writers long for recognition. "Yes," I said and felt myself flush. My article had appeared in the Sunday magazine of one of the newspapers.

"Neat," Jamie said. "I'd like to go into computers. I'm not very good at math, though. But I'm better than I used to be."

"Is being good at math a prerequisite for being a whizbang at computers? I shouldn't think so, since everybody under the age of ten seems better at it than the rest of us."

"Being good at math doesn't hurt. But like I said, I'm better. Mom isn't here. She went up to St. Cuthbert's. She was going up there to see that Mr. Joliad, the guy who wants to buy St. Cuthbert's."

"Oh—" For a moment my mind was blank. Then I remembered Claire telling me that the man representing the Swami Gupta Nanda was a Mr. Martin Joliad. Then the rest of what Jamie said registered, and a chilly feeling trickled down my spine. "St. Cuthbert's is not the safest place, I'd think, after Mr. van Reider's death and the body I found up there."

"That's what I told her, but she never listens to me. I even said she ought to stay home and keep me company, since I have this code, but she had Lucinda, our cleaning lady, come here today instead of tomorrow. I'd have gone with her, but she didn't ask me." He sounded aggrieved. "Are you going to do a piece on the deaths at St. Cuthbert's? That'd be cool, like a real-life crime."

"Death at St. Cuthbert's," I said, trying to push aside a growing unease and to enter into the spirit of the thing. "That'd be a good title. By the way, when did she go up there?"

"She took off around eleven. Said she'd be back for dinner. Can I give her a message?"

"Just say I called, thanks. Feel better."

"Get her?" Simon asked when I got back to the table.

"No. She went up to St. Cuthbert's to meet Mr. Joliad."

"Who's Mr. Joliad?"

"He's the representative of the people that the church's been dickering with about St. Cuthbert's. I guess it's good news for them."

"Who are they? A foundation?"

"Not exactly. They're an ashram, or at least, their leader, a guru, wants to have St. Cuthbert's for his East Coast ashram. I don't have to tell you that the church's congregation, according to Claire, is less than joyful about that, but a sale is a sale and they need the money." I drank off the remainder of my coffee and started to get up.

"Where are you going?"

"Strange as it may seem, I'm a little tired after all our rousing adventures and want to go home. By the way, what did you do with the syringe you picked off the balcony railing last night?"

"Put it in my suitcase. I thought I'd take it to O'Neill, fingerprints and all. Sit down and have another cup of coffee and some food. You probably need it, and I want to talk some more about what's going on." As I hesitated, he said sharply, "It won't commit you to anything."

I sat down. It was true about my needing food. I had picked at breakfast and passed up the plastic snack the airline offered.

Simon summoned a waitress. "What do you want?" he said.

I settled for a scrambled egg and an English muffin.

I was nibbling at that when Simon said, "What kind of guru?"

"How would I know? There must be dozens floating around the woods. I suppose they're the Orient's answer to Western nineteenth-century missionaries."

"According to what you said, that's what Joris was setting out to be."

"He was setting out to find the Way, the Truth and the Path —as have many others."

"After what we know, you're still defending him?"

I didn't answer for a moment. Then, "I'm not sure that the case against Joris is entirely proven, but—no, I'm not sticking up for him. He obviously wasn't the person I thought he was. Or he's changed drastically."

Simon sat back. "Or you never saw him as he really was." He paused. "Kit, I'd like to talk about Joris for a few minutes. But not the way we have before, with me on the attack and you on the defense. Let's talk about him as though he were somebody neither of us had an emotional investment in, either good or bad. Can we do that?"

"Here? Today? This minute?" I was aware that my mind was dragging, not willing to go where Simon led.

"Yes, here, today, this minute. I have a growing feeling that your friend Claire's safety might depend on that."

"What on earth are you talking about?"

"Remember some of the games that the three of us—you, Joris and I—played? It was frequently some form of pig-in-the-middle, with me as the pig. But we also played others, such as anagrams, in which, *mirabile dictu,* I sometimes beat both of you."

I felt a queer stirring. "Anagrams," I said. "Yes, I remember."

"What was Mr. Joliad's first name? Martin, by any chance?"

"Yes. Yes it was." Claire's voice came back to me: *"Mr. Martin S. Joliad, to be accurate."* I asked now, "How did you know?"

"And what was the angel's name? Dan Troilais? There has to be a J there somewhere, and an M. Dan J. M. Troilais."

I stared at him for a moment, then fragments from my unconscious came together where I could see them.

"Oh my God!" I said. "Joris! It's Joris!"

"Having fun and games, as he always did."

"But if he is the guru that's going to buy St. Cuthbert's, he must have millions—a big organization of some kind."

"He probably does, but not with offices in the Twin Towers or Rockefeller Plaza. Or if he does, it's all very legit and called something meaningless like Construction Consultants, Inc. The millions come from his drug connections, but people like that don't incorporate themselves."

"You mean he wanted St. Cuthbert's as some kind of drug hangout?" The moment I asked, I knew how stupid a question it was. "Of course, with the ashram as cover."

I put my head in my hands and stared at my plate. "Then, for some reason I don't understand, he's responsible for van Reider's death, for the death of the man whose body I stumbled over, and Crystal's death too."

"Maybe."

I raised my head. "What do you mean, 'maybe'? You're the one who put this together."

"True. All I meant was that it's possible van Reider killed the guy you found. If the guy had been pushing his son around, it's not impossible. You know what a temper he had. But Joris is responsible for the others."

"And Claire's gone up to see him!" I said. "We have to go up there immediately."

"Why not call O'Neill? He can get the local police in on it."

I was already on the way to the pay phone. But frustration hit me again. O'Neill wasn't there.

"Can you tell me what it's about?" the voice on the other end of the phone said.

There was no way I could telescope my reasons for thinking

Joris was up at St. Cuthbert's with Claire and representing a real danger. "When will Lieutenant O'Neill be back?" I asked.

"Maybe in a couple of hours. Can somebody else help you?"

"No," I said and hung up. Then, digging in my bag for my notebook, I found St. Cuthbert's number and dialed. It was a long shot, because the house was enormous, so I was disappointed but not completely surprised when there was no answer.

"Well?" Simon asked.

"O'Neill wasn't in."

"But I bet they could reach him if they wanted to."

"They didn't sound as if they wanted to, and somehow it was too complicated to explain. I'm going to go up there, Simon."

"How?"

"I'll rent a car. There's a rental agency at the terminal."

"We'll take mine."

As I hesitated, he said, "Don't worry. Once this is over, I'm not going to force my company on you."

"Where is it?"

"Outside the terminal, in the parking lot."

We were barely onto the expressway when Simon said, "In view of van Reider's murder, that place will probably be crawling with cops, which should be some kind of protection for your friend Claire."

"But he was killed in his New York apartment."

"Nevertheless, they have a lot of funny things to put together. There was the guy you found there, plus van Reider's son being hit on the head."

"Plus the fact that the Krauses have gone."

"Who are they?"

I told him.

"Sounds like they might have been bribed. I wonder why. Why would they want them away from the place?"

"So they can hide the drugs there?"

"Probably. Which means that they must have a lot of stuff to warehouse in an ostensibly innocent place."

"Van Reider did say he'd heard noises that he couldn't account for, and when he returned each weekend swore there were signs of vandalism."

Simon grunted.

We drove for a while in silence. Simon seemed to have withdrawn, and for the first time he reminded me a little of the time we were married. I glanced at his profile and was struck suddenly with his resemblance to Joris. I also tried to remember how long he said he'd been off alcohol.

"How long have you been sober?" I asked.

"Nine months."

"Not a single drink in that time?"

"Not a single drink." He glanced swiftly at me from the corner of his eye. "And I'm not about to pick up a drink now, however much this kind of a mood used to go before a binge."

"What kind of a mood is it?"

"It's not important and I don't think at this point you'd be interested."

I decided to go back to my own corner. I told myself that he was right. As far as I was concerned, it wasn't important, and I wasn't interested . . .

With all my strength I forbade myself to ask any further questions. I would keep my own counsel till we got to St. Cuthbert's.

As I thought of that bleak, abandoned mansion built by the first van Reider and taken over by St. Anselm's, a trickle of fear and . . . and horror went through me. Suddenly, in my mind again, I saw the body sprawled out on the floor, and experienced again that flash of recognition of the man as the one who watched my apartment. As though I were being led through all the events in that house again by a force outside myself, I saw the boy . . . and I saw the cat next to him, its back arched, its mouth drawn back . . .

I glanced up at Simon's face again, hoping . . . what? But now there might as well have been a glass wall between us. So I pulled my gaze down again, looking through the windshield, where the rain was streaming, and where the wipers were swishing rhythmically left, right, left, right. That seemed mesmerizing, so I transferred my gaze to the dashboard. And then to Simon's key in the ignition. Dangling from it was a chain and medal swinging back and forth, back and forth, back and forth . . . and I remembered then the thing Claire had said, rather had asked me, that had been at the back of my mind, scratching for attention: "Have you ever been hypnotized?" And as she had asked me that I had seen something bright, like a pendulum, swinging back and forth, back and forth.

"Did Joris ever play around with hypnotizing people?" I asked.

"Yes. That was one of his sidelines. He used to try it at school. There were a few boys it didn't succeed with, but quite a lot it did. Joris wasn't stupid. He specialized in boys who were younger than he was and were devoted fans. As I say, every now and then he'd take on a tough nut, somebody who didn't fall at his feet each time he came around. His success with those wasn't as high. I suppose he tried with you—and succeeded, of course."

I was about to object to the "of course" when I saw that he had a certain amount of justification on his side. I was Joris's most devoted acolyte. I trailed after him. When he laughed, I laughed. When he made fun of somebody, I joined in . . . There was that fat child who came to ride one of our horses. Joris and I would sit on the fence. He'd say something malicious, and I'd giggle, and then override any stab of conscience I might have by telling myself that if Joris did it it was all right.

Malicious. Never before had I admitted to myself how malicious he could be. Because he never turned his tongue on me. "You're the princess and I'm the king, I'm the lord and you're the page . . . Come, Kit, let's run over the fields and far away to the sapphire kingdom, where you will ride a milk-white horse and I shall help all the people in the world. There'll be no more hunger, no more war, no more corruption . . ." He looked so much like a priest-king, a savior, that I believed every word. Then he'd change abruptly. His eyes would dance. "I sound like a cleric, don't I? Just as my revered father would like me to be."

"I don't know," I said now to Simon in the car. "If he did hypnotize me, he must have done such a thorough job that I don't remember it. The funny thing is, when Claire asked me if anyone had, I said no, that that would mean I would have given control over me to someone, and I'd never do that."

"You gave Joris control over you all the time."

I winced. "Are you sure that's not a biased view? You weren't one of Joris's admirers—or mine."

"I'll certainly admit to bias against Joris—I had plenty of it. But if I was so biased against you, why did I marry you?"

"Because I had, as Joris's follower and coconspirator, a sort of unattainable status. I think you were proving something to yourself. I don't think it necessarily meant you loved me."

"You may be right. I've come to wonder about that myself."

Even as he agreed with me, coolly, dismissingly, I realized that I was hoping he wouldn't. "Whatever," I said, trying to sound indifferent. "Did Joris have control over me? To the point where I would let him hypnotize me?"

"If you mean, did I see him do it? No. But he did carry that shiny medal which he would swing in front of his chosen subjects, and once when I was coming towards the two of you and you didn't see me, I noticed him putting it in his pocket."

"Medal? Like this?" And I pointed to the key in the ignition.

"That shape, but shinier, and not the same metal."

Bending forward, I turned the medal over in my hand. It was a pewter color. On one side were the praying hands. On the other:

> God grant me the serenity
> To accept the things I cannot change,
> Courage to change the things I can
> And the wisdom to know the difference.

"I think I've read that somewhere before," I said, "or heard it."

"Yes. It's a well-known prayer."

I turned the medal over in my hand for a moment. "What kinds of things can't you change?"

"Other people, places and things."

"That's practically everything. What *can* you change?"

Suddenly he gave a grin. "Myself. That's the hard one."

"You've changed a lot," I said without thinking.

I saw him flush. "Thanks. Or at least, I suppose you mean that as a compliment."

"Yes. I do."

There didn't seem to be anywhere to go from there. I looked

at the medal, and tried to think about the medal Simon said Joris used to hypnotize people. I'd seen it done in movies, and read about it in books. Maybe, I thought, feeling suddenly drowsy, I should just let my mind go blank. The sound of the wheels on the parkway, the rhythm of the car, all contributed to my sleepiness. It had been a long day . . . And then, suddenly, I saw the medal, only much brighter, in fact almost like a light, or something shining with light, swinging in front of me, and behind it a voice . . . It was like walking through a tunnel that was my own mind . . .

"Are you asleep?" Simon asked.

I woke up suddenly. "Yes, I was, sort of. By the way, I think you're right."

"That's nice. But before you tell me what I'm right about, please tell me where I turn in the next few minutes. I haven't been here before, and we're coming to an intersection."

I directed him past the intersection and got him onto the next main drive up to St. Cuthbert's.

"Okay," he said. "Now tell me what I was right about."

"I think Joris did hypnotize me. I can't exactly remember, but when I was dozing there for a moment, I sort of recalled the medal swinging back and forth like a light, and I felt, rather than thought, that there was something there, hiding." I didn't say anything for a moment, and then, "How awful it is to find how wrong you are about somebody . . . somebody you've loved."

"Yes, it's not pleasant or easy."

We made it in record time. It was not much past four when we eased into the drive in front of the huge mansion.

"No cops," I said. "But that could be Claire's car." I nodded in the direction of a car parked on the other side of the circular drive.

I was about to get out of the car when Simon reached out and took my arm. "You realize, don't you, that if Joris is here and your friend Claire is with him, she's going to know him as Mr. Joliad, and as long as she believes that, she's in no danger. But if we go in and identify him as Joris, then she joins the growing list of those who have been or could be killed."

I shivered. "What's the alternative?"

"The alternative is to drive into town and inform the police of what we know."

"I can just see us succeeding in that. The police officer who arrested me wasn't at all happy when they couldn't pin anything on me. Would they believe my wild tale of a half brother back from the dead and into drugs, put together by a bunch of half hints and thready clews?"

"They convinced us."

"But we knew Joris."

I sat there, thinking over what Simon had said, because he had made good sense. And I didn't want to put Claire's life in jeopardy. But an overwhelming urgency was gripping me, and I knew that I wasn't going to drive away again.

"Why don't you let me out here and go yourself to the local police, or call O'Neill?" I said, opening the car door.

"Of course. I'll just drive away safely while you go in and talk to Joris." Simon got out his side and closed his door.

I glanced at him for a moment, then started for the front door. When we got there, I put out my hand to ring the bell but decided not to. Instead, I pushed the door open as I had before and walked in. Simon was right behind me. There were voices coming from one of the rooms on the right, and I followed them into the living room. Joris and Claire were standing there. They both turned.

"Oh, hello, Kit," Claire said. "What are you doing here?"

"Hello, Claire." I looked at the man standing near her and forgot about putting Claire's life in danger. "Hello, Joris," I said.

11

He looked, at first, the same. There were the brilliant blue eyes, the aquiline nose, the tawny hair. But there was something different about his face, although I would have had a hard time defining what it was. Perhaps, I found myself thinking, it was a difference in tone. Astonishingly, he hardly seemed a year older, let alone twenty.

Claire was looking at me in an odd way. "Are you saying that this is the Joris Maitland—your half brother—that you were telling me about?"

"Yes. He may have introduced himself to you as Mr. Martin S. Joliad, just as he introduced himself to Piers Somerville, of *Public Eye* magazine, as Mr. Dan J. M. Troilais. But we—Simon and I—know him as Joris. Don't we, Joris?"

Joris smiled in the engaging way I remembered. "What a spoilsport you've turned out to be, Catarina! It was just a joke. I'd have told you when we finally got together. Why did you have to ruin it by coming today and showing the bad taste in bringing Mr. Me-Too with you?"

"You haven't changed much, have you?" Simon said.

"Unfortunately," Joris said acidly, "the same can also be said of you." And he turned his head and winked at me.

It was, under the circumstances, such an incongruous, even clumsy, thing to do that I felt as though time had been suddenly telescoped. The three of us were back in Virginia.

I waited for Simon to say something, but he had leaned back on the arm of a sofa and was watching Joris and me.

"How long have you known that Mr. Joliad and your half brother were one and the same?" Claire asked, her voice strained.

"Not just Joliad and Joris, but Troilais, Joris and the guru, I suspect," Simon said.

I understood now why Claire had given me that strange look —as though she had trusted me and then discovered that I was not trustworthy. "Claire, I've known that Joris and Joliad were the same since about fifteen minutes ago, when Simon and I got to putting things together and he caught onto the anagrammatic names—Simon used to be the best when the three of us played anagrams. We knew, or suspected, that Joris was behind a lot of drug goings-on here and on the Coast. I told you about Crystal's talking of the Archangel. Well, Joris is the Archangel. Until a few minutes ago during our drive up here, we didn't realize he was also Swami Gupta Nanda of the Golden Flower." I looked at Joris. "You are, aren't you?"

He raised his hands. "Each of us has many roles to play. I am different people for those at different levels."

"A religious leader who deals in drugs?" Claire asked.

"That's a typical attitude of establishment clerics who seek to prohibit the only spiritual escape open to ordinary people."

"What bilge!" I said angrily. I was suddenly bitterly angry— angry at this collection of charades that was Joris, angriest of all at myself for my lifelong gullibility. "Simon and Mother were right! You're crazy!"

His face seemed to change. His eyes became flat and opaque, as though painted on china. "No," he said. "I'm not. And don't say that again. Now," he went on in his old, cajoling voice, "what am I going to do with you? It was really very stupid of you, Catarina, to come here. You've complicated things. The Reverend here was going to go home in a few minutes, the sale would be completed within the next week or so, and everything would slip into place. But now—"

Belatedly, I realized what I had done. And it wasn't for lack of warning. "Claire's a priest," I said. "She knows how to respect confidences."

Joris smiled. "Come on, Catherine. Do you take me for a fool? I gather that you two geniuses didn't figure out that I was the swami until you were on the way here. So you haven't had a chance to tell anyone." He looked at Claire. "You told me you came from home, not the church, although I suppose you could have informed a secretary you were coming here. It doesn't matter. The tragic accident you're going to have will take care of everything there."

I opened my mouth to say that Jamie Aldington, Claire's son, knew, but saw Claire's eyes on me with an intent expression. She might well have guessed that I had found out from Jamie where she had gone and was silently pleading with me not to mention him. I closed my mouth without saying anything.

"Which means," Joris went on, "that the three of you cannot return. You, Reverend, will have that accident on the way back to the city. Your fate, Simon, is easily told: you lapsed back to the bottle and stumbled onto a busy road. Oh, yes," he said almost gleefully, "I know all about your drinking and your recent abstinence. I have connections everywhere, and I have made it my business to keep up with you."

"How did you happen to become Piers's angel?" I asked.

"I heard through various grapevines that he needed money. And I like to have a finger in the arts. Besides, you often work for the magazine, and I thought it would be amusing to be controlling your destiny without your knowing."

"Your business must be very successful," Simon said dryly. "But then, the import and sale of drugs is, and all tax free."

"As you say, successful indeed."

"Even if a little immoral," I added.

He shrugged. "The strong won't suffer, and they're the only ones worth bothering about."

"I take it you have partners," I commented, thinking of some of the things O'Neill had said.

"Of course," he spoke impatiently. "They do the legwork. I do the planning."

"Tell us," Simon said. "Why did you suddenly disappear twenty years ago? What was the purpose of that?"

"I had things to do, and it was important that I do them in private. Besides, I'd had a little trouble before graduation. The bourgeois administration of the college took exceptions to some of my—er—experiments. Even in the sixties, though, when the faculties were into rebellion against the administration, they hesitated about expelling, just before graduation, the son, grandson and great-grandson of powerful alumni. Dropping out of sight solved all my problems."

"Even if it did break your father's heart," I said.

He shrugged. "He didn't understand my great potential."

I stared at Joris, realizing at last and far too late that he was like a dazzling amoral child, which probably accounted for his power. There were no shadows there, no consciousness of vulnerability or doubt. Suddenly he reminded me of the knave in playing cards—all the colors primary, all the lines clear and sharp. No wonder he stood out next to my parents: my mother, with her attention divided and subdivided by responsibility and lack of funds; my father, stilling any questions he might have had by poring over his theological studies . . . Simon, with his chronic self-doubting, which, trailing after Joris, I had mistaken and mocked for weakness . . .

My God! I thought, how cruel and stupid and wrong could I have been? Simon may have been flawed—as who wasn't? But he was a decent and honorable human being who had had the guts and perseverence to pull himself out of his problems. Drinking, he had hit back at me when provoked. It was terrible and wrong, but he had tried to make amends. Whereas Joris—

Words that my mother had spoken, words I had pushed to the bottom of my mind, sounded in my head: "Always remember, Kit, that Joris is insane, certifiably insane . . ."

But I had chosen not to believe her. "Mother was right," I said. "You really are insane."

"That's the second time you've said that, Catherine. Don't say it again. Your mother said it to me once. I told her she would regret it, and she did."

"What are you talking about?"

"How do you think the fire that destroyed her and her

horses and her house started?" His eyes were brilliant now, demanding my admiration for the burning farm. The picture was so horrifying I felt sick. "You are also," I said, "truly evil. I can't understand how I didn't see it when I was a child."

Claire, who had been standing with her hands in her pockets, straightened, took them out and said, "I have to get back. I have an appointment." And she started toward the door. It was a brave gamble and she almost made it. But Joris was quicker. His arm flicked out, the hand flat and lethal, striking her on the head. She fell.

Both Simon and I started forward, and then stopped. In Joris's hand was now a pistol pointed at both of us.

"I don't think so," Joris said in an even, almost cheerful voice. "You didn't believe me when I said the three of you are not going to be able to go back. I'm sorry about the lady priest, but that's your fault, Catarina. I always told you not to listen to Simon. He's not good for you. It's more than time I was back in your life, since you were foolish enough to marry him. When I was around, you wouldn't have spat on him. Now you, Catarina, are going to come upstairs with me—"

It was at that moment that a ludicrously ordinary thing occurred. A ginger-red cat strolled in from the door leading to the hall.

"There's that animal again," Joris said. "I never could stand cats—"

An old pain and an old memory leaped in my mind. This time I knew what he was going to do.

"Ssss—scat!" I yelled at the cat. It jumped back through the door, missing the bullet that roared from Joris's gun.

"At least it would have been a more merciful end than the one you gave Lucifer. You tormented him to death," Simon said.

"Yes, what did happen to Lucifer?" I asked, and felt the stab of pain I had felt before.

"Nothing important. I used him for a small experiment. I told you at the time. It was necessary to kill him after that. Unfortunately, you made such a fuss, that I had to hypnotize you into forgetting it."

And I saw again that shiny medal, swinging back and forth,

back and forth, the same kind of medal, I noticed now, that I could see under Joris's open shirt.

He was smiling. "Catarina, come here. I want us to go where we can talk privately." He held out his arm.

"Not on your life," I said. "I'm not a lonely, bewitched child any more and that won't work."

"Oh, yes, it will. You've always been my creature. I can do with you what I like. You will do as I say. Come along now."

"You heard her!" Simon said and moved in front of me.

This time I didn't think fast enough. "No!" I yelled and pushed Simon with all the strength I had. But the second bullet blazed from the gun and Simon went down, blood oozing from his head. I knelt beside his unconscious form.

"That's enough!" Joris said. "You'll come with me."

"Simon," I whispered. "Simon!"

"All right, Catarina, if you won't come now . . ."

I felt myself pushed away and saw the gun go down toward Simon. I jumped up. "I'll come with you—right now. I promise! But let me see how badly he's hurt."

"If you don't come now, he'll be dead. I mean it, Kit!" and Joris lowered the gun again. The telephone started to ring. Joris frowned at it. Then he picked it up.

"Yes?" he said into the receiver. Then, "I told you to wait until later." He was turning his back toward me, but the gun was still in his hand. I moved, and he whirled around again, the gun pointed at me. "Oh no you don't. No, I'm not talking to you," he said into the receiver. "Just to—er—a guest who's here. All right. I'll see you later." He hung up. "Now we're going to have a nice chat, you and I. But first, I have to do something with these . . ." And he shoved Simon's body with his foot. Then looked over towards Claire.

I didn't even think. I picked up an ashtray on the end table beside me and flung it at Joris's head. His gun went off but missed me. I started to run.

"Stop, Catherine! Stop or I'll shoot!"

But I was at the door to the hall by then and I ran through and slammed it behind me. It wasn't courage. I felt somehow that Joris would not kill me, at this moment, in this particular way. To do that would be to him a defeat. He had to act out his role first. He was intelligent and fiendishly clever, but I was now fairly sure that he was what the neurologists and head-shrinkers once called a psychopath, later renamed a sociopath. Like most journalists, I had a smattering of information about various fields of knowledge on which I had done articles. And I had written one on a sociopath who had finally been caught after leaving a trail of dead women behind him. One of the characteristics of such people, I had learned, is grandiosity. I saw now how my adoring trust had provided the stage on which Joris strutted. He would need to get that back, to show off to me his brilliance and power before he finally got rid of me.

As I tore up the stairs, I heard him wrench the door open and his feet pounding after me. I should, of course, have gone out the front door. But it was closed, and it was much farther away than the staircase. Even so, as I heard him gain on me, I knew what a mistake I had made.

He caught me, of course, and with one of his long, strong hands around my neck, he pushed me into a bedroom and onto a chair.

"Now," he said. "We can have that little talk. But first—I'm sorry to have to do this, Catarina, but you really mustn't wander around." And while I was still taking in what he said, I saw his hand, flat again, coming toward me. I tried to fling myself away, and that was the last I remembered.

When I woke up, I was lying on a bed. Outside it was dusk. I lay there for what seemed like a long time, because I couldn't remember how I'd got there. Then, slowly, it came back. Finally I sat up, and as I did, something soft hit me, and then rubbed against my leg. Trembling, I turned on the light over the bed.

There, its back arched, was the red cat, the one from downstairs, the one I had dreamed about, and undoubtedly the one I saw on Bart van Reider's bed. What was it van Reider had said? That the cat was a stray that had become attached to Bart. So much for my fear that my mind was playing tricks on me, I thought. Nevertheless, Simon's words went through my mind: "Joris always said his familiar was a cat." I shook my head as

though to clear it; then I took a deep breath and reached out
my hand. A second later I had withdrawn it, and a line of blood
appeared along the back of my fingers. Happily I sucked the
wound and decided there was no question about the reality of
the cat . . .

Then I remembered Simon and Claire, and what Joris had
done to them. Something my mother once said to me flashed
through my mind: "There are no victims, only volunteers." I
had been furious with her at the time, because I had com-
plained—most rarely—of some high-handed treatment by
Joris. "You asked for it," Mother said bluntly. "You let him do
whatever he wants. So don't complain to me when you don't
like it . . ."

What a criminal, idiotic fool I had just been! How many
warnings had I had about what kind of person Joris really was?
And now, going back to my childhood, reseeing certain inci-
dents, conversations with Joris, wasn't I then, even for a child,
an easy dupe? Why? That part of it was not hard to figure out.
How many times had I heard or read that any female child
growing up with a rebuffing father was ready prey for any man
who paid her attention? And I wanted so much to believe that
Joris was the demigod I thought he was . . .

So I had remembered only what I had thought were the
"good things" about Joris, the moments when he seemed
tender and loving, and carefully did not allow myself to notice
anything that would argue a motive different from kindness
. . . And I had done the exact opposite with Simon. All I
permitted myself to see there was what Joris so carefully
pointed out to me. The versions that Joris held up to me not
only fed my need for love and attention, they also fed my ego
. . . And how very good Joris was at that. As for Simon—I did
not see, because I did not want to see, his pain and humilia-
tion, his faltering self-esteem, his need—as great as mine, if
not greater—for love and attention. Most of all, I didn't recognize that with all his faults he was basically decent, and with all
his brilliance, Joris was a monster. After all, I thought now,
sitting with eyes closed, wasn't Satan just a fallen angel?

And now—

The door opened abruptly, and Joris backed in, carrying a

tray. He put it down on a small table near the fireplace opposite the bed. Out of the corner of my eye I saw the red cat
disappear under the bed.

"Let's have a private dinner up here. Just you and me. I've
brought a fabulous wine to tempt you."

"I'm not hungry, Joris. But I would like to talk to you."

"It's a '69 vintage," Joris went on as though I hadn't spoken.
"I left it in the cooler just the right amount of time." He busied
himself sinking the corkscrew into the cork of a tall, slender
bottle of white wine.

"Joris, where are Simon and Claire?"

He was slowly pouring the wine into thin-stemmed glasses.
"There are those who say '67 was a better year for this, but I
don't agree—"

"Are you deaf, or stoned, or just oblivious?"

He lifted the wineglass and took a small sip. "Perfect. You
were right to refuse to believe that I was dead all those years.
You knew I would come back, didn't you?"

"Joris!" I pounded the bed with my fists.

He never changed expression. Suddenly I couldn't take any
more. Going over I struck the glasses off the tray onto the
floor. Then I snatched up the wine bottle and flew across the
room to the window. I had almost thrown it out when powerful
hands gripped me from behind and spun me around. "You'll
play according to my rules," Joris said, "and in whatever play I
write."

He took the bottle from my hand, then drew back his other
hand and slapped me hard across the face. "You'll do as I say.
You'll either drink this wine and eat the dinner on the tray
there, or you won't eat at all. Oh, don't act so wounded! Simon
knocked you about a bit, didn't he? At least that's what I have
been told. And you seem to have forgiven him."

"Simon was an active alcoholic then."

"And that makes it all right? Well, cheer up, with me supplying the wine, you may become one yourself. You'll have plenty
of time, and not much to do with it."

"I'm leaving here as soon as I can get out," I said. "And
what have you done with Simon and Claire?"

"All taken care of and quite safe. Now, do we play according to my rules and have a pleasant dinner? Or do you need reminding again of who controls whom?"

It was foolish, but I saw a clear space between me and the door and rushed for it. It was locked, of course. I fully expected to feel Joris's hand on my shoulder again. But when I turned around he was sipping another glass of wine. The floor was carpeted, and my throwing the glasses down did not seem to have damaged them.

"It's locked," Joris said. And then he smiled. "As you might have guessed."

I stood there, feeling desperate and frightened and a fool to boot. "I didn't see you lock it."

"I didn't intend you to."

"Joris, you're mad. You can't keep me here."

"Why not?"

"Because people would start looking for me."

"Who would? Your trusty lieutenant? He won't find you. Simon? He won't be in any shape to find you or anyone else. Also your friend the Reverend Aldington."

"But why?"

"Because all three of you insisted on interfering with my affairs. If you'd just let well enough alone and not dragged the other two in. But no, you all had to snoop around to see what happened to Crystal Mahoney. You started to put things together, tracking down bits of information from Crystal, Britton and others. You're right about one thing—I wasn't quite straight with you before. I am an importer, a businessman." He smiled. "Drugs, of course. Much the most profitable commodity."

If I needed any proof of Joris's insanity I had it now. Since I couldn't get out, something told me that the best thing to do was to keep him talking. "You knew about our efforts, then?"

"Of course I knew. My—er—business associates don't care much for people who try to winkle out bits of information about our affairs."

"Is that why you had somebody watch my apartment from across the street?"

"Yes. You may not believe this, but I was trying to look out for your safety. I knew my partners would be quite happy to

remove you altogether. They really did not like your snooping.
So as soon as I knew you were onto Crystal's story, I hired a
former—er—employee of mine to look out for you and to
follow you and keep a watch on you."

"Well, he certainly fulfilled his mission. He was there every
morning, watching my apartment. But he was never there
when I ran downstairs to find him."

Joris grinned. "He was carefully trained. Stay so long and
then split. He probably could see your curtain or blind move,
and got away before you could come pelting downstairs. Too
bad van Reider had to kill him."

"Why did he?"

"Because I gather it was your would-be bodyguard who
knocked van Reider's son on the head. Since they're both
dead, I can only guess. But I told Ramedos—your guard—to
follow you, which means sometimes going ahead of you.
There's another road here that comes up the back of the garden and leads into the drive that winds around the house. He
knew you were coming here, so he came in before you and
probably bumped into the van Reider boy. So he knocked him
on the head and was caught doing that by van Reider, who
chased him down the little stairs and killed him. Then drove
his car away."

"How did you know I stumbled over the body?"

"Good heavens! It was in all the papers. Poor Ramedos!"

"And what about the man who almost knocked me off the
platform?"

"I don't know anything about that, but I do know that my
business partners were not at all happy with your investigations into Crystal's death, which, by the way, they arranged—"

"How?"

"Don't be tiresome and naïve, Kit. There could have been a
dozen ways. They probably forced her to swallow the suicidal
dose. It can be done—and without leaving a mark."

"And they scattered the documents, the van Reider papers,
around her motel room? Why?"

"It seemed a good red herring. It kept everyone's attention
on van Reider's pet obsession: the house and the publicity
surrounding it, and on him and his family."

"But you wanted her dead too, didn't you?"

"Let's just say she was in everybody's way—"

I interrupted him. "Because—my God! of course—because she recognized you at the party. She saw that you, Mr. Dan Troilais, Piers Somerville's angel, was also the Archangel and drug connection she'd known."

He smiled again. "Precisely. In addition to all of which, having Crystal around lessened the odds on the success of our exercise. And then she sealed the matter by behaving very foolishly. After snooping around the grounds here and trying to get into the house, she went into the village to eat and ended up in a bar where she talked freely and unwisely about her project. I guess she was overheard by some of my partners' —er—employees. It was the night after that that they made sure she didn't talk any more . . . So when you started investigating up here, and after van Reider killed poor Ramedos, they put their own guy onto getting you. Which was what I was afraid they might do."

"Why? Why were you afraid? Why did you *care?*"

"I told you. You belong to me. Right from the beginning you were mine."

"I'm not anybody's, Joris. Certainly not my half brother's."

"I've never considered you a sibling. We're soul mates."

"Incest, too?"

If I thought to jar him, I was mistaken. He shrugged. "Why not? The Pharaohs thought nothing of it."

"Did you kill van Reider?"

"I arranged to have it done. Time was a-flying. The shipments are coming in. We were tired of having to fit our schedules around his weekends. Besides, he wasn't even going to let the church sell."

"And now that you're going to have the house—what's it going to be? Drug capital of the Northeast?"

"Something like that. But also an ashram."

"You're totally cynical, aren't you? Once, I thought you were really seeking—as you called it—the Path."

"And as I said once, why spend thirty years sitting in contemplation when there are quicker ways? My business dealings help me to finance the place."

"How in God's name did you connect up with these drug people?"

"Don't be an innocent, Kit! You connect up with these people, as you charmingly put it, when you become a customer. When you start supplying other customers, you become a partner. Besides, when I traveled in the East and elsewhere, I was helpful to them in setting up new supply lines."

I stared at Joris. My mind was beginning to clear and teem with more questions. Joris had been missing for twenty years. To me, except for being a little thinner, he seemed almost the same. He had always seemed the same, beginning . . . beginning when? Beginning when I was seven, when I saw him for the first time. I'd barely known of his existence, although afterward I remembered Mother saying something about Father having a son by his first wife, a son who was now at school . . . so I met him for the first time when he came home from school. He was seventeen. At the age of seven I never questioned why I hadn't seen him before, why he hadn't come home for school holidays . . . And after that it never came up.

I said now, "Joris, why didn't we meet until you were seventeen and I was seven? I never thought about it before, but surely you would have come home from boarding school before then."

"Well," Joris said, "it was a very special kind of school." He smiled to himself. "It was called St. Jude's."

"But St. Jude's was a—"

"A psychiatric institute? Yes. Otherwise known as a loony bin. More fools they! What the stupid don't understand they call ill." He laughed, and his laugh had an almost metallic quality.

"And, all the time, you've been storing drugs here? Where do you put them?"

He smiled. "Since you're going to be with me, there's really no reason—is there?—why I shouldn't tell you. In the gazebo or folly or whatever you want to call it. It's where we keep our supplies."

I remembered the broken-down little building in the grounds. "It doesn't look in very good shape."

"That's camouflage. Actually, inside the broken frame and sagging blinds it's as strong and safe as a vault."

"But didn't van Reider know about this?"

"We did our thing during the week, when he wasn't here. Unfortunately for his dog, he started sniffing around the gazebo when he was here on weekends with van Reider. We realized if he kept doing it it was only a matter of time till van Reider would come over for another and more careful look. So we had to take care of the dog."

Joris spoke casually, as though talking about an office memo. I had a flash of memory of van Reider's face as he said, "He was a good dog. I was very fond of him . . ." It made me both angry and sick.

"Still," I said, "he did notice the vandalism in the house, because he spoke to Claire and me about it."

Joris took another sip of wine. "People are careless. They shouldn't be, of course. But they are."

"But the carelessness could undo you and your friends. People notice things like cigarette stubs."

"Who are people? You? But we're on the same side—or soon will be. And Claire—well, as I told you, she and Simon will be taken care of." He smiled.

No! I thought, and then prayed for some way to make it true. I knew Joris was watching me. Better to switch to another subject.

"I suppose you—or your friends—bribed the Krauses."

"Couldn't have been easier. And they left us the keys."

"Doesn't it bother you that your previous—er—place, ashram, whatever you want to call it, destroyed at least one boy?"

"I suppose Britton told you that."

I didn't say anything. The network that Joris seemed to have built up could operate anywhere. Why endanger the good doctor?

"I just heard it."

He shrugged. "There were several who were not strong enough to take our training."

"And you—or someone of your group—'helped' him in his

so-called suicide." It wasn't even a question. I remembered the mouse, sliced to death, Lucifer the cat, the boy—and me.

"The weak are expendable. You know that. It's the history of evolution. The weak are always pared away. It's only today that we take such trouble with them . . . But I couldn't waste time that way . . ." He held up his glass of wine and looked at it in the light.

"And I suppose that syringe that Simon picked up off the terrace railing outside Cleveland was meant to dispatch me."

He leaned over and tapped my cheek. "Only temporarily. As I've said. I have plans for you."

"You're insane! Sick!"

His magnificent eyes became, suddenly, like frozen glass. "Didn't you hear me? What the stupid don't understand they call ill. I was afraid downstairs that you might have become one of them."

"And do you include your father and Mother among them? He adored you."

"Of course I included him. And your mother. You would have been entirely stupid too, unaware, if I hadn't taken you up to a high mountain and shown you a few things . . . and taken a hand in your life. You didn't know that, did you?"

His face broke into that meaningless smile.

"When your not very bright friend Mr. Somerville took me out to lunch and tried to pump me for information about how I knew Crystal and when, it was I who suggested that he assign you the job of doing an article on St. Cuthbert's—after all, I'd taken care to follow your career, and it was now time to bring you back in my orbit."

As I stared, he put back his head and laughed. "So you see, my dear Catarina, the whole thing was my idea from the beginning and you didn't even know it."

"And you—or your goons—stamped all over my apartment!" The thought made me feel literally ill. "Looking, I suppose, for any research I might have come up with."

"I didn't want a repetition of that little book I took away from you."

And let Topaz out, I thought but didn't say. Superstitious it might be, but I didn't want even to mention Topaz's name in front of Joris. Finally, I did say, "Why me?"

"Because, my dear, you were my first and most perfect creature. I didn't want to lose you."

"As I keep telling you, I'm not your creature. I may have been once. I'm not now."

"No? You will be again. I assure you. We belong together."

I shuddered uncontrollably. "I would truly rather be dead."

"That, too, can be arranged."

"If this was really your idea, right from the beginning, how come you didn't know I would pick up information about you from Britton, Simon and the others?"

"I didn't think you were that bright. A mistake, I see now. And an even greater mistake was my not thinking you would bring Mr. Me-Too into it. Your taste really deteriorated when you married him. I had originally thought that when the time came, probably up here, I'd simply let you know that I was here, and everything would fall into place. And then that nosy harlot, Crystal, had to screw it up by coming up here—"

Suddenly Joris's head went up, and he appeared to be listening to something. Then I heard him—the sound of a car and footsteps on the gravel. My heart lifted. I opened my mouth to give a loud scream, but didn't get it out through the napkin that was suddenly thrust almost down my throat. I gagged and heaved and then gagged again. I tried to get my hands up to my face, but they were being twisted behind my back.

"No, my dear. I have every reason to think that those steps belong to a friend—one of mine, not yours. But I'm not taking any chances. We're due for an extra import tonight, and this is no time to take risks."

As I gagged and tried to catch my breath, I was thrust onto a chair, and a rope, taken from a small chest at the foot of the bed, was wrapped around me. Frantically I made as much noise as I could. If Joris left me that way, I would suffocate. I kept on making the noises, faint as they were, and tried to plead with my eyes.

"Yes, I expect you are feeling a little frantic, my dear, aren't you? And if I take the gag away you'll promise you won't make any noise?"

I nodded vigorously.

He laughed again and the sound chilled me. "You really must think me a fool to believe you. However, it isn't part of my plan that you should die now. I do have other uses for you —you've always been such a gloriously willing instrument for me to practice on, Catarina." And he chucked me under the chin, shoving my chin up and making me gag again.

"All right," he said. "I'll relieve it a little. Just remember something. If those footsteps belong to who I think they do, your life will suddenly be worth nothing. I have a use for you. My partners, businessmen to the core, don't." He pulled some of the gag out; then, taking his handkerchief, he tied it around my mouth, holding firm there the remaining portion of the napkin that was in my mouth. "Ta-ta," he said airily, and left, slamming the door.

12

"You've always been such a gloriously willing instrument . . ."

For a moment, surmounting even the awareness of what a mess I was in, the words taunted me. And they produced, as night follows day, the memory of my mother's words: There are no victims, only volunteers. It was a harsh saying and, as Mother would be the first to admit, there were obvious exceptions: victims in war, persecution and crime. But, with ordinary people in ordinary circumstances, she insisted, the words held.

I stared back over my life and realized and accepted, for the first time, that what she said held true for me. I closed my eyes as memories I had suppressed, memories of Joris's anger, his occasional scalding sarcasm, his cruel indifference to everything but his own pleasure, crowded in now. There was the mare whose sides he had ripped with a spiked spur. When I cried about it, he shrugged and said that Mother shouldn't have forbidden him to ride her. She was Mother's horse and Mother allowed no one on the mare but herself, and sometimes me. How I could have come to accept his statement that by forbidding him to ride her, Mother herself was responsible for the torn flesh, I couldn't now remember or even imagine. But I did. The whole thing became the fault of an unfeeling woman. There was the time I jumped from a high branch in a tree and hit my head on stone . . . Joris, standing below, had told me to trust him, that he would prevent my hurting myself. And when, weeping and furious and bleeding all over my shirt, I asked him why he hadn't, he said that I had not jumped in the direction he had told me and that my lack of faith interfered with his power.

"What power?" Mother exploded when I was foolish enough to confide this to her. "Listen, Kit, I haven't told you this before, but Joris wasn't in school, he was in—" If she had been able to finish that sentence, my life might have been different. But Father came into the kitchen then, white and furious.

"You break your promises easily," he said to Mother in the hoarse, whispery voice that was a sign of his anger. He turned to me. "You will leave us."

Naturally, of course, as soon as I could get back to Mother I asked her to finish what she was telling me. But she was vague about it. Then, turning to me, her hands on either side of my face, she made me promise that I wouldn't trail after Joris, when he next came home from college, the way I had before.

I promised, because I didn't know how not to. And I made a small attempt to keep it, even going so far as to tell him the beginning of what Mother was telling me.

"What did she mean?" I asked. "Where were you instead of school?"

"In a monastery," he said. "Father was furious. The family has always been Anglican, but here I was going to a Roman establishment!" He laughed. "I can't think of anything that would make him madder. He loathes the Catholic Church. He claims it's made up of Irish servants." (That much was true: I'd heard him say it.) Then Joris looked at me. "But you won't tell anyone, will you?" Curiously, he, too, put his hands on either side of my face. Only, it meant more when he did it than when Mother did. I promised, of course, and never pursued the matter further . . .

Why? I asked frantically now. Why on earth, given the petty

cruelties, the malice that even I knew was destructive and yet laughed at with him—why did I block out from my memory all the episodes that, involving anyone else, would have been more than justification for my undying hatred?

The answer was obvious: because when Joris was not being cruel or mean, he was warm and loving, or at least he seemed that way. My father had no love to give me. And Mother—poor Mother was herself brought up by undemonstrative parents and didn't know how to express love without embarrassing herself and the other person; added to that was her frantic efforts to keep the farm going. When a horse was sick, she sat up all night with it; when I came down with some childhood ailment, she sent for the doctor, gave me whatever medicine he prescribed, put a book in my hand and went back to her work . . .

So Joris had plenty of edge in my lonely and grudging heart. And he used it. When he saw me, he hugged me and kissed me. When I wrote something—a poem, a little story—he praised it lavishly, dwelling on every good line. He also, occasionally, gave me good criticism. Mother, to whom I gave some of my things, gave them back to me saying, "Very nice, darling. Now, have you cleaned out Buttercup's stable this morning?"

"Have you read them?" I asked once, angrily.

"Of course I have," she said. "How can you ask such a thing?"

But I had crept into her bedroom one night after I had put a sheaf of papers in her hand. There she was, the papers strewn about the bed, her head back against the pillow, sound asleep. I never again showed her anything else. Everything went to Joris . . .

"My God!" The words which I couldn't say out loud strained against the gag. "What a stupid, dumb, buyable fool I was and am . . ."

With any other family, the fact that Joris had been at St. Jude's would have been known in the family. But with my father's pride, that would be the one thing he could not bring himself to mention.

Without thinking, I pulled at my wrists. The rope was thin and smooth but strong, and was tight enough that my wrists were already beginning to swell. I thought of all the books I had read in which the culprit managed to expand his or her wrists so that when the villain left, he/she could relax the wrists and slip them from the bonds. So much for that, I thought. I stopped tugging at them and tried to think of another way.

Then I nearly jumped in the air, taking the chair I was bound to, with me, when something, coming from behind, plopped on my lap. I looked down. The red cat sat there, sniffing around, and periodically brushing against my bound arms. I couldn't even say anything, but I did try to make the whimpering sounds that emerged from behind my gag. Why I tried, I didn't know. Perhaps to establish some human-animal contact.

To my surprise, Red made a miaowing sound back, and rubbed again against my bonds. This was getting neither of us anywhere.

I sat there, coming to grips with my total helplessness. To accept it, I felt sure, was to accept death. If not today, then tomorrow. With every reason not to believe Joris about anything, I did believe him about the indifference of his partners to my life and welfare.

On the other hand, to make any kind of noise, to attract attention, was just as likely to bring about my own end. I closed my eyes and tried to word some kind of prayer that would help me make a choice. But now there were no words.

Then, as though it were being made for me, I did the one thing I had it in my power to do. I raised myself up and slammed the chair down. I did it again and again, which turned out to be tiring. When I tried it for the fourth time, the chair tipped over to the side, and I made more noise falling than I had bargained for. It could have been a catastrophe, because if my head had come in line with any furniture, I would have been powerless to avoid it. Fortunately, it didn't.

I lay there, mouthing the sickening dryness of the handkerchief trying to work it out of my mouth. Red, of course, had been flung off my lap long since, and I wondered where he was. It was then that something seemed to be pulling the gag. Of course, the small napkin that formed the gag was three quarters out of my mouth, under the handkerchief that bound it across my face. But a red-ringed paw was making passes at one corner that rode above the handkerchief, outside my mouth. I closed my eyes. Those claws were coming perilously near them. They were certainly scratching the skin around my mouth.

Then he got hold of the handkerchief corner in his teeth, and pulled, growling as he did so, reminding me of a Siamese cat I once briefly knew. When the napkin would refuse to be moved, he'd go back to his clawing of the material around my mouth—and the skin.

But the gag had loosened. I concentrated on pushing it out with my tongue. Finally it was out of my mouth. I could taste my own blood from the scratches, and wondered when I'd last had a tetanus shot.

Some minutes later, by jiggling my head and using the carpet as a lever, I got my chin free of the handkerchief.

"Thanks," I said hoarsely to Red. It was nice not to have the gag, but where did it all get me? I could, of course, scream. But wouldn't that be bringing more hostile attention to myself than I wanted?

I pondered the options. It was somehow hard to get my breath, lying like this with the gag just under my mouth. Making an extra effort, I breathed in, and sneezed from the dust on the carpet. Then I sneezed again, threatening once more my ability to breathe at all. And my condition was not helped by my fright and pounding heart.

I lay as quietly as I could, while I tried again to make some choice. I had been breathing normally for a minute or so when I was aware of a new element: the air I was breathing smelled of smoke. I breathed in again quickly, and choked. Then I saw the faint coloring to the air coming into the room under the door, and smelled burning.

The choice was made for me. I strained my head away from the floor, took as deep a breath as I dared, and yelled, "Help! Help! Help!"

I half expected to hear running feet, but there was no sound at all. I cried out again and again and again. Then rested. And then started again.

Somewhere along the line, I was coming to face the horror

of death by burning, like my parents, like Buttercup . . . "Oh God!" I moaned into the carpet. The smoke coming under the door was stronger now, and there was no way I could raise myself to avoid it.

"Red," I called, wondering what had happened to the cat. One of my arms, resting under the chairback, was now numb. I tried to move a little, and cried as the numbed arm began to have a little feeling. I was now crying out of a combination of terror and rage when suddenly something or somebody touched me, and I felt an abrupt strain on the rope tying my hands.

"Who's that?" I yelled.

"Who do you think it is?" Simon said. "Hold still, this knife is not the sharpest I've ever seen."

"Oh, Simon!" I said, still crying. "Are you all right? How is your head?"

"Sore. Luckily, only the scalp was grazed. But it knocked me out briefly and I bled like a pig. It's not serious."

"And Claire?"

"Okay. Joris tied us both up and dragged us into another room."

"Where did you come from now? The door is locked."

"The window, and before that, the roof. I would have been here sooner, but I had to find some kind of a rope. This roof is not flat, and there was no point in us both falling off. Jesus! These things are tough. Don't wriggle!"

"The place smells like it's on fire."

"It is. Cousin Joris always had a bit of the arsonist in him—especially if he was angry or cornered."

"Yes, I know. He burned the farm and the horses. I can't even bear to think about it. Do you think they—my parents and the horses—might have suffocated before the fire reached them?" I asked hopefully. "And Buttercup?"

"Let's hope so. There, I think your hands are done. Now I've got to do the rope around your feet and the one tying you to the chair. Here, I hadn't noticed this before. It's a fruit knife on the tray here. Maybe you can help."

With my free hand, I sawed away at the bond binding my

body and arms, slipping the knife under the rope over my chest and rubbing it up and down.

"Where are Joris and all his business partners?"

"I don't know about the partners, but I left the police tracking Joris down through the house."

"The police?" I turned around in surprise, or at least I turned as far as my rope would let me. "They came here?"

"They did. Apparently Claire's son got worried when she didn't turn up, so he called O'Neill, whom he had met before and knew as a friend of his mother's. O'Neill called the Dutchess County police and himself flew up in a helicopter. He showed up after the first lot arrived. They untied both Claire and me, and then everybody started a systematic search for you and for Joris. I knew this place was big. I couldn't believe the number of rooms, anterooms and walk-in closets. By this time we knew that Joris had set fire to his wing of the house, and also to the stairwell."

"Because he was angry or cornered or both?"

"At this point, both. Even to Joris it must appear that his dazzling and wonderful plans have blown up in his face. The police tried to call the fire department, but the phones were dead, so the cops called from their cars. They should be here any time now. But Kit, we're going to have to go back by roof. Both the center stairs and the staircase at the end of one wing are out. We can slide along the gutter to the opposite wing and come through one of the windows and down the stairs at the far end."

By this time I was free. Shakily, but quickly, I got up. "Simon, you're always rescuing me," I said.

"Yeah. Okay. Get yourself through that window. There's a ledge you can step on. Before you step out, though, take hold of the rope that's there. It's tied around one of the chimney stacks."

I had my foot on the windowsill when I turned. "What about the cat?"

"What the hell—this is no time for that. Get your damn foot on the sill and take hold of the rope."

But I stepped back and, avoiding Simon, looked under the

bed. There was the cat, crouched next to the wall at the far end.

"You'll have to shove him from that side," I said, looking up. "And give me your coat. I'll wrap him in that, or he'll jump away and tear both of us to pieces."

Simon stared, then got out of the coat and threw it at me. Then he plunged under the other side of the bed.

We eventually got the frightened cat out, with long scratches on both of us to prove it. Finally, I somehow got him tied up in Simon's coat and hauled him again to the window ledge. The flames in the hall were becoming audible now.

"If you're going to take that with you, give it to me first while you get onto the rope."

I got myself, clinging with hands and knees and ankles, to the rope. How I was going to take the cat I didn't know. But when I was ready, I said, "Okay. Give him to me."

"No. You go up. Then, when you're up, shake the rope and I'll come up with him."

I felt I should insist. Taking Red was my idea. But I went up and stood on the gutter that surrounded the house. Then I shook the rope. It was at that moment fire engines, summoned from the nearest town, came shrieking up. "Thank heaven!" I said and shook the rope again. "Simon," I screamed in the clatter. "Come on up!"

"I don't think so," a voice said behind me. I turned, almost losing my balance. There was Joris, just a few feet above me on the edge of the roof.

"Coming down," he said, and then was beside me. "Now," he said, "we'll just cut this." And without an extra movement, he slipped a large pair of scissors from his pocket and started sawing away at the rope.

"Stop it," I screamed, and lunged for his hand holding the scissors. He pushed me away as though I were a child of three.

"Simon," I yelled. "Don't come up the rope. Joris is here, cutting it off."

The firemen and assorted policemen were below. The fire department started raising its ladder toward the window where Simon was. I couldn't see him from where I was struggling with Joris, but I could hear his voice. Then suddenly he stuck his head out the window.

"Kit, are you all right?"

Joris stopped sawing at the rope, put his hand in his belt and produced a pistol, which he now aimed at Simon. In the only effective action I accomplished the entire evening, I lowered my head and bit his hand as hard as I could. He dropped the pistol. Then I got a chop on the head that would have stunned me worse if Joris hadn't lost his balance and nearly missed me. I watched, half dizzy, as he slid to where the pistol had fallen and started groping for it.

Suddenly a voice I recognized yelled, "Jump, Kit! jump quickly."

The firemen had a canvas stretched below. I knew that though I might break my head, my leg or my neck, no good could come to me where I was. I slid along the gutter a few feet from Joris, who made a lunge for me. Then I jumped, and remembering my efforts in high diving at school, somersaulted twice, landing harmlessly on the canvas.

"You ought to think of going into the circus," O'Neill said dryly as he helped me out.

I looked up. Simon was climbing down the ladder, and the fireman beneath him was carrying the thrashing bundle. Then I saw that Joris had taken aim at Simon.

"Stop him," I screamed, and as I did so, heard the shot.

For a moment, I thought that Joris had shot Simon again, but Simon, standing on the ladder, seemed to be unharmed. Then I saw, near where Claire was standing, a policeman holding a rifle. I looked up. Joris stood poised for a moment, lighted by the flames that were coming out of the windows below and on either side. The firelight lit up his face, now exalted with some inner vision. Then, quite suddenly, he screamed and fell.

Simon, Claire, Red and I drove back together in Simon's car. Claire's, which had been put in the garage by Joris, was damaged by the fire. Simon drove, I sat beside him, and Claire sat in the back. We had found a box and punched holes in it for Red. He had finally gone to sleep in the box, aided by an eighth of a sleeping pill donated by the local doctor, who turned up to see if he could help.

For a while none of us talked. Then, after a while, Claire said, "I've always wondered what pure evil looked like. I now know."

I tried to answer the question that neither of them asked but which was filling the silence.

"I never saw the evil, or at least don't remember doing so, until tonight. Now I wonder how on earth I missed it."

"It's called denial," Claire said, her voice ragged with fatigue. "You had too much invested in believing him to be wonderful to let yourself notice anything else about him. If you saw it, you undoubtedly repressed it."

"Yes. When I was upstairs, thinking I was going to be burned alive, as my parents were, an awful lot came clear to me."

"That would certainly serve to concentrate the mind," Simon said dryly.

I turned and looked at Claire. "Why did you go up today? Was something more afoot about the sale?"

"Apparently Martin Joliad, alias Swami Gupta Nanda, alias Joris Maitland, called and said he was going up to St. Cuthbert's and would like to meet one of us up there to make final arrangements for the sale. Sally told him that the rector wouldn't be back till next week, but he was impatient and said he'd like to have the details ironed out before the rector arrived so the sale would go forward immediately. I went up there basically to make soothing noises and promises if the place was in as bad a condition as van Reider said it was. I didn't want the sale to slip through our hands this time. Our need for money for the outreach program grows apace. So—I went up. If you two hadn't arrived when you did, I would have finished my business with him and been none the wiser."

"How did you react to him?" I asked.

"Well . . . the fact that he seemed unfazed by the general shabbiness sort of won me over. At least, it did at first." She hesitated. "Telescoped, I'd say that my first reaction was that he was astonishingly good-looking. After a while I realized I didn't really like him, which surprised me. I like most people.

But the feeling became so strong that it startled me, and made me wonder why I felt that way.

"It took me a while as he and I walked around the wings, but finally I saw what I disliked so much: it was my sense of being manipulated. There was really no reason for it. I was perfectly willing to do what I could to shove the sale forward. But he had a way of looking at me out of those hypnotic blue eyes, as though what I said, or even grunted, was the most important thing in the world to him, as though he were trying to call something—I didn't know what—out of me. It made me so uncomfortable that I was on the point of leaving when you arrived. Let the rector deal with him, I thought."

"Maybe that was why you felt—for a moment—that I had known who Joliad was and had betrayed you by not telling you."

"I think so. Sorry! After that, I saw the best thing I could do was leave and get hold of the police, only the so-called Swami —Joris—saw what was in my mind." Claire paused. "It's a terrible thing to be glad when someone's dead. But I'm glad he is, and out of your life."

"Amen," Simon said.

"Did he and his thugs kill van Reider?"

"Yes," I replied, and told them what Joris had told me. "But it was van Reider who killed Ramedos, the body I found up there. He was the man Joris had hired to follow me and serve as a sort of bodyguard. Van Reider had killed him because Ramedos had bumped into Bart, van Reider's son, and then whacked him over the head."

After a moment of silence I asked, "Could Joris's scheme have worked if Simon and I had arrived half an hour later, after Claire had gone? . . . Of course not, how stupid can I be? Simon and I knew about his multiple roles and would have confronted him."

Simon interjected, "At which point he would have tried to kill us. Even if he had succeeded in the short run, I think the flight of the Archangel was about over. There'd have been too many questions by too many people, including the police— thank God. Because if by any chance he had dodged us this time and we had gone back to New York, he would have tried to draw Kit in, and then he'd have had to deal with me."

I touched his arm. "But I thought you said we were finished, or words to that effect."

"I'd planned to stop bothering you. I certainly wouldn't lose sight of you." He glanced sideways at me. "He did plan to keep you around, didn't he?"

"Yes. But I told him I'd rather be dead."

"That must have been a blow to his titanic self-esteem." After a pause, Simon glanced at Claire through the rearview mirror. "How is that wildcat doing?"

Claire looked down at the box, whose lid she had taken off. "He seems to be breathing normally. What are you going to do with him?"

"I don't know," I said truthfully. "I think he'd kill Topaz. I'll see if I can enlist Letty's help."

"She's your psychic lady?"

"Yes."

"Do you feel less haunted, Kit?" Claire asked. "After all, you didn't see a supernatural cat beside young van Reider. He was and is real. And the rest of your problem came out of your own dreams."

"True. But I think that Joris did hypnotize me so that I wouldn't remember what he'd done to Lucifer, our cat at home. But it must have lain at the bottom of my mind all along. And when I saw Red here, the whole thing, including the associations with Joris, must have been activated in my dream." I paused for a moment. "You remember, Claire, you once asked me if I had ever been hypnotized and I said haughtily that I'd never give control of myself over to anyone. But I was wrong—on both counts. I think Joris must have used that medal he wore. I do remember he was fond of dangling it."

"It sounds like the kind of thing he would do."

"What is the church going to do about St. Cuthbert's now?" I asked. "It certainly won't bring the money it would have— especially not after the fire."

"I'm happy to say that that's a problem for the rector and the vestry. I don't care if I never see it again."

"Amen," Simon said again, and then I echoed it. For a

moment I saw Joris's exalted face as it had looked on the roof. "He *was* evil," I said. "There's more I must tell you about what he said to me. But not now."

We dropped Claire off at her house and went on down to the Village. It was almost light by now. Letty's kitchen light was on, so I asked her to take the still-sleeping Red in his box. "I can't wish him on poor Topaz," I said to Letty, "not after all Topaz has been through, and he's been an only cat for so long. Do you think you could find a home for this one? He's a holy terror."

Letty looked at him and stroked his red coat. "Yes, I'll take him. If he's too wild for my lot, then I know a couple of people who'd be interested. But I'll try and work some magic on him."

"If anyone can, you can," I said and kissed her.

Simon and I went upstairs to my apartment. "Are you all right now?" he asked. "It's been a stirring evening and I think I'll get home."

"Yes, thank you, I'm okay."

"Are you still surprised about Joris?"

"No, Simon, I'm not. And my self-esteem is not feeling too healthy for the persistence with which I believed him, even until today—yesterday," I said. It was now 4 A.M.

"Don't be too hard on yourself," Simon replied. He sounded tired. "I'll admit I wasn't too happy about the persistence of your devotion. But considering the amount of manipulation he did when you were a kid and vulnerable and starved for affection, it isn't too surprising."

"The same could be said of you," I said slowly. "But you didn't collapse at his feet."

"Not the same thing. I was almost Joris's age. I'm male, not female, and I did traipse along. I don't think either of us had much backbone. But I'll give you this, you didn't make the royal mess of your life that I have."

"But alcoholism is a disease."

"Yes. Still, I have to remember, that no one put the booze in my mouth—I did. And it's up to me not to put it in again. To all of which purpose, I'm going home and getting some sleep. I've had it."

He started toward the door.

"Simon," I said. "If I asked you to spend the night—what's left of the night—here, would you accuse me of playing games? Because I'm not."

"I'm not interested in gratitude—at least not from you."

"I *am* grateful. But to my knowledge it's never been known as an aphrodisiac." I continued to sit on the couch, absentmindedly stroking Topaz. For some reason it was a point of honor—my honor—not to go over and use stronger persuasions. Not because I thought they were wrong, but because I wanted him to feel free to choose. Neither he nor I had ever really been free. And I wanted us both to be. "Please," I said.

After a minute he came over, put his hand under my chin and tilted up my face. There was nothing I could do about the tears that were on it. "All right," he said. "Let's declare a new scratch and start. Okay?"

My nose was beginning to run, so I dug into a pocket and produced a tissue and mopped up. "Yes," I said, when I could. "Let's do that."